THE WORLD BENEATH

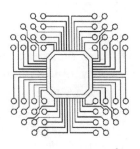

REBECCA CANTRELL

ALSO BY REBECCA CANTRELL

Mystery/thrillers in the award-winning Hannah Vogel
Mystery series set in 1930s Berlin:

A Trace of Smoke
A Night of Long Knives
A Game of Lies
A City of Broken Glass
On the Train (short story)

Gothic thrillers in the Order of the Sanguines series
(written with James Rollins) set in ancient and modern day
times and following the adventures of an order of vampire
priests.

The Blood Gospel
Innocent Blood
City of Screams
Blood Brothers

Young adult novels in the iMonster series
(written as Bekka Black).

iDrakula
iFrankenstein

Happy reading!

THE WORLD BENEATH

REBECCA CANTRELL

Copyright Information

This book is a work of fiction. All of the characters, organizations, and events portrayed in this novel are either products of the author's imagination or used fictitiously. Any similarity to real person, alive or dead, is completely coincidental.

THE WORLD BENEATH

Copyright © 2013 by Rebecca Cantrell

Cover Design by Kit Foster www.kitfosterdesign.com

Dedication

For my husband, my son,
and my (non)psychiatric service cat

PROLOGUE

November, 1949
Presidential train
En route to Grand Central Terminal, New York

Dr. Berger looked into the long dark mouth of the tunnel. This tunnel would lead to another and then another until they stopped at a secret platform under New York City's Waldorf Astoria hotel. Only one train had permission to stop there. This one—the presidential train car. It hadn't been used by the president since the war and, despite its original purpose, the car was surprisingly utilitarian—simple wooden cabinets, a stainless steel counter bearing four liquor decanters, and leather chairs bolted to the floor.

He clutched his precious briefcase with nervous fingers. The train had almost arrived at its destination, and nothing had gone wrong. Yet.

Darkness engulfed the train car as it pulled inside. The train slowed to a crawl. To see why, Dr. Berger adjusted his round spectacles and peered through bulletproof glass so thick that it had a green cast. Dim, electric lights hanging from the ceiling revealed a field of silver tracks merging together again and again as the tunnel narrowed. The engineer had slowed to switch tracks. The car was deep underneath the city now. Close.

He cast a sidelong glance at his sole traveling companion: the uniformed soldier who was tasked with protecting him and the secrets he carried. What did he know about the man?

What was there to know? The man sitting straight-backed and alert with a Thompson submachine gun flat across his lap was merely an ordinary American soldier. A soldier much like the one who'd taken Dr. Berger prisoner in Bavaria a few years before. Another square-jawed man with close-cropped hair whose narrow eyes told Dr. Berger how much he hated all Germans. Of course he did—because of the war. These American soldiers held him personally responsible for all the deaths caused by Hitler's madness, as if these soldiers could have influenced Roosevelt's decisions themselves, as if his adherence to orders was so different from theirs.

In the end, he had defied his superior's orders when he'd packed up his notes and gone to meet his destiny on a train not unlike this one, fleeing west, praying only to surrender to the Americans and not the Russians. He'd been lucky. The troops who'd stopped his train were sturdy and well-fed, chewers of gum and crackers of jokes—American through and through. Their orders regarding high-level scientists were clear, and they hadn't mistreated him.

They'd brought him to the United States, interrogated him respectfully, and paid him a good salary to continue his research. They'd even retrieved his yellow parakeet, Petey, and the upright piano he had inherited from his father. His specialized knowledge had put him in the president's own train car on a special and secret mission that would change the future.

Funny how things turned out.

"Near now," Dr. Berger said.

The soldier jerked his head. Almost a nod, but not quite. The man had probably been given instructions not to speak to him. As kind as they seemed, the doctor doubted his American colleagues trusted him. A mutual state. The wounds from the war had not had time to heal.

Dr. Berger's fingers tapped out a song on his briefcase, but instead of helping him play music, the notes in its leather interior helped him to play the human mind. The trials were promising indeed, though protocols in the United States were more complex than they had been in Germany. Here he spent too much of his time talking about safeguards, about how to minimize risk and wondering if his funding would be canceled.

He hadn't worried about such things in Germany.

The SS valued only results.

He tilted his head, certain that he had heard a familiar sound. The clacking of steel wheels against track filled his ears. The reassuring rhythm told him that every second brought them closer to their destination. He closed his eyes and relaxed.

The sound came again—like Petey's soft warble when he tapped his mirror with his rounded beak. This sound wasn't quite the same. Seeking its source, he scanned the front of the car. A small hand emerged from behind the door of a cupboard at the front of the car, and tiny brown fingers with dark nails groped the frame.

"*Gott im Himmel*" The precious briefcase slid unnoticed to the floor as the doctor sprang to his feet and brushed past the startled soldier. The little hand vanished behind the wooden door as if it had never been there. But he had seen it.

Dr. Berger lurched toward the cupboard. It was impossible. It couldn't be there. It must not be there.

"Come out, little one." He eased the door to the side. Its nerves were probably on edge, too, and he had no wish to startle the creature.

The soldier stood behind him, gun trained on the half-open cupboard. "What's in there, doc?"

So, he could speak.

Dr. Berger reached inside the cabinet with one cautious hand while speaking in a gentle singsong voice. "No one will hurt you. We are all friends here."

Leathery fingers curled around his wrist, and a slight weight dropped onto his forearm. Slowly, he pulled the creature out.

"A monkey?" asked the soldier.

Not just any monkey. The animal on his arm was a female rhesus monkey. Short brown fur covered her plump body, except for the inverted pink triangle of her face. Huge brown eyes stared up into his.

"Do I know you?" Dr. Berger crooned.

He touched her soft ear and felt for a tag punched through the cartilage. His heart sped with fear, and the monkey tensed, too. He took a deep breath and hummed a few bars of *Eine kleine Nachtmusik* to calm them both. With one hand, he tilted her to the side to study the small piece of metal that would determine his fate.

The orange tag bore the number sixteen. The worst of all.

He wanted to throw her out the window, as far from him as possible, and pretend he'd never seen her. He could. The soldier didn't know what the tag meant. She'd have a few days, perhaps weeks, of precious freedom before she succumbed, and he would be safe.

"How'd a monkey get in here?" The soldier seemed charmed by the little creature. "He's a cute little guy."

"It is a female monkey." As if that mattered.

The thick bulletproof windows had a complicated latch, but the soldier would undo it for him, if he asked. He could not ask. He was a scientist first. This monkey must never be freed. Indeed, she must be contained at all costs.

Because she was infected.

She'd been infected only a few days before, but the infection ran its course quickly in primates. The danger already swam in her rich red blood. Incurable.

He remembered her now, recognized the distinctive shock of golden fur above her brows. She had been the most docile of animals, before. But she might not be docile now. He must not agitate her.

"Find a cage," he said quietly.

He stroked a finger along her warm cheek, and she followed the movement with round eyes the same shade of brown as the soldier's. Smiling, he hummed to her, while she relaxed in his arms. He drew her close to his chest and cradled her like a baby. She reached up and left an oily smudge across the right lens of his glasses.

The soldier looked blankly around the car. The doctor watched him go through the cupboards with methodical efficiency. The young man pulled out paper, pens, liquor, snacks, a towel, but nothing to contain the monkey.

If they could not imprison her, they would have to kill her. The doctor could have done it easily, but a deep wound ran along the palm of his hand where he had cut himself yesterday when slicing bread. If the monkey's blood entered his cut, he might become infected, too.

"You must kill her." He lifted the animal up toward the soldier. She weighed about five and a half kilos—he translated the metric measurement because he was in America now—twelve pounds, not much more than a human newborn.

"It's only a monkey." The soldier made no move to take the warm furry body.

"Take her," the doctor ordered.

The monkey's eyes widened as if she knew what he intended. Lightning fast, she sank her teeth into the doctor's thumb. Her sharp canines grated against his phalange bone, and his grip weakened. She squirmed free of his wounded hand and landed on the floor on all fours like a cat.

Holding his bloody hand, the doctor stumbled back against the wall of the car. He cursed. Pain throbbed through his thumb, but that was not the worst of it.

A harsh screech rose from her throat. His blood dripped from her bared fangs and fell onto the floor. She trembled and swiveled her head from side to side as if she saw enemies everywhere. She probably did.

While the soldier gaped at the angry creature, gun lax in his hands, she leaped onto his knee and climbed him like a tree, little hands and feet gripping the folds of his uniform. When she reached the top of his head, she leaned down to sink her teeth into his ear before leaping off his head and grasping a light fixture hanging from the ceiling of the car.

Nimble and quick, she swung along the wire toward the back door. The soldier's bullets stitched a neat line behind her, never quite catching up. Bullets ricocheted around the car, and both men dove to the floor.

When they stood, the monkey had disappeared.

The soldier cupped the bite on his ear, and Dr. Berger gripped his bleeding thumb.

"We may be infected," Dr. Berger said. "We must follow protocols."

The train engineer's surprised face stared at them through the thick glass window separating the engine from their car. The engineer was protected from them, and from the monkey. He lifted a black object with a curly cord. His radio. Good. He would explain what had happened, and proper protocols would be in place when they arrived. The danger would be contained.

Dr. Berger nodded his approval, and the man turned around again.

The doctor lifted the heavy top off a cut glass decanter that stood next to the compact steel sink, and the harsh smell of gin billowed out. That would do. He sloshed gin over his thumb. The alcohol burned like acid in his open wound, but it was not to be helped. It ran down the drain, colored pink with his blood. He tore a strip from the bottom of his white lab coat and used it to fashion a crude bandage for his thumb. Then he cleaned and dressed the soldier's wound, slow and fumbling because of his bandaged hand.

The monkey stayed hidden, and neither of them attempted to find her.

The soldier put down his gun and poured them each a glass of gin. He pointed to the bottle of vermouth, and Dr. Berger shook his head. The soldier didn't bother with any, either. Some things called for liquor straight up.

The gin burned a warm trail down his throat. His aching thumb would heal, and the chances of cross-species infection were minor. It was a mere inconvenience, but they would both have to be quarantined for a few weeks to make certain. Fortunate, indeed, that he had brought his notes. Perhaps the time in isolation would let him truly concentrate. At least there he would be spared the drudgery of meetings. He drained his glass, and the soldier filled it again.

The train jerked to a stop. Dr. Berger peered into the gloom. The row of orange light bulbs hanging from the ceiling cast faint light on ten armed soldiers standing in formation around the car—four on each side and two behind. These soldiers looked like the soldier inside the car, except that their Thompson submachine guns were raised and pointed at the train.

With his hands raised above his head and a meek expression plastered on to his face, Dr. Berger stood. He knew how to surrender. He walked toward the back door, to open it and explain to them they had nothing to fear from him or from the soldier.

"Don't open the door, sir," barked one of the outside soldiers.

Dr. Berger stood still and called through the door. "It is not airborne. You could only be infected by transfer of blood. There is no danger."

The soldier kept his weapon up.

Clanking at the front of the car told the doctor that a worker was unhooking the engine, but he could not see him. Half the lights were burnt out. Postwar rationing.

He'd have to wait until an intelligent man arrived to whom he could explain the situation properly. In the meantime, he sat and drank more gin while a new engine pushed their car down the tracks from behind after the old engine had left. There would be time to explain when they reached their destination.

He hoped.

A spike of paranoia rose in his brain, but he quashed it. He posed no threat to these men, and they posed no threat to him. They were no Nazis. Human life mattered to them.

The engine pushed his blue railroad car into a dead-end tunnel, then pulled away.

Darkness cloaked the car at the back and on both sides. He stared at the mouth of the tunnel. Soon they would send a doctor to whom he could explain the risks, and they would be released into quarantine.

Lit from behind by the lights strung from the ceiling, the silhouette of a tall man moved in front of the men with guns. The tall man carried a triangular blade and a bucket. A smaller man carrying the same curious items walked behind him. Were they setting up to disinfect the car with chemicals from their buckets? That was unnecessary, and they must know it. They wore blue overalls like workmen, not white lab coats, so they must be here to perform a different task.

Dr. Berger pressed his face against the cold bulletproof glass to watch.

The first man fumbled with rectangular objects on the

ground, covering them with something from the bucket and slapping them with his blade. He'd already completed one row before the doctor realized what they were.

Bricks.

The two men were walling them in.

The gin burned through his system in an instant. Blind panic replaced it.

He yanked open the train door and jumped onto the tracks. Dank underground air hit him like a wall. The soldiers standing outside the shed raised their guns to point at him.

The bricklayers gave him frightened looks and increased their pace.

"There is no risk," the doctor said. "None. You are all safe."

He took another step toward the soldiers, tripping on a train tie.

"Don't move, sir," said a voice behind him.

He faced the soldier he had been drinking with a moment before. The man stood on the steps of the train, gun leveled at the doctor's chest. Blood had seeped through the makeshift bandage on his ear, but his dark eyes were determined.

"We are ordered to stay here. We must stay," the foolish soldier said.

"Those are bricks." The doctor pointed a white-clad arm at them. Already there was a second row. "They wall us in here now."

The soldier stared at the bricklayers as if he had never seen one. Perhaps he hadn't. He was young.

"We will follow orders," he said.

The men worked quickly and methodically—laying in a brick, covering it with mortar, and adding another next to it. If he ever built another house, he would want to hire them. He pulled himself together—his mind could not be allowed to wander, not now.

"We will die in here," the doctor said. "Together with that damned monkey."

The soldier lowered his weapon a few degrees.

That was enough. Dr. Berger walked toward the light.

"These are not the correct protocols," he called. There was no scientific reason to brick him in here. His heart sank. There might be political ones.

"Don't take another step, sir." This time, the soldier who spoke was on the other side of the bricks. His weapon aimed straight at the doctor's chest. The doctor did not doubt that the man would shoot him.

Already, the wall was up to his knees.

"I am an important man," the doctor said. "I come on the orders of your president. In his very own car. Do you not see his seal?"

The soldiers didn't seem to care about the seal. Dr. Berger waited precious seconds while more bricks were fitted into place. They did not understand him. They would not. They were burying him and his research. Something had gone wrong, and it had nothing to do with the errant monkey. Someone wanted him out of the way. His research was unpopular in certain circles. His enemies were burying it—and him along with it.

He spoke to the soldier he had just tended. "Give me your weapon."

The man looked between the German doctor and his American compatriots beyond the wall. His loyalty was clear. "No, sir."

"Do you want to die in here?" The bricks had reached waist height and climbed higher.

"If those are my orders." The young man looked shaken but resolute. There was no time to win him over.

Dr. Berger would not die in the darkness here. He must

find out who had put him here. He must escape. He sprinted toward the growing wall, keeping low.

The soldier outside opened fire.

A bullet ripped into the doctor's shoulder near his neck. Another tore a bolt of fiery pain through his leg. He fell heavily to the hard ties. Steel track struck his temple. Warm blood ran down one cheek. Full darkness blinked in his head, but he fought it.

He must keep his wits about him.

His broken eyeglasses fell to the ground as he crabbed toward the entrance, using his good arm and leg. The smell of his own blood filled his nostrils like water filled those of a drowning man. He gagged on it, spit onto the wooden ties, and crawled forward.

They could not kill him. He was an important man. A doctor.

As a doctor, he must stop the bleeding in his neck, must assess the damage to his leg. But he was an animal first, and if he did not reach the ever-narrowing crack of light, his wounds would not matter.

Another row of bricks was added. Already, he would have to stand to climb through it. If Petey were here, he could have flown to freedom. The thought of his small yellow body flashing through the room and out into the light cheered him. Petey flying free.

Weakening with each motion, he dragged himself one body length, then another, until he reached the base of the newly built wall. The odor of wet cement overpowered the smell of blood. It reminded him of the summer he built his house, after he was appointed head of his research lab at the beginning of the war, when everything had seemed possible.

He grunted in pain as he hauled himself upright. His good leg took his weight, and his fingers found holds in the wet cement slopped between the bricks.

Then the light vanished.

The last brick was in place.

September 8, present day
Former Naval hospital
Guantanamo Bay, Cuba

Dr. Dubois jerked his head up at the crash of breaking glass. The windowless room held two battered steel desks, his and Dr. Johansson's, both occupied; old wooden cabinets full of beakers and flasks; a stainless steel table with a microscope and other equipment; and an incinerator in the corner to dispose of medical waste. In his immaculate lab, glass did not randomly break. Nothing was amiss here.

A distant scream, swiftly cut short, told him that the trouble was nearby.

Had a test subject escaped? He'd locked them in carefully after their last mission, when they were still tired and docile. Most of them were sick, practically dead on their feet. None of them could have gotten out.

Another crash, closer now. Something, or someone, was heading straight toward this room, and fast.

Dr. Johansson drew in a sharp breath and pushed thick glasses up on her freckled nose, magnified eyes rounded with fear. One hand touched the bright pink locket she always wore, a gift from one of her young daughters.

Dr. Dubois examined the room again, as if another appraisal might yield better results. It didn't. The only exit was through the door, and it led to a long corridor lined with more windowless rooms. All those doors were locked and those inside would not help him.

Based on the sound, the test subject had already reached the middle of the corridor. He and Dr. Johansson couldn't get past him. They were trapped in the lab.

He glanced at the thick steel door to the room. It had a stout lock, but it would not help them because the door only locked from the outside.

"Hide," he barked.

They both leaped to their feet and searched for a secure hiding place. If he emptied one of the medical-supply cabinets, he might be able to cram himself inside, but the test subject would notice medical supplies all over the floor. The creaky wooden file cabinet? It wouldn't offer more than a second of cover. Under the desk? Likewise.

He picked up a scalpel. The subjects were younger and stronger than he, with advanced combat training, but that might make them overconfident enough that he could get in a quick slash to an artery.

Dr. Johansson crossed to the massive incinerator recently procured to dispose of medical waste when this cell had been repurposed into a laboratory. It was the only place in the room large enough to fit a body. Her gaze met his, her unspoken question clear. She was a young military doctor with twin daughters in preschool and a brilliant research career ahead of her—she had much to live for. Dr. Dubois was years older than she, and his children were grown; they didn't need him like hers did, but he was a far more valuable researcher than she. He recognized opportunities that others missed. Scientifically, he was a greater loss.

Taking advantage of his hesitation, she swung inside the incinerator. He reached in and grabbed her long hair. She braced herself against the sides with her arms and legs. A handful of blond hair came loose in his hand.

He reached for the scalpel in his pocket to slash at her arms, but stopped when a thud against the outside wall warned him that young Private Henderson had fallen. He was the last guard in the corridor. The subject was nearly in the room. No time remained to fight with Dr. Johansson.

Dr. Dubois ran for the door and stood next to the door's hinges, gripping the scalpel. When the door opened, it would conceal him. If the test subject ran far enough into the room, or got distracted, the doctor might be able to slip out into the corridor and run. Not much of a plan, but he could think of nothing else. Maybe this test subject wasn't one of the brighter ones.

The steel door slammed open and crashed to a stop less than an eighth of an inch from his sweaty nose. He held his breath.

"I've come for you," said a hoarse voice.

Dr. Dubois recognized it at once—Subject 523. Not good. Subject 523 was intelligent, with formidable strength and training.

Quick footsteps crossed the lab, stopped by the computers, and resumed. A crash from the corner told him Subject 523 was breaking open an old wooden filing cabinet. He seemed to know what he wanted.

No decompensation yet, still high functioning in spite of exhaustion and illness. Dr. Dubois stopped himself from continuing the diagnosis. Not the time for that, either.

He peered around the edge of the door. Across the room, Subject 523 faced away from him. His dark hair was neatly cut, his uniform clean and pressed. From this angle, as he reached inside the broken file cabinet, he looked like a courier picking up a routine file.

He was anything but.

Subject 523 pulled an old manila folder from a wrecked drawer. The yellowed documents within were highly classified. They'd been kept hidden for decades, and for good reason. The doctor wasn't about to fight him for them.

Subject 523 stuffed the folder inside his desert camouflage jacket and half-turned toward the door. Dr.

Dubois ducked below the wire glass window, straining his ears for the sound of Subject 523 moving toward him.

Silence.

He needed to distract the man for only a second, long enough to get into the corridor so he could make a break for the exit to the outside. A smooth rectangular object in his pocket had all the answers. Quickly, he lifted it out. His cell phone.

He called the only person who could help him right now. Her phone chirped.

From the incinerator.

Subject 523's footsteps hurried to the sound. Dr. Dubois slid out from behind the door and made for the corridor.

Dr. Johansson's shrieks sounded behind him.

He stumbled over the soft hand of Private Henderson in mid-corridor. The young soldier lay flat on his back on the polished concrete floor. A red slash ran across his throat, a wound so deep the knife must have gouged his spine.

His head rested at an impossible angle in a pool of blood, and his sightless eyes stared at fluorescent lights embedded in the ceiling. The meaty smell of a butcher's shop hung in the air. Five minutes later and the private would have been on his lunch break.

Dr. Dubois ran past the corpse and two more blood-soaked bodies sprawled on the hard floor, throats slit. Blood had splashed against the brown doors on either side of the corridor. Those doors led to secured rooms full of other test subjects. He would find no safety there.

Men pounded against the steel doors, hurling profanities at him.

A crash from behind him. Subject 523 was close.

His foot slipped in a pool of blood, and he fell against a door. The man inside smashed his fist into the thick glass inches from Dr. Dubois's head. The glass held. He pushed himself off and ran, expecting to feel Subject 523's blade against his throat at any moment.

He burst out the exit door and into the humid Cuban afternoon, glad of the sunshine on his face and even gladder for the armed soldiers running toward him.

The door slammed back against the side of the building as Subject 523 cleared the corridor behind him. Two options: He'd leave Dr. Dubois alone, or take his revenge before the soldiers could stop him. The doctor redoubled his pace.

His right leg gave, and he collapsed onto the stinking tropical dirt. With a cry, he rolled over onto his back. Red spread across his thigh. He'd been shot. Subject 523 had shot him. The bastard.

Dr. Dubois looked back toward his building. The freed man sprinted into the jungle, his own safety clearly more important than his need for vengeance against the doctor, at least for the moment.

Hot pain shot up the doctor's leg. His heart raced and skipped in his chest. Was he having a heart attack, too? He was a middle-aged man who hadn't taken care of himself the way he should. He should have spent more time in the gym as Dr. Johansson always nagged him to—his mind sheered away from her final moments in the incinerator.

Armed soldiers surrounded him, shadows falling across his face.

"Orders, sir?" asked a burly sergeant whom he didn't recognize.

"Follow," he wheezed. He pointed in the direction Subject 523 had taken into the trees. "Don't let him leave the island."

"Yes, sir." The soldier saluted and pivoted to direct his men.

One man dropped to his knees next to the doctor and

dropped a first aid kit onto the ground. A medic who barely looked old enough to be out of high school. "Are you OK, sir?"

"No," the doctor yelled. "I'm shot. Shot in the leg."

"I see that, sir." The young man's voice was infuriatingly calm. His hands fussed with a hypodermic syringe.

"Hurry, God damn it!"

"Yes, sir," he said.

The doctor barely felt the needle, but he felt the drug enter his system. The pain gave way to warmth, to a feeling of well-being. He couldn't give in to it. They had to catch Subject 523.

But he was too smart to be caught. If he didn't come back for revenge, Subject 523 would be off the island in hours. He had the training to evade capture, and he'd figure out a way to steal a boat or a plane or God knew what else. He was a skilled man, still.

Dr. Dubois must control this situation—starting with dealing with the rest of the 500 series, then hiring a man to find and sacrifice Subject 523. As bad as things were now, they would soon get much worse.

Subject 523 was infected.

And the file in his shirt would lead him to the most-populous city in the United States—New York.

1

Subway tunnels breathe. They exhale when trains come and inhale when they leave. Their concrete lungs fill with smoke and soot and rubber and the scents of a hundred ladies' perfumes. When trains aren't running, the tunnels hold their breath. They might let wisps of warm air drift into the cold night, draw in slow nips of bracing frost, but mostly they sit still, waiting for trains to bring them back to life.

A thousand times a day their breath coursed over Joe Tesla's body. It was not so warm as human breath, nor yet so cold as stone. He was used to it, now.

Because he lived here, underground, in the tunnels of New York City.

He had not felt sunlight on his skin for 181 days, and he might never feel it again. His skin, long pale, had whitened. He looked like a vampire, except that he didn't have the teeth for it.

He didn't have the teeth for a lot of things these days.

Not so long ago, he'd had plenty of teeth. Sharp ones. Now he wasn't much use to anyone.

Edison nudged his hand with a cold nose, brown eyes concerned. Edison was his psychiatric service animal—a patient and affectionate dog who'd inherited the best genes of his Labrador mother and golden retriever father. When Joe got upset, the dog brought him back, brought him home.

Edison pulled Joe through the darkness. He'd have been lost without him.

He scratched Edison in his favorite spot behind his ear. The dog's tail thumped the hard train ties. As always, Joe counted, and with each number its corresponding color flashed through his mind: the number one was cyan, two blue, three red, four green, five brown, six orange. Edison stopped wagging his tail, and the colors and sound faded. This late, quiet filled the empty tunnels, broken only by the occasional squeak of a rat, or the rustle of tiny paws across paper blown down from a platform.

No passenger trains ran this late—Joe had long since committed their schedules to memory. Of course, trains were occasionally moved to new stations or out for servicing at night, so his system wasn't foolproof, but with Edison's keen hearing and Joe's knowledge of places they could hole up along the tracks while trains went by, it had been pretty safe.

Joe didn't need much to keep them safe down here: a metal flashlight he'd discovered on the mantel of his new home, a pewter badge to show transit workers, and the heavy ring of old-fashioned keys hooked to his belt and covered with a polar fleece bag to quiet the jangling. Those keys were said to grant him access to every underground door and platform. So far, they had.

Right now he stood in a vast room deep underground northeast of Grand Central Terminal. Here the tracks merged together under Manhattan before reaching the station's forty-four platforms (green, green). Since they had been built a century before, many of the tracks were no longer electrified. It was a good place to let Edison explore without worrying that he'd electrocute himself on the third rail.

Joe rummaged through his backpack. His questing fingers

found a roll of duct tape, a bag of dog treats, and, at last, the glow-in-the-dark tennis ball. He pulled it out. "What do you think, boy?"

Edison's tail wagged in approval, brown eyes glued to his hand.

Joe tossed the ball in an arc across the old sidings, and Edison ran after it in a streak of gold. The dog returned with it, and he threw it again. He liked watching the glowing ball career off tracks and roll under parked train cars, liked to see Edison having fun.

Edison bounded about, abandoning himself to every moment. Joe couldn't remember a time when the same could be said about him. Maybe Edison could teach him that, too.

Ball in his mouth, the dog loped back again. This time he didn't drop it at Joe's feet. Instead, he dropped the wet ball in his hand, a sign that he'd lost interest in playing. Joe tucked it into his jacket pocket and wiped his hand on his pants.

Above, tons of rock hung between him and the sky. It was very different from his beginnings—he'd spent his childhood with only the thin metal skin of a travel trailer separating him from the elements, and often not even that. Whenever he could, he'd slept outside in a sleeping bag. He'd gazed at the night sky from fields across the Midwest, sleeping with quiet stars above and the circus animals moving in their cages around him for company, everyone waiting for the next performance. Now he, too, was trapped in a cage, because his brain, once his greatest ally, had betrayed him.

Enough. No self-pity.

Joe adjusted his night-vision goggles and turned toward home, Edison ranging ahead. The world glowed an eerie green, the best the goggles had to offer. He found them more reassuring than a flashlight. The white beam felt out of place down here, more unnatural than night-vision green.

He'd bought Edison canine night-vision goggles, too. Not hard to find. War dogs used them, but Edison didn't like them. He'd wear them with a weary air of resignation if Joe made him, but Joe didn't force the issue. Edison's eyes were good in the dark. Turned out, dogs could see almost as well in darkness as cats. The *tapetum lucidum* at the back of a dog's eye refracted the light back through the retina, like a cat's or a bat's.

Joe swept his gaze along the tunnel. This one was cut and cover. It had been built by tearing up the street above, cutting the tunnel, then covering the top back up and replacing the street on top. Most of the tunnels this high were cut and cover.

He liked them better than the deep-bore tunnels because they had more room on the sides to get out of the way of trains. Deep-bore tunnels were drilled with a big round drill. They were barely large enough for the train cars. He and Edison could be spread across the walls like tomato paste if they got caught there off guard at the wrong time. Even there, if he flattened himself against the side, he'd survive a passing train. Edison would be safe, too, so long as he didn't panic, and Edison was never one to panic.

Counting each step, Joe marched toward home. He used the short strides he'd developed for walking in the tunnels. Instead of measuring his stride by the length of his legs, he measured it by the distance between train ties. It had felt awkward at first, but now it was his natural gait down here. When he went back to the stations and shops topside, it took him a few minutes to switch back to the same gait as everyone else.

Edison stopped to sniff a foul-smelling object on the ground, probably a dead rat.

"Don't roll in that!" Joe called.

Edison had, before. He often brought the odors of dead rats or rotten food into their home, and Joe had to toss him in the giant claw-foot tub and scrub him clean with Balenciaga soap. Edison didn't like the scent any more than Joe liked the stench of dead rats, but since Joe had to do most of his shopping at the luxury stores in Grand Central Terminal, Edison had to take what he could get.

The yellow dog gave him a hurt expression, as if he would never think of coating himself with the stink of a dead rat, and trotted to stand next to Joe's leg. Joe bent and ruffled the animal's soft ears. "Good boy."

The dog stayed close to his leg as Joe walked toward home. He'd warned Edison about the dangers of the third rail, but Joe didn't like to take chances and kept him to heel when he could.

They arrived at a round metal door faced with an ornate pattern molded into the Victorian-era steel. On it, Joe tapped his own addition—a high-tech electronic keypad. Nineteenth-century security combined with twenty-first-century technology kept people, and the occasional floodwaters, out of the most personal part of his domain. He entered an eight-digit code on the keypad. At the green light, he inserted an old-fashioned key from his key ring, turned it, and pushed open the heavy door.

He took off his night-vision glasses and entered a large tunnel floored with wooden planks long worn gray with dust and soot and lit by amber bulbs strung along the ceiling. The bulbs looked old enough to have come from the workshop of the original Edison—Thomas himself.

His Edison bounded ahead. Joe followed along the planks toward home. As always, he paused before entering his house, amazed that he lived there.

The amber lights illuminated the neatly painted facade of a full-size Victorian house. Surrounded by stone, it looked as if someone had chiseled a house-shaped cavern into the schist, then teleported a building into it. He blinked, but the house was still there when he opened his eyes. Even now, his mind had trouble fathoming it. It was completely incongruous, but it was real. A three-story Victorian house built deep underground.

Nearly a century before, the eccentric lead engineer on the construction of Grand Central Terminal had been granted the weirdest perk Joe had ever heard of—a house buried in the tunnels far below Grand Central Terminal, deeded to his family in perpetuity, combined with access to all the tunnels in the system. It was his key ring that Joe carried on his belt, and the keys on it had opened every underground door that he had come across.

The engineer and his wife had raised their children in this fantastical house in the world beneath, taking them up in the elevator each day for school and outings. A few articles about their unusual living situation had appeared in turn-of-the-century newspapers, and then the world had moved on and forgotten.

The engineer's children had opted for lives aboveground. Following generations had used the family house only for parties. Joe's ex-girlfriend Celeste Gallo and her twin brother, Leandro, Joe's college roommate and old friend, were the final heirs to the house. Ever since Leandro had told him about it, Joe had itched to see it, but had never found time until he became trapped in New York not far from the house's entrance.

Tonight, Joe gazed at the house. The wooden facade glowed bright sulfur-yellow with clean white trim and gingerbread accents picked out in brick red. It resembled the famous painted ladies lining Alamo Square in San Francisco, except that this house stood a hundred feet below where it ought to.

Buried treasure.

He could see why Leandro had fought so hard to keep it after September 11, when the government had tried to have it closed down as a security risk. But Leandro's great-grandfather's contract had proved ironclad, and the house had stayed in Gallo hands.

He was just grateful that he'd persuaded Celeste, with whom he shared a complicated romantic history, to let him live here. It hadn't been easy, and Leandro had fought it. Leandro had claimed, "Digging Joe into a bigger hole is just enabling him." Leandro had told Joe that what he really needed was a good kick in the pants. That would cure his agoraphobia, and he could fly back to his life in California.

That wasn't going to be possible.

Celeste had won in the end because, like everyone else, Leandro couldn't deny her anything she wanted. So, the house was Joe's.

Edison stood in front of the front door, wagging his tail. He was ready to sack out. So was Joe.

As he walked up the stairs to open the door for the dog, he had an uneasy feeling. He and Edison had been exploring the tunnels for months, and they'd encountered only the occasional maintenance worker down this deep. Tonight, Joe had come across unfamiliar prints. They'd had pronounced ridges, more like hiking boots than the simple straight-line treads of the shoes worn by most transit employees, and they had ranged across dozens of the lower tunnels.

He'd met homeless people underground before, of course, clustered near subway platforms or in the upper tunnels, but no one had ever dared to come as deep as Joe's house.

Until now.

And Joe didn't like that at all.

2

November 27, 4:25 a.m.
Carrie Wilbur Home for Adults with Special Needs
Oyster Bay, New York

Ozan Saddiq loved coming to New York because he could
visit his brother, Erol, in the home. He couldn't care for
Erol in his own home, because he didn't have one, and both
of their parents were dead, so he paid a fortune to keep him
in this expensive facility, and Erol repaid him by being
happy. Erol excelled at being happy.

Erol liked Ozan to stay by his bed while he slept, so that
was where he sat. The home didn't allow overnight visitors,
so Ozan had to break in at night, after everyone left—a
simple task for a man with his talents.

Ozan studied the familiar room, the one constant in his
nomadic existence. Erol had his own room, for an extra fee,
decorated with manatees and sea turtles. The carpet was
aqua blue as were the walls. Even his comforter had an
aquatic theme—sea turtles swimming on a blue background
with bright yellow fish nibbling on their shells. Ozan
watched his brother breathe—almond-shaped eyes closed,
yellow-framed glasses folded on the nightstand, body
abandoned to a deep sleep Ozan could only imagine.

Chance had given Erol a genetic blueprint with Down
syndrome. It could just as easily have been Ozan in that bed.

Ozan tucked the cover under his brother's soft chin and turned to the demands of his latest client—Dr. Dubois. He wanted the job done immediately. He always did. Ozan had worked for him a few months before—driving a Navy boat laden with cargo he was forbidden to look at to a certain GPS location and then scuttling it. As the ship had sunk beneath the oil-black waves, he'd untied the motorized dinghy and piloted it across miles of open ocean to Florida.

Before he'd sunk the vessel, he'd examined the cargo. Corpses. One hundred and three of them. One hundred had had no visible wounds and might have died of natural causes. Three had had their throats slit with a savagery that spoke of great anger and strength, one of them burned beyond recognition. When the doctor had contacted him again this time, he'd doubled his fee.

He took a teacup from its place on Erol's nightstand next to a picture of the two of them together at the New York Aquarium. Ozan had brought his own thermos of Turkish tea, brewed strong like their mother used to make. It would be a long night for him.

He inserted the memory stick into its port in his laptop, aware that he would be unable to copy anything from it and the data would erase itself twenty-four hours from the time he viewed it. He could memorize details quickly, another gift he'd received from their parents that Erol hadn't. It was a useful talent in his business.

Because Ozan's business was killing.

Like many men, he'd learned to kill in the Army. Like few, he was very good at it. People noticed the care, if not the pleasure, he took doing it, and those people put him in touch with others who would pay for his unique gifts.

He was an aficionado of death. He could be quick and brutal, or slow and elegant. What he was, above all else, was discreet. His murders were viewed as accidental deaths when required, or pinned on others if necessary. He rose to the demands of each occasion.

His prey always underestimated him. A slight man, he didn't seem like a threat. With black hair cropped short, compact small hands, graceful movements, wide brown eyes—he looked like a waiter.

Erol snorted in his sleep. It sounded like a laugh, and Ozan smiled at him before returning to his reading. For this job he must locate the target, known only as Subject 523, and kill him. That part was straightforward.

A moth fluttered against Erol's bedside lamp. Ozan's hand flicked out and caught it. He held the creature against the hot bulb with his forefinger. It waggled its tiny legs as if it could escape him. He held it there, ignoring the pain in his finger until the faint smell of burning hair reached his nostrils, then he let it go. The dead moth fell to the nightstand, and he brushed it to the floor.

He read the next paragraph of the file, twice, surprised by the requirement that he send the doctor a very particular kind of proof that he had completed the job. He wasn't squeamish, but the strangeness of the request startled even him.

He read on. If the subject possessed classified documents, they must be returned unread. If the subject had shared those documents with others, then additional targets might need to be defined. But he didn't think on that yet. He would deal with each challenge as it came, examine it thoroughly, then let it go.

A few minutes of research on his laptop dug up a press report that told him Dr. Dubois wasn't telling the whole truth about his target. Clients rarely told the entire truth, but the flash of disappointment made him frown. It wasn't that they lied, it was that they thought him naïve enough to believe them. As if he were Erol, open and trusting.

He scanned the article. A homeless man had beaten an unidentified businessman to death with a hammer outside the Grand Central Hyatt a few weeks before. The businessman need not remain unidentified—Ozan recognized his picture in the newspaper. They ran in the same circles, competed for the same jobs, although his fees were reportedly lower than Ozan's. Regardless, he wouldn't have been an easy man to surprise or overpower, even by a hammer-wielding crazy man.

Ozan must assume that the murdered man had pursued the same quarry as he, and he'd not only been killed while doing so, he'd also attracted attention, which made Ozan's job much more delicate. The target had been on the run for an indeterminate amount of time before the murdered colleague had found him. Then the target had killed the man sent to kill him, and more time had gone by.

For this man he should take his time, be even more thorough and careful than usual. The man was dangerous, and Ozan wanted to know all the variables in play.

Instead, he was to rush, as the doctor had made it clear that the subject must be dead within four days. After fumbling about for months, they had given Ozan ninety-six hours.

What could possibly be so urgent?

3

Vivian Torres drew in a deep breath. Sure, it smelled like smog, but it was still good. The cold winter sun shone on her long-sleeved running suit as she tightened her shoelaces. She stood at the Manhattan end of the Brooklyn Bridge, watching random tourists amble across its iconic span. They were bundled up in jackets and scarves, breath frosting out in front of them.

She gathered her black hair into a ponytail. She'd just gotten it cut, and it was barely long enough. When she did a few quick stretches, she drew admiring glances from a couple of passing guys. At six feet tall and Army strong, she was used to the attention and ignored them.

"Just a short run, right? Nothing competitive," asked Dirk. He'd come to run with her. They'd served together in the Army before her discharge, and he knew she was competitive.

"More like a stroll than a run." She stood and stretched first one leg and then the other.

"Sure," he said sarcastically. Dirk, with his honorable discharge and family connections, had gone straight from the Army to the police. Vivian, with her dishonorable one, had been stuck working private security.

"Ready?" He ran a hand through his short blond hair and bounced from foot to foot. He was an inch shorter than Vivian but a faster runner.

She counted down from three, and they took off. She took an early lead and lengthened it. In a straight line, she was slower than he was, but she was better at dodging obstacles, which is how she thought of the tourists. His well-muscled physique, kept in top form through daily weight lifting, looked good, but it meant that he couldn't get around people as quickly as she could.

She poured on more speed when she hit an open stretch, knowing he'd make up time on her when he got clear of people. Crisp air cooled her sweaty cheeks.

The Brooklyn end of the bridge beckoned, but she slowed to let Dirk catch up. They both knew she would have won, and that was all that mattered.

They reached the end and stopped, both breathing hard. She stared up at the Watchtower, the Jehovah's Witnesses building in Brooklyn. As usual, she felt as if someone in the tower was spying on her, and a shiver ran down her back.

"How the hell did you pass the lady with the double stroller?" Dirk sounded winded.

"Matrix-style," she told him. "Same as always."

They headed back across the bridge, walking without talking, catching their breath. She'd missed this—the easy camaraderie of soldiers. She was close to her family, but it wasn't the same as the bond she shared with Dirk.

"So, what's bothering you?" Dirk asked. His sea-blue eyes met hers, and he waited.

He'd see right through a denial. "About six months ago, I lost a guy I was supposed to be following."

"Happens to everyone sometimes. Even you."

While they walked, she told him how she'd been assigned to babysit a Silicon Valley software executive. He wasn't supposed to know she was there. It had started out easy, but then he'd left his hotel and disappeared in the column in Grand Central Terminal—the one inside the famous clock. She could still see it in her mind—she'd been across the concourse, checking out the time on its four opal faces, when he'd stepped into the information booth and then actually gone inside the pillar.

"I never knew the pillar had a door," Dirk said. "Don't see how that's your fault."

"Maybe." She shrugged. When you were tailing people, sometimes they got lost. But it usually happened to other people, not her. "Anyway, he came out a couple of hours later, totally trashed."

"Drunk?"

"Something like that," she said. "I dragged him back to his hotel, had an altercation with another guy along the way, and tucked the executive into his own little bed."

"Altercation?" Dirk grinned. "Did the other guy walk away?"

She paused to stretch her hamstrings, muscles gone stiff from the air outside. "Actually, the jerk was kind of curled up in a fetal position when I left him. But he had it coming."

"What did he do?" Dirk put on his jacket.

"He jumped me by the shoe-shine benches in front of Grand Central. You know the spot?"

"I do."

"I was coming out practically carrying my guy, and this teenager comes up and asks for our money. Nicely, he said he was collecting for charity and needed a donation."

"And so late at night, too. That shows dedication." Dirk moved aside to let a teenage couple pass, their hands in each other's back pockets.

"He flashed a knife to make sure I contributed the right amount."

Dirk winced. "Poor kid."

"I disarmed him," she said. "Without doing any permanent damage. I couldn't turn my back on him, so I made him aware that it takes one hundred ten pounds of pressure per square inch to rupture a testicle."

"Does it?" Dirk moved a step back.

"So I've read," she said. "Sadly, I was forced to apply about eighty pounds of pressure to the aforementioned area."

"I bet that subdued him."

"He gave me no further trouble while I took my client back to his hotel."

Dirk laughed. "Sounds like you did a hell of a job protecting your client, even from himself."

"That's what worries me." Vivian pulled the most recent issue of *Forbes* magazine out of her backpack and handed it to Dirk. "It's the cover article."

Tesla's face smiled from the front cover. He was pale, like software engineers were supposed to be, with high cheekbones and well-formed lips, the top one dipped in the center like a bow, almost feminine. Curly black hair was cut to his jaw line. He wore a light blue suit that matched his eyes. And he grinned like he'd played the greatest trick ever on the world.

Dirk read aloud as he skimmed it. "Joe Tesla, software millionaire...set to ring the bell at the New York Stock Exchange on the day his facial-recognition software company, Pellucid, went public . . . software uses a revolutionary algorithm . . . CTO never showed up . . . has disappeared from sight . . . rumors are that he has developed agoraphobia and not left the Grand Central Hyatt for six months."

Vivian sighed.

"This was your guy?"

She stared down at the green water flowing far beneath the bridge. "Something happened to him down there."

Dirk stood close to her, his warm form sheltering her from the wind. "How do you know?"

"He had no trouble going outside when I was following him. He trotted right over to the terminal and stumbled back. He didn't have agoraphobia then, but he does now."

"Weird, but not your problem."

"What if it is?" She shifted from one foot to the other in the cold. "What if something happened to him down there, something that wouldn't have happened if I'd been there, and that's what changed him?"

"Even if," he said. "He's a big boy. Not your job keeping him out of trouble all the time."

"That night, it was." She clenched her jaw. "And I blew it."

"What are you going to do about it?" Dirk asked. She liked it that he didn't try to talk her out of anything, just asked questions.

"I don't know yet," she said. "But something."

"You'd be better off letting it go."

"Sure," she said. "You're right."

They both knew she wouldn't listen to his advice.

4

Edison's warm nose nuzzled against Joe's knee, and he looked up from his laptop. "What, boy? Can't you see I'm busy?"

He wasn't really busy. He was never busy these days. On the day of his first panic attack, he'd quit work. Now he just screwed around online.

The dog looked pointedly toward the door. He wanted to go outside. The poor guy had been watching Joe stare at his laptop screen and pound on the keys for hours. Dogs must think humans are completely strange.

Joe checked his laptop's clock. Just after three. Time for Edison's walk. It was as if the dog had his own built-in chronometer. Joe stood up and stretched, causing Edison to make a break for the door. Joe loitered and looked around the room. It had originally been called the parlor, and it existed in a kind of time warp. Crimson velvet curtains, drawn on two walls, seemed to shut out the light of day. But, of course, they didn't. The light of day never made it down here. The curtains hid stained glass windows backed by stone.

He'd been sitting in a leather wingback chair with his

laptop. In front of him an electric fireplace crackled like the real thing. He turned it on most evenings, for the warmth and the soothing noise. Even though the fireplace looked modern, the mantel built around it was an antique treasure made of hand-carved mahogany. He counted the sea shells scattered atop it—cyan, blue, red, green, brown, orange, and slate flashed in his head. A human skull rested among them and a statue of the Egyptian cat Goddess, *Bastet*, carved from black basalt. It had been collected by the Victorian gentleman who'd insisted on living here, in the midst of his greatest creation.

Joe envied him. As much as he loved the house, he didn't live here by choice. If he could have gone, he'd have been outside in a heartbeat, living in a glass house with the ceiling open to the sky. But he couldn't.

Joe turned off the fireplace and walked past the floor-to-ceiling bookshelves filled with leather-bound volumes and passed a large oil painting of a girl in a gauzy white dress. He found Edison waiting in the front hall, holding his leash in his mouth, next to an umbrella stand made from an elephant's leg. Joe made sure that Edison got outside in the sunlight and fresh air every day—he wasn't about to force the dog to stay in his underground prison all the time. Like everyone else in New York, he'd hired a dog walker.

They closed the door and walked along the planks to the elevator. The house sat in the middle of a long tunnel. Both ends of the tunnel were capped by giant metal doors accessible only by entering the eight-digit code and using the key in Joe's pocket. Near one end of the tunnel was an elevator that would take him up into the famous clock at Grand Central Terminal. He also knew of a fourth exit—a secret passageway behind the bookcase in his bedroom that he'd discovered quite by accident—but he rarely used it because he had to scramble through it on his hands and knees.

He pressed the button, and the elevator doors opened automatically. Since he was practically the only one who ever came down here, the elevator was where he'd left it.

The doors opened on an antique birdcage elevator of curling wrought iron. The wall beyond was visible through the metal lacework. This contraption was older than Joe, his mother, and probably his grandmother.

He tried not to think about it. With Edison at his heels, Joe stepped inside and pulled the metal grate closed, before moving the elevator lever to the side. He had to hold it in position all the way up, or the car would stop.

Stone walls slid by. He imagined poking his finger through the fancy iron, pulling back a bloody stump. Elevators had come a long way in the last century. Now they had safety features, like walls and extra cables. Even with those safety features, twenty-six (blue for two, orange for six) people per year died in elevators. What'd those numbers been like when they built this behemoth?

As usual, though, the creaky old elevator functioned flawlessly, and the doors opened onto a tiny room with a spiral staircase. At the top of the stairs he lifted a hatch and climbed out with Edison close behind, carefully closing the hatch before turning to the next door. It opened into the round information booth underneath the clock in the center of Grand Central Terminal.

"Good afternoon, Miss Evaline," he said to the cheerful black woman sitting on the chair there.

She gave him a quick nod before returning to dispensing rapid-fire advice to a lost traveler. She had an extraordinary memory and was unfailingly polite and patient even as she had kindly refused him admission to the information booth over and over until he'd gotten his paperwork in order to move down below.

As always, his eyes were drawn upward to the giant rounded ceiling, background now restored to greenish blue with Zodiac constellations painted on it. It was the only night sky he ever saw anymore.

No self-pity.

He glanced toward the square pillars standing along one side of the concourse and at each of the large staircases flanking the giant room. One set of stairs led to a giant American flag and a restaurant, the other to another restaurant with no flag. He'd eaten at both.

Straight ahead in the hall, people darted back and forth like ants across the polished marble floor. Some headed to the giant information board that listed scheduled trains. Others walked down to the train platforms. He and Edison wove through them to the interior hall leading to the Grand Hyatt Hotel.

Unlike the terminal, the Hyatt was modern. It made no attempt at old-fashioned architectural style, just dark glass walls and a flashy silver front at street level. Functional, straightforward, uncomplicated. Its only nod to color was the red slash through its logo. Joe remembered these details from when he'd checked in, six months before.

Joe had to take a few deep breaths to cross through, because one side was a wall of glass lit by sunshine. He could deal with windows, but only if they weren't too big and had substantial frames. He pulled open the heavy door and stepped inside the opulent lobby, the genteel patter of a fountain the only sound, the room empty but for a few seats occupied by well-dressed travelers.

He and Edison headed straight to the wooden coffee shack housing Starbucks. Tiffany already had his coffee waiting. Service with a smile, every afternoon.

A spray of freckles danced on the bridge of her nose when she smiled. The distinctive pattern of those freckles set her face apart from anyone else's on earth. He tipped her, bought today's *New York Times*, and sat to read it. His new daily routine—the refuge of the unemployed or the early retired—crossword puzzles.

He scanned the lobby for Leandro. Some afternoons, if Leandro was free, he would join Joe for coffee. After giving up on the battle for the house, he'd been surprisingly sensitive to Joe's condition.

No Leandro today, which meant Joe had nothing to distract him.

According to the *New York Times*, his erstwhile company was doing well without him. On the day Joe had freaked out, Sunil Raghavan, Pellucid's chief financial officer and Joe's best friend at the company, had managed to get Joe back to his room and then cabbed it to the NYSE himself in time to watch the chief executive officer ring the bell that Joe, as chief technology officer, was supposed to have rung.

Joe had retired that very day. The new CTO still called him with questions, and every month or so the other executives mounted a campaign to persuade him to come back. What use was a man who couldn't even go outside?

He was grateful that one of the Gallos, probably his friend Leandro, had run down a fiber-optic cable to wire the underground house for Internet. Joe'd hooked it up to a couple of Wi-Fi routers so that he had Internet all over the house and for some distance into the tunnels outside. Being fully connected gave him access to a giant trove of time-wasting media.

A woman in black spandex pants and a green jacket jogged across the lobby. She passed the escalator and sprinted down the stairs, auburn ponytail bobbing. He counted to ten (cyan, blue, red, green, brown, orange, slate, purple, scarlet, and cyan plus black). She was probably outside by now, running down the dirty sidewalk, buildings leaning in toward her, hundreds of people jostling against her. He willed himself to think of something else, to calm his breathing, to still his racing heart.

He'd tried to go outside again, several times. Each time he'd reached the bottom of the escalator, he'd known he would die if he took another step. The psychiatrists labeled his feelings a panic attack. An attack of panic. True, but not useful. It failed to capture the intensity of the experience, how his brain short-circuited and drove him back from the door.

He'd always trusted his brain, but now it was betraying him.

No one could tell him why. In the first days, he'd grilled the doctors and scoured the Internet, searching for a reason why he was incapacitated if he tried to do something he'd done every single day of his life—go outside.

His sources said that sudden onset agoraphobia was not unusual. A little over three million (red followed by six beats of black) people in the US suffered from agoraphobia, and no one knew why it sometimes appeared out of the clear blue sky. There were theories, but none stood up to careful scrutiny. His psychiatrists, and he'd been through a few, seemed to agree that he needed to work on controlling his panic attacks, that the first attack was probably triggered by the stress of taking Pellucid public and perhaps a genetic predisposition passed down the Tesla line. Joe's father, too, had agoraphobia, and a few had speculated that their most-famous ancestor, Nikola Tesla, had had it, too.

Joe had asked them if his condition could have been triggered by a chemical, if a person might have slipped a drug into his drink at the party he'd attended the night before his agoraphobia struck. This suggestion had been met with a universal "no." Long-term tranquilizer and alcohol abuse might cause agoraphobia, but nothing they knew of could do it in one shot. He'd demanded, and gotten, blood tests that had revealed nothing and caused the psychiatrists to brand him as paranoid.

His hands trembled as he opened the newspaper. The shakes came from the last dregs of the antidepressants. He'd been through a couple of regimens designed to calm him down enough to get his feet onto the sidewalk outside. None had worked, and each one had made him stupider than the last. He had to think clearly, so he'd stopped the drugs.

He'd stay inside forever before he'd poison his brain.

Besides, he was managing just fine. He had plenty of room to roam. An internal walkway linked Grand Central Terminal to the Hyatt, so he could get there without going through the front door and outside. The giant complex contained restaurants and all the shops he needed. It was big enough to give him exercise, and he'd joined the Vanderbilt Tennis and Fitness Club on the third floor of the station. He didn't play tennis, but it had a decent gym and a window looking out onto the street below, under the giant statue of Mercury he'd admired on the last day he had been able to go outside. Plus, he had his new house and the tunnels underneath New York—train tunnels, subway tunnels, steam tunnels, coal chutes. He had a bigger range than most people chose to exercise.

But he lived in fear that it would get worse. That his brain would betray him again, make him terrified of more things, shrink his world into smaller and smaller circles. Moving down into the tunnels was his attempt to fight back. It would have been too easy just to stay at the Hyatt forever, waited on hand and foot, but down here he had miles and miles to explore.

Whole afternoons were spent wandering the platforms underneath Grand Central Terminal, breathing in the smell of soot and engine oil, and watching people board trains and head off into the wider world. It cheered him up. He had things under control. He was fine.

Right now, though, he had nothing to do but wait for the dog walker, and he was bored. And a bored Joe was trouble. A little bit of hacking would make him feel better. Nothing big. Or maybe something big was what he needed.

He clicked on the picture of a seagull nestled behind several of his on-screen windows. He'd downloaded it the night before, thinking to do something with the image to make Celeste smile—maybe an animation of it flying.

Now he had a better idea. He grinned as he opened his laptop. He'd already cloaked its IP address so that it was difficult to trace, but he bounced through a few computers before he got to an illegal iPhone-monitoring site he'd heard about. With a few clicks, he checked Times Square for iPhones. Plenty to choose from.

He brought up a live camera view of Times Square to see the precise location of those phones. Some were right where he needed them. By the billboards.

As he'd expected, most of the billboards used Wi-Fi feeds with simple encryption. Not a problem. He hummed as he took control of one billboard after another, beaming the image of a seagull through his network of borrowed phones and onto the electronic billboards.

He smiled as the seagull in flight appeared next to one person and then another when he shifted the image from phone to phone. It looked as if a flock of giant seagulls flew in and out between the billboards. Slowly, people noticed. Then, they stopped and stared. Even the ones whose phones he'd hijacked had no idea of their role in the drama unfolding around them.

A stir in the lobby drew his attention from his laptop. A few quick keystrokes disconnected him from the phones and computers until his laptop looked ordinary and honest. He bet the seagulls would make the news. He'd have to tell Celeste to watch for it. Seagulls were her favorite birds.

Edison stood and wagged his tail, and Joe followed his gaze. Andres Peterson, a half-Estonian artist, was walking across the lobby toward them. A long woolen coat that looked as if it had been through a mysterious Eastern European war or two flared out behind him. He had light blue eyes and artfully disheveled brown hair. Celeste had recommended him as both an artist and a dog walker. Joe liked the photos he'd seen of his melancholy giant metal sculptures, and Edison adored him.

"Good afternoon, Mr. Tesla." Andres took Edison's head in his hands. "And Edison the Dog."

Edison's eyes shone and his tail wagged furiously. Edison was usually a somber dog, but Andres turned him into a puppy.

"Today we go to Central Park, bury some bones?" He lifted an eyebrow to ask. A scar bisected the eyebrow, perhaps from a fight or a long-ago piercing. The scar worked as a distinctive identifying mark. With his air of mystery and sexy accent, Andres was more Celeste's type than Joe had ever been, and Joe wondered again if the two had dated.

"Central Park sounds good," Joe said. No point in being jealous of the past. He liked Andres—the man was good-natured, smart, and great at his dog-walking job.

"One day, you come with us," Andres said. "Not always working."

Joe suspected that Celeste hadn't told Andres about his condition. If she had, Andres never let on. "Maybe."

He handed Andres the leash and watched the pair walk across the lobby on their way outside. For them, it was as simple as that.

Once they were out of sight, he dialed the number he'd dialed every day since he'd become trapped in New York.

He held his breath waiting for an answer. One ring, cyan; two rings, blue; three rings, red.

"Hey, Joe," said a weak and breathless voice.

"Celeste." Relief flooded through him. She was well enough to talk on the phone.

"Think me a number," she said.

"Seven," he said. "Slate blue, like your eyes."

Only Celeste understood about the numbers. A talented abstract painter, she loved blocks of color. She danced them around in her head as he did numbers.

"A cheap line," she whispered. "I'll take it."

"Your eyes are cerulean," he said. "Blue with a wash of gray, like slate or the sea before a storm—and the number seven."

A tiny laugh came down the line, and he laughed with her.

When they'd been together, she'd painted him a giant canvas using shades of blue and gray, and called it Joe's #7. It hung on the wall of his house in California. By the time he'd thought to buy it, it had cost a fortune. He made a mental note to get the painting shipped to New York.

"Is it a strong day?" he asked.

"Minus one," she answered.

Celeste had amyotrophic lateral sclerosis, commonly known as Lou Gehrig's Disease. It was slowly paralyzing her. Eventually, it would reach her respiratory system, and she would die. Most people who contracted it died within three to five years. He reminded himself every day that Stephen Hawking lived with it for more than fifty years (brown followed by black—a big, reassuring number).

"Minus one," he said. "Cyan for one, but pale because it's negative."

"You make me smile," she said.

"I made you a present today."

"Oh, God," she said. "Have you taken up knitting or

papier-mâché?"

"Not yet." He smiled. "Check the news. Look for the seagulls."

She laughed, a short wheezy sound. "As soon as I get off the phone, but I wish you were here to show me in person."

His stomach clenched. "If I could, I'd get a cab at the curb and see you in ten minutes."

"Best you don't," she said. "My hair looks awful."

"You always say that." He remembered the last time he'd seen her, how her wavy blond hair had blown into his mouth when she hugged him good-bye at an airport. "And it's never true. You have the most beautiful hair I've ever seen—like butterscotch syrup with strands of honey gold."

"Remember the chocolate syrup at my parents' house in the Hamptons?"

"Till my dying day." Messy for the sheets, but worth every frantic second of cleanup after.

"It should have been butterscotch."

He closed his eyes and wished that he could arrive on her doorstep with a jar of butterscotch syrup and a smile. Of all the things the agoraphobia had taken from him, this was the worst.

"Joe?"

"Just thinking." He would order a butterscotch sundae sent to her penthouse apartment. It was New York City, and he was a multimillionaire, how hard could it be? It wasn't what he most wanted to do with that syrup, but it was better than nothing.

"Any progress on breaking out of your prison?" she asked.

He hesitated. She rarely spoke of his illness, or of her own. "You have it a million times worse. I know that."

"Do I?" she asked. "Everyone pities me and cares for me, and no one ever blames me for this. No one tells me to buck up and stop being such a pussy. Even when I am a pussy."

"I'd trade you," he said.

"Only because you want to cure me, because you're a hopeless romantic."

"Hopeful romantic," he said.

She sputtered into the phone.

"You OK?" he asked.

"The nurse Googled seagulls," she said. "Times Square? You rogue."

Joe smiled. The risk of the hacking had been worth it to hear lightness in her voice again.

5

Rebar reached the half-empty train platforms. The numbers twenty-three and twenty-four told him he'd found the right place. He liked to go down into the tunnels from Platform 23. It felt right. He ducked to the side, away from a familiar silver train with blue stripes, and made for the far end of the platform, centering himself between the rows of fluorescent lights that hung from the ceiling next to the tracks and avoiding the yellow stripes installed on the floor to tell people when they were getting too near the trains. He didn't like the color yellow anymore, although he couldn't remember why.

In Cuba his door had been painted yellow. Maybe that was it. There, the doctors had called him Subject 523, but here, in the tunnels and streets of New York City, the homeless called him Rebar. He liked the name. Ramrod straight, hard iron, invisible—but at the center of everything, giving it shape and strength.

Not a lot of folks came down here this late. Once the train left, the platform would be empty, and no one would notice what he did. He walked by people stumbling on to the train. Late-night smells assailed his nostrils—beer, onions, and wet wool.

A couple leaned against the railing by the entrance with their arms around each other and their tongues down each other's throats. The sheer animal need of them brought memories—girls he'd kissed and girls he hadn't. He hadn't kissed enough of them.

He walked until he reached the end of the subway platform. The train made ready to leave, and the amorous couple hurried aboard. Two men slurred insults at each other, but neither seemed to have the energy or the passion to act on them. He made himself small against the wall and waited.

It was warm here, and safe. Maybe he should just sit here for a while. He was tired all the time since Cuba. Maybe he just needed rest.

The train pulled out and away, red taillights growing small.

The platform was empty. He could have dropped a grenade in here without hurting anyone. White light beat down on flattened gum, forgotten newspapers, an empty paper cup.

He dozed and woke with a jerk. He had to go down. It was his mission. Without checking to see if anyone had come onto the platform, he vaulted the metal divider and trotted down the stairs without breaking stride. No shouts behind him, but he didn't slacken his pace until he was fifty yards in and invisible to anyone in the station.

He walked through the graffiti, broken beer bottles, and used condoms that gathered by the platforms, half-hearted attempts to assert ownership over the dark tunnel. Most desperate people's tolerance for darkness extended about a hundred feet in.

He had a much higher tolerance than other people. For a lot of things.

He stopped next to the second pillar unmarked by graffiti

and picked up his tools. He hefted a sledgehammer in one hand, a battery-powered lantern in the other. The pockets of his filthy jacket bulged with maps and papers, some old and others new. Since he'd left Cuba, he'd carried them with him everywhere. He needed to keep them safe, but also to reread them often to remind himself that he wasn't crazy. Everyone was wrong about that. And he had to do it soon. He'd overheard them talking about December. December first was an important deadline for them. He wasn't sure why right at this moment, but he would remember it again.

The yellowed pages crinkled when he moved. They were important. That's why he'd stolen them from a filing cabinet in the Naval hospital. They described experiments carried out years before he was born by scientists taken straight from Nazi Germany and put to work for the US government. Even they had abandoned this research because it was deemed too risky.

Years later, however, another doctor had started the research back up. On him and five hundred men like him. He just had to prove it.

Even in the cool tunnel, sweat dripped off his nose, and he slowed his pace. It was the fever. He was weaker than he used to be. Before, he'd hiked for hours without faltering, but not anymore. Not since they infected him. The tiny organisms swimming around in his blood were eating away at his strength, his control, his identity.

He was too weak to protect the papers now. He must find a place to hide them. That way, if he were ever caught, they wouldn't get the information. But what if he forgot where he hid them? He forgot so many things these days.

Setting down the heavy hammer, he patted his pockets. The papers were there. A big man had tried to take them from him. Rebar thought that he'd killed the thief, but he couldn't remember. Whatever had happened, the thief hadn't bothered him again. The papers were safe.

A far-off rumble warned him of an approaching train. He picked up his hammer and stepped over the third rail, being careful to keep clear of the tracks' points. They might snap together as a train approached, shunting the train off in a different direction. If his foot got caught in one, he could lose it. Or be killed by the train.

He couldn't be hit, and he couldn't be seen. If the train engineer saw him, he'd call it in, and transit police would be down here with flashlights and baying dogs. It'd happened once before, and only his knowledge of the tunnel layout had saved him. He worked from a map that was older than theirs. It showed extra tunnels, and access doors that led to long-unused rooms. Places to hide. He needed a place to hide right now, from the train.

Two sets of tracks separated by concrete pillars ran up ahead. If he hurried, he could take cover behind a column on the side away from the approaching train. Good enough. Not caring about his fever or his weakness, he ran and ducked behind a pillar before the train's headlights came into view. He leaned his back hard into the cool concrete.

The sound and shaking reminded him of night combat, of the aftermath of an IED, except that this went on and on, noise and light and the ground heaving under his feet. He'd fallen to his knees by the time the last car passed, the faces of dead friends swimming before his eyes as the red taillights winked out in the distance.

He fought back against the memories and forced himself to his feet. He was in New York, not Afghanistan or Cuba. His buddies weren't here. And he had a lot of tunnel to walk tonight. Hours.

He would not think about how he was searching for objects that might not exist.

According to the papers in his pockets, the scientist

who'd done the first experiments after World War II had last been seen on a train heading from Washington, DC, to New York, but the car had never arrived. The official version was that he'd escaped with the files and taken them back to Europe to sell to the highest bidder. The project had been shut down after that, deemed too risky to continue even with another scientist.

But Rebar didn't believe the doctor had fled. He would not have fled. The United States was the safest place for him to be. Someone had taken the man before he'd arrived and silenced him. And, if he had gone back to Europe, what had happened to the train car? No, a bad thing had happened to him on the way to New York.

If someone had taken that car from the open tracks between the cities, Rebar would never find it. So his only hope was that the car had been abandoned underneath the city. He had a map on which he'd marked potential tunnels in red and crossed them off in black after he'd cleared them. For weeks he'd been walking through old passages, checking walls, seeking decades-old clues. It was crazy, but no crazier than anything else.

And his best chance lay up ahead. He knew it. Sometimes, he forgot what he was looking for, but not today. Today he was looking for answers.

He felt stronger than he had minutes before and whistled as he walked on the train ties, stepping on every other tie as if it were a game that he could win. The lantern didn't weigh much, and even the sledgehammer didn't slow him down anymore. Today was a good day.

6

November 28, 2:35 a.m.
Tunnels under Grand Central Terminal

Joe closed the heavy metal door behind him and moved through the dark tunnel. He donned his night-vision goggles, settling the strap behind the back of his head. The round contours of the tunnel jumped into sharper focus. He ran his fingers along the rough stone wall. In a few yards it would join with an active train tunnel, and he could already make out the lighter entrance where they met.

"Ready for another night out?" He looked down at Edison's bright shape.

The dog didn't seem to hear him. He stared off to his right, his head cocked to the side as if he were listening to a far-off sound. Joe stood still, straining his ears. He heard only the wind through the tunnels and the faraway rumble of a single train.

Whatever it was, it bothered Edison, so Joe might as well check it out. It might be the person whose boot prints he'd begun to see in the tunnels. Joe felt proprietary about the tunnels, as if they belonged to him, instead of just the house and the small tunnel that ran between the two doors.

"Find it!" he ordered Edison, and the yellow dog trotted forward. He didn't put his nose to the ground, but instead held his head up and his ears pointed forward. Whatever he was tracking, he was tracking it by sound instead of scent.

After a few minutes' walk, Joe heard it, too. A thud echoed down the tunnel. It wasn't a train—too slow. It was rhythmic, like the beat of a sad song. He'd never heard a sound quite like it, and he wanted to know what it was. It might be dangerous, but he had to know.

He trotted forward for about a quarter mile until the tunnel ended at a vast well-lit chamber where the tracks came in from outside and merged toward Grand Central Terminal. He and Edison often played fetch here.

The thuds changed to a clanking sound. It drew him to the left, to an unlit siding. A quick glance at the ground told him that this was the person who had been leaving the footprints. Feeling like one of the children who followed the Pied Piper to their death, Joe turned sideways and slipped between black-painted columns.

He had to know, and he had to share knowledge. This trait had cost him dearly at Pellucid when the CIA began to insist that only they should get the high-powered version of the facial-recognition software, while the rest of the world got a dumbed-down version. The demand, a veiled threat really, had resulted in bitter discussions between Joe and the other chief executives at Pellucid. They were all for giving the CIA what they wanted and not risking the IPO. That way everyone could make money and be happy. Even dumbed down, the software was still the best on the market. But Joe had insisted that the software was too powerful to leave in the hands of a single agency—if they were going to release it, everyone should have a right to use it.

His insistence on making the knowledge free to everyone had alienated everyone except for Sunil, but Joe had the majority shares, so they had to go along with him. In the subsequent legal battle, Pellucid had prevailed, at least for now. The upshot was that Joe had lost his closest friends.

Still, he'd been right.

He hefted his heavy metal flashlight in one hand. A weapon in a pinch.

He crept forward, trying to make as little noise as possible, keeping to the wooden ties. A yellow glow led him on. A minute later the source of the sound was illuminated by a battery-powered lantern set on the rocky ground—a scarecrow of a man pounding a brick wall with a sledgehammer. With each stroke, he mumbled a word. Gradually, Joe realized that he was counting. A man after his own heart.

The man's ragged pants and filthy jacket resembled desert-style camouflage, although it was hard to say through the thick coating of dirt and soot. The man struck the wall again, back straight, form perfect. His posture said that he was military.

Whoever he was, he was taller than Joe, and looked stronger, too.

Joe debated leaving him alone. The man was only damaging an old wall, and the wall wasn't Joe's business. No point in messing with a man with a hammer. But Joe had to know why.

Before he could decide what to do, the man wheeled around, hammer held high. Edison growled a warning.

"It's just me," Joe said, as if the hammerer knew him.

The man's glassy blue eyes came into focus. His eyes were set farther apart than average, one a few millimeters higher than the other, and his face gleamed with sweat. "They call me Rebar. Or Subject 523."

The numbers flashed in Joe's head: brown, blue, red.

"Joe," he offered, trying not to let on that he was frightened. "Nice to meet you."

Rebar lowered the hammer, and Joe relaxed. The man stood well over six feet. Joe bet he could do serious damage if provoked. Even without the hammer.

Rebar put the hammer head on the ground and leaned the handle against his baggy pants. His clothes hung on him as if he were a coat hanger instead of a man, as if he'd lost a lot of weight over a short time. His pockets bulged with dirty papers.

"Interesting wall you got there, soldier," Joe said, inanely. How did you strike up a conversation with a crazy man in the middle of a dark tunnel in the middle of the night? You didn't. You ran. But the unsolved problem kept him there.

Hefting the hammer, Rebar half-turned back to the wall. Joe followed his gaze. Soot had settled on the mortar between the broken bricks, and black lines streaked down the side. That wall had been put up a long time ago, probably before Rebar was born. Why was he knocking it down?

"What are you after?" Joe drew himself to his full height, deliberately echoing Rebar's military posture.

"Completing my mission, sir." Rebar rasped his hand across dirty brown stubble on his receding chin. "The month is almost up."

"Mission?" Joe stood straight, legs apart, hands loose by his sides, ready to run if he had to. Edison kept his distance from the man, too.

Rebar gestured with the hammer's wooden handle. "Been looking for what's back there for a long time."

"Mind if I stick around to see?"

"No, sir. I do not mind," Rebar said, but the scowl on his face indicated otherwise.

Joe leaned against the cold steel pillar and waited. Rebar picked up the hammer again and smacked it into the bricks, the noise echoing down the tunnel. Brick chips caromed off the wall, one slicing a thin line into Rebar's stubbled cheek. He didn't seem to notice.

Brick dust, soot, and crushed cement swirled around the

hammering man. He looked like a genie emerging from the glowing lantern in a cloud of red and gray dust. Rebar coughed, spit next to the rusty tracks, and went back to hammering, counting each blow.

Should Joe offer to take a turn? What was the etiquette on performing public acts of vandalism with an accomplice? Lookout or criminal, those were the roles. That made him the lookout. He should sneak off. But he stayed.

A section of wall at Rebar's shoulder height gave, toppling forward to create a dark hole. Joe blinked in surprise. He pushed off the pillar and stood straight.

Joe fidgeted from side to side while Rebar pounded the broken section until it was big enough to climb through. Joe wanted him to stop so that he could peek at the secret behind the wall, but he kept his peace. After all, the mission was Rebar's, not his.

Rebar picked up the lantern and held it above his head like an old-time lighthouse keeper, warning ships away from the rocks. The man's grotesque shadow leaped across the pillar and fell on Joe's hand.

Without turning around, the man thrust the lantern through the hole. The tunnel around Joe went dark. The silhouette of Rebar's head against the yellow light blocked Joe's view inside.

Joe moved next to him, leaning forward eagerly. He couldn't wait to see it.

"Permission to see inside?" he asked.

The horse-like smell of Rebar's sweat blanketed the air, reminding him how much bigger, stronger, and crazier Rebar was than he. Rebar leaned away with a grunt, leaving the arm holding the lantern in the bricked-up room.

Joe peered through the hole. In the center of the room stood a single blue train car. Rust bloomed along its steel side like dark lichen. The window glass looked more than twice as thick as normal train windows, watery green behind a patina of dust. Bulletproof. A familiar circular seal adorned the car's side—an eagle bearing a laurel branch in one clawed foot and arrows in the other. He didn't need to read the words above it to know what they said: Seal of the President of the United States.

A legend in the tunnels. He had heard of a special train car that had carried Franklin Delano Roosevelt to New York during the Second World War, stopping two hundred feet underneath the Waldorf Astoria, a short walk from a freight elevator used to carry FDR and his automobile up to the hotel parking lot during the war. After the war, the car had vanished.

Until now.

Rebar had found it. But why?

A flash of ivory drew Joe's eye to the top of the car. Thick dust blanketed old bones. A tiny skull, long arm bones, fragile-looking ribs. A child's skeleton.

A train passed a hundred feet behind them. The ground shook. A piece of broken brick clattered into the room, and the skeleton on top of the car shivered. Rebar's arm twitched. Moving light scattered shadows around the room as if a thousand ghosts danced there, finally set free.

Joe shifted his gaze from the dancing shadows to the left wall. Olive-green fabric covered with dust leaned against the stone. On the train ties next to the green pile rested a pale orb with a hole in the back.

A skull.

The green rags? An Army uniform covering a skeleton. At the end of one green arm a dusty gun lay atop the rusty train track. The man had shot himself in the head.

On the ground between the skull and the uniform-clad skeleton lay a set of round wire-framed eyeglasses, one lens a spider's web of cracks. A man died there, long ago. Not just one (cyan). Two (blue). Close to the wall, a second skeleton wore a long coat that looked as if it had once been white.

He realized it from their postures—the men had been walled in alive.

As much as he was repulsed by their terrible deaths, the mystery intrigued him. Who had walled them in here? And why had Rebar searched for them and brought them to light?

Rebar's arm trembled. Shadows formed and broke. Joe withdrew his head.

"I found it," Rebar whispered. "It will save me, the treasure in there."

"Treasure?"

Rebar lowered the lantern to the dirt. He fingered the greasy handle of his hammer. "It's mine, sir."

Joe's heart raced. They were alone down here. No one to stop Rebar from doing whatever he wanted. Possibilities clicked through his head, but it came down to fight-or-flight. Rebar was bigger than he was, armed with a hammer, and insane.

He took a careful backward step. "I understand that. It's yours."

Rebar cocked his head as if listening.

The tunnel was silent. Joe backed up, eyes on the hammer. He came up hard against the pillar.

"We need to tell them, sir," Rebar said. "Before the end of the month."

"Tell them what?" Joe asked. His heart thudded against his ribs. He wasn't an action hero, he was a nerd. He couldn't disarm a man with a hammer. Next to him, Edison growled.

"You don't know?" Rebar asked. "What's your name? What are you doing here?"

Rebar's muscles corded in his neck. He lifted the hammer and advanced on Joe.

Joe ran. He focused on the tracks in front of him, the tracks that had carried FDR's train here all those years ago. If the silver rails tripped him up, he was dead. Rebar was crazy, and he'd use that hammer if he could.

Think, he told himself. Find a safe place. He headed back for the open room. Trains pulled in and out of there, sometimes, at this time of night. A driver might see him, help him.

He wasn't a brave man. Cowardice was to be ashamed of, he knew. He'd always tried to think his way out of fights, and run if he had to. Standing and fighting was never his favorite option. And Rebar had a hammer.

Joe veered off into an unlit tunnel. He had to make sure that he wasn't being followed. Edison loped silently next to him, calm as always.

No sound of running footsteps on the tracks. Not even the grumble of a train.

Farther down the tunnel, he and the dog slowed. Joe kept glancing over his shoulder to see if Rebar followed them. No one did.

He took a shuddering breath before continuing. This tunnel connected with another not too far ahead, and he could follow that one back to the door that opened onto his own tunnel and his house. He'd be safe there.

What had Rebar uncovered? How had he known to look there? Joe might not be a brave man, but he was a persistent one. Once something piqued his interest, he wouldn't give up on it.

He would return to the brick room later to pry out the secrets that Rebar had kept from him. He would go back. He wouldn't be driven away from the truth.

He entered the code and unlocked the metal door. Gesturing for Edison to go first, he hurried inside and closed the door. The green light told him that the system had armed itself again. He leaned against the inside to catch his breath and wait for his heart to slow. This was real fear, not the product of misfiring brain chemistry.

Another feeling had joined the fear. A feeling he hadn't experienced in a long time.

Exhilaration.

Joe let the feeling wash over him. Ever since he'd become trapped inside, his world had diminished. He'd lost his job, his friends, the sky. He tried not to dwell on it and keep going, but his new life had weighed him down in a thousand ways.

Tonight he'd caught a glimpse of something new, something exciting—a mystery that was to be found only in the world beneath. He had to solve it. He had to figure out who Rebar was, why he was there, and how the train car came to be bricked in. It might be dangerous, but he'd risk a lot to keep feeling this alive.

As he followed Edison toward his front door, he couldn't stop grinning.

Things were going to change for him.

7

November 28, 4:04 a.m.
Bricked-in train car under Grand Central Terminal

Rebar watched the man with the yellow dog sprint away from him across the rows of shiny tracks and into a tunnel. He didn't bother to chase them. They didn't seem dangerous, just curious. He didn't have time to bother with them. He had to concentrate on his prize.

He had found what he had long searched for. He wasn't crazy. He was right. He'd almost given up back there on the platform, but he hadn't. And now he had found it.

With one dirty hand, he touched the brick wall and muttered a quick prayer, surprised that he still remembered one. This brick train shed wasn't just the source of the secrets he sought. It was also a tomb for the doctor who had started it all, and a hapless soldier who'd been ordered to accompany him on his final journey. His papers said so, and he would find proof.

He wiped his hand on his filthy pants and picked up the lantern again, then leaned against the cold wall and stuck his arm through the hole. Reverently, he gazed into the room. The lantern light shone on a blue car that had once carried the president himself. The car had been lost for so many years. Everyone had given up on it. But not him. He knew that he would find it. And he had.

The doctor must have been trying to get out. He lay crumpled against the end of the tunnel where they had laid the final bricks. Dark stains on the back of his coat told Rebar that he'd been wounded, probably shot to keep him inside while they finished the wall. He hadn't given up.

The soldier had obviously chosen to eat a bullet rather than die of dehydration or from running out of oxygen. A brave choice. The other skeleton looked like it belonged to a monkey. It hadn't been mentioned in the papers that Rebar had come across before.

Rebar climbed through the hole he'd created in the wall and walked over to the long-dead doctor. The man had died before Rebar's own parents were born. Hard to believe that he might even now hold the secrets to Rebar's own life and death. Funny.

He studied the white-clad figure on the floor. The man had nothing in his hands, and the ground around his body was clear. If he'd carried anything with him, he hadn't brought it all the way to this last resting place.

Holding the light at waist level, Rebar turned in a slow circle, looking for clues. The skeleton in the uniform listed against the wall. His skull rested about a foot from Rebar's boot.

He didn't have the papers on him, either. That left the train car.

Rebar set the lantern inside, then hefted himself up into the old car. Sooty dust lay velvet thick over everything—chairs bolted to the floor, a cabinet in the corner with an old sink, and empty glass decanters.

He searched the floor, and spotted what he was looking for next to a chair. A grimy rectangle. A briefcase? He wiped the dust off the top with the sleeve of his jacket, uncovering a cracked leather surface.

Rebar lifted it up with trembling hands.

The briefcase's hinges had long since rusted, and they screeched and broke as he lifted the top off. He stared down at a stack of yellowed papers inside.

He sat down on an old chair that had perhaps once held FDR and began to read. The papers didn't make sense, yet. They discussed clinical trials, strains of the parasite, side effects. Nothing about a cure. There must be more papers.

A clink outside caught his attention. Probably a train. Or a man working far away.

He couldn't be sure. He needed to take the papers somewhere safe and hide them until he had time to read them carefully. Before that, he needed to check the rest of the car out to make sure that there weren't other papers hidden there.

He emptied the papers and maps from his own pockets into the briefcase, smashing them in until he could put the top back on. Then he took off his belt and wrapped it around both halves of the broken case. Nothing could fall out now. He tucked it under his arm and lifted the lantern.

The room was, as he'd expected, empty. He climbed through the hole he'd opened up. He swung the lantern in a slow circle, shadows chasing each other across the walls. No one out here, either. Hadn't there been a man and a dog earlier? Were they back? He didn't think so.

The uneasy feeling wouldn't go away. He took the lantern and walked along an unused track, counting his steps. At just the right spot, as if he'd known it all along, he stumbled over a stack of broken train ties that looked as if they'd been tossed there before the Korean War. Quickly, he cleared a space in the pile, placed the briefcase in the middle, and then restacked the ties haphazardly atop it.

Then he went back toward the car. He would find the other papers, the ones that the doctor must have hidden.

The ones that told how he could be cured.

Dread consumed him. What if they weren't there?

He half-ran back to the brick tomb and climbed inside. He ransacked the car, finding no papers concealed in the cupboards or fastened under the chairs, nothing on the floor or walls. The ceiling held nothing but a wire and pockmarks from bullets, nothing useful at all.

With a curse, he threw the glass decanters one after another against the thick glass windows. The square bottles shattered, and shards of glass glittered against the thick dust.

He jumped from the back of the train and ran to the doctor's body, ripping the coat from the skeleton, hands delving into the pockets, searching even his pants pockets. Nothing. He repeated his actions with the soldier's corpse, pulling them both into the center of the room so that he could see them better.

Sweat ran down his back, and his breath grew tight. Calm down, he ordered himself. Think. The papers had to be here somewhere. After all, the men were trapped in this room. Nothing could have left the room.

He started at the far end of the room and walked from one end to the other, lantern in one hand, peering at the dirty ground. When he got to the brick wall, he turned, took a step to the left, and walked back the other way. His footprints formed straight lines in the dust. He was walking a grid. If it was here, he'd find it.

An hour later, he collapsed on the steps that led up to the car. He'd found nothing. There was no hope. He dropped his head into his hands and wept.

8

Ozan hated train tunnels. They smelled like oil and rat piss.
The third rail ran electric death along the side of each track.
One kick to the wrong spot, and Erol would be alone. Ozan
walked on the train ties, both to avoid the third rail and to
keep from leaving prints in the dirt.

He'd brought a flashlight, but hadn't had to use it yet.
The tunnels were illuminated well enough that he could walk
without one. The light would draw attention, and he never
liked to draw attention.

It was inconvenient that he had to come down here, but
inconveniences were necessary on a job like his—as were the
uncomfortable too-big shoes he currently wore, even though
he had a pair that fit perfectly in his jacket pocket.

A train rumbled up and Ozan slipped behind a pillar,
taking cover. When he came back out, his target was gone. A
shadowy figure headed back to the platform. Ozan tracked
it. He caught up just as the man neared the platform. The
man paused by the stairs, as if he sensed Ozan's presence
behind him in the tunnel, then hurried into the light. He was
several inches too short to be Subject 523, so Ozan
retreated.

A few hours later, he was ready to call it a night.

The trains started to run again at 5:30. That gave him only thirty-eight more minutes to search. After that, he'd head topside for a shower and a long sleep, and start again in the evening.

The man should have been distinctive—tall, dressed in dirty fatigues, looking like a homeless man but walking like a military one. Ozan had spotted six men who fit that description in the first few hours of staking out Grand Central Terminal. He'd followed each one, eliminating each one as his target.

Sometimes, jobs were like that—many false trails had to be followed before the right one revealed itself. Ozan didn't mind.

He'd first spotted Subject 523 when he had walked into the terminal just before the last trains left for the night. He'd gone straight down to Platform 23 and headed into the tunnel where Ozan had lost him. Ozan had a feeling, based on the man's easy, comfortable stride, that he always used Platform 23 to access the tunnels. He'd probably be back there the next day.

Ozan passed through a maze of tracks where commuter trains converged on Grand Central Terminal. Security swept this area often, and he had to appreciate the target's stealth. Had the man been coming down here for months without being caught? Ozan hoped that he himself would be so fortunate.

He was ready to turn back when a glimmer of light twinkled far ahead in the tunnel. A golden orb bobbed up and down—a lantern, not a flashlight. Subject 523 had been carrying a lantern.

Ozan pocketed his own flashlight and closed in on the light. Mindful of stones and debris on the ground, he chose each step carefully, footfalls whisper quiet. It was a matter of professional pride that no one ever heard him coming. And it kept him alive.

The target walked furtively, shoulders hunched, head on a swivel. Whoever the man was, he was nervous. His steps, too, were cautious. The target clearly had training in moving undetected. Nothing about this background had appeared in the dossier Ozan had received, so he had to assume the worst—that the man was trained as a deadly killer and no one had bothered to tell Ozan. Any other assumption was foolish.

Ozan crept closer. The man's head turned far enough to one side that Ozan recognized his receding chin. Subject 523. In one dirty hand he carried a battery-powered lantern that radiated light in a giant circle. That lamp had drawn Ozan to him as brightness drew so many predators to prey.

The man stopped and held the lantern high, searching in all directions. Ozan stopped, too. The light from the tunnel behind might silhouette him, but he could do little about that now. He eased himself against the stone wall and waited.

Seeming satisfied, the target turned around again. Ozan lagged behind. Once the man chose a tunnel, there were few places where he could turn off and, even for those, his light would make him easy to find—as long as he didn't become suspicious and douse it. But he was a careful man, Subject 523, so Ozan could take nothing for granted. He didn't let him out of his sight.

The light bobbed along in front of him like a will-o'-the-wisp. It promised magic and excitement. Because tonight Ozan hoped to kill the man who held it.

He fingered the knife in his pocket, then touched the hard steel Glock he carried in a shoulder holster. Both weapons were suitable, but he hoped to come across an object at the scene that he could use instead. A rock. A brick. A discarded board. On-site weapons were impossible to trace and made the police think of crimes of passion instead of premeditation. That would lead them down blind alleys.

The light ahead stopped abruptly, then jerked up with tiny quick movements as if the man were climbing over a low wall. Ozan noiselessly closed the distance between them. He smelled the target's sweat and the clay-like odor of disturbed brick dust.

The beam angled toward the ceiling as if it had been put down. Ozan drew his knife. The Glock was a better distance weapon. Considering how the last man on the job died, the more distance the better, but he didn't enjoy it as much when he killed from a distance. He liked to be close enough to feel their muscles go slack, see death dull their eyes, and let their last rattling breath whisper against his cheek. He stroked the knife's hilt with his thumb, waiting.

The target had climbed through a jagged hole smashed into a brick wall. Footprints in the dust told him that the target had come to this place and left at least once.

Among the target's tracks he spotted another set. Whoever had left them was a person of interest, might have met Subject 523 here. Ozan studied the prints, about a size ten, but that meant little. Plenty of short men had large feet, and large men had small ones. The stride would tell him more. He left Subject 523 alone in the brick room and circled back to follow the other man's prints, careful to keep to the train ties and leave no prints of his own in the dust here.

Based on the length of the strides, the man who had left the prints was tall, around six feet, and had been running. Maybe he'd come across Subject 523 here, too, and 523 had chased him off. A quarrel like that might prove useful to Ozan. He'd prepared an alternate scenario for Subject 523's murder for the police, but would he use this one instead? The footprints might be years old. Better to stick with what he had. Still, he would track those footprints back to their source later, to be sure.

He crept back toward his target. He didn't want to lose sight of his quarry tonight of all nights. This was the perfect place. They were alone down here, and he could work without fear of detection, away from the people and surveillance cameras that plagued him. And he'd been told that he must do it soon.

He moved until he could see through the jagged opening into the room where 523 had disappeared. A rusty blue train car sat inside. A curious Ozan slipped closer, glimpsing a small skeleton resting undisturbed in a layer of dust atop the car. Another skeleton lay on the ground a few feet from the car.

The target sat down on the rusty steps, sweat plowing furrows in the dust and grime coating his face.

Ozan didn't have much time before the trains started running and the security sweeps came by. Someone might hear the man's screams. And Ozan believed in acting with caution. This man had killed a skilled colleague. He was probably trained to withstand interrogation, at least for a time, and he was large and possibly armed. The best option was to kill him and search for the papers later. The contract had said that their retrieval was desirable, not mandatory. Ozan had no intention of risking his life on lower-level priorities.

He spotted a sledgehammer leaning against the outside of the broken wall, and the decision was made for him. A thin layer of dust coated the hammer, as if it'd been used long ago and then set aside. Maybe 523 himself had brought it here to break the wall. A perfect weapon of opportunity. He closed in on it quickly.

The wood felt slippery under his gloves. It had seen good use, this tool.

The light stayed still in the car, and the target still sat on metal steps that had been folded out from the side of the car as if it had stopped at a station. He leaned forward, hands clenching and unclenching in his pockets. "It has to be here," the man whispered over and over.

It didn't matter what he was talking about. Ozan had a job to do. He leaped over the broken bricks and into the room. He landed with each foot flat on a different train tie. The time for stealth was past.

The hammer arced down.

The target lifted his head, quicker than Ozan expected.

Hammer met bone. Bone gave. But not the skull. The man had deflected the blow with his right arm.

The man's left fist connected with the side of Ozan's head. Ozan's ears rang, and he stumbled back.

The man was on him then, knocking him to the dirt.

Ozan rolled to the side, but the man fell onto him. His wounded arm dripped blood in Ozan's open eyes. Ozan blinked it away and twisted the man's wounded arm. It felt hot, as if the man had a fever. Broken bones grated against each other. The man screamed and reared back.

Ozan pulled away from him and reached for the hammer. The man tried for it, too, but Ozan was quicker. The hammer connected with the side of the man's head. Blood and gore spattered up onto Ozan's hands.

The target fell backward against the side of the car. His hands jerked once, and then he was still.

Neatly done. Efficient. One blow.

But this shouldn't look efficient.

Ozan brought the hammer down five more times. The man's head stopped looking as if it had ever been human by the third blow. That was what crimes of passion looked like—too much force, wasted energy.

Ozan released the hammer and let it drop into the thick dust next to the body. He did a quick inventory of his own injuries. Nothing serious. A bruise on the side of his head and a cracked rib. He could finish the job and walk away.

No danger now. Without moving his feet, he surveyed the room. The skeleton on the floor belonged to a soldier. Based on the uniform, the man had died here before Ozan was born. Next to that skeleton rested another wearing a stained white lab coat with a dark hole in the shoulder surrounded by a dark blotch. An old bullet hole. What had brought these men to this place? What had brought 523 here?

It must not be relevant to his job. If it were, then he would have been informed.

The artistic part of the job was done. All that remained now were loose ends. First, he searched 523's pockets. He found, and took, a map of the tunnels and a wad of crumpled one-dollar bills. He didn't find any other documents, classified or otherwise, but he searched inside and underneath the train car just in case. He found broken alcohol bottles, pens, and a few sheets of aged blank paper with the White House seal. He took those, too. But he found nothing interesting, and nothing modern.

That was a problem. He'd hoped to find those papers.

He had one more task, one he'd almost forgotten because it was so out of his usual routine. He flipped a plastic bag inside out and used it to scoop up a sample of 523's warm brain tissue. He turned the bag right side out again and sealed it, then put it inside a second bag. He'd have to get the sample into a special chilled container and mail it to his client, proof that the job was complete. Brain tissue seemed an odd choice for DNA testing, but he couldn't imagine what else they might want it for, unless they'd messed with the man's brain.

Ozan drew a twenty-dollar bill from his front pocket. He'd never touched it with his bare hands so it wouldn't have his fingerprints. He folded it and tucked it into the dead man's pocket. He dropped another bill on the floor.

Three more bills were in Ozan's pocket, and he fished them out. Dropping his right hand into the man's blood, he held the bills with his bloody fingertips, careful to smear them enough that it would be hard to tell if he'd worn gloves.

After a murder like that, the killer would be frightened, running. Ozan sprinted toward the door, lengthening his strides to appear taller. He already wore shoes a size too large. The inserts crammed against his toes made it easy to run in them.

Bending, he swept away the prints of the third man, the one who'd stood and watched the target and the room. If the body were ever found, he didn't want things to be complicated. Whoever that man was, he was lucky.

Ozan smashed the lantern against the wall, and it went dark. Then he headed for the outside by the shortest route, making sure to step in the dirt to leave a good print here and there. If it ever came to it, the police should be able to track the panicked killer aboveground.

Soon he'd be outside. He took off his gloves, carefully turning them inside out and tying the ends closed. He wiped his face and hands with his antiseptic wipes and secured them all in a paper bag. He'd drop it into a dumpster with his ripped and dirty jacket. He'd be an ordinary man out for a stroll in the early morning quiet. He'd leave the too-large shoes he'd worn for the murder and a few bloody bills next a homeless man who slept near this very exit. Then he could go home.

Contentment filled him. He'd completed his task early, and he'd never killed a man with a hammer before. He'd liked it. If only he had someone to share his joy with, but there was just Erol, and he would never understand. Erol must be protected from this side of his brother, always.

Still, he'd done a good job. As much as he knew that he could demand the rest of his fee and move on, a niggling doubt in the back of his mind told him that he must stay a few more days and search for the papers. He would play with Erol and enjoy the pleasures that New York had to offer.

A bark broke through his concentration. Ozan froze, listening.

Another bark. Someone with a dog was behind him, by the murdered man.

Now he had a difficult decision to make. Should he stick to his original plan and leave, or should he go back?

If the man with the dog was a friend of 523, he might have passed him the classified papers.

Their retrieval wasn't mandatory, but Ozan liked to be thorough.

He turned around and headed back down the tunnel toward the barking dog.

9

Edison at his side, Joe hiked through the tunnels toward his destination. The only illumination came from his flashlight— a bubble of brightness that disappeared a few paces ahead of and behind them. Unlike the tunnel on which his house sat, which was covered with simple planks, sharp stones covered the ground here. Two lines of silver tracks ran down the tunnel's center, and a third rail sat to one side. Remembering his training, Edison avoided the third rail and walked by the opposite side track.

Joe had paced around his house for a couple of hours, wanting to go back and check out the abandoned train car again, but afraid that Rebar would still be there. Then he'd tried to sleep. Eventually he'd given up and convinced himself that he would just go and take a peek. If Rebar was still there, he'd go to bed and try later. The trains would be running soon, and that would probably chase Rebar back outside.

It seemed like a good plan in his well-lit parlor with the electric fire crackling by his feet and stout steel doors between himself and danger. Now, in the tunnels, where a crazy man with a hammer lurked, it seemed like the worst kind of stupidity.

Still, for the first time in a long time, Joe had a mystery to explore.

As they drew closer to the field of tracks where he and Edison usually played fetch, he slowed. Edison stuck close to his heels, as if sensing that this was serious business.

He'd run. At the first sign of trouble, he'd run. If he maintained enough distance between them, Rebar wouldn't catch him. Besides, the man was probably long gone. Joe wished that he believed his own words.

When he reached the tracks, he examined the spot where he'd seen the abandoned train car. It was dark. He relaxed. Rebar had taken his lantern and gone home, wherever that might be. Joe could poke around the skeletons and the train car and try to figure out why a homeless veteran had known about it and broken it open. He'd even be able to film it for later analysis.

Then he would call the city and report it. Someone ought to identify the dead men. Their families might have been waiting decades to learn their fate.

Joe walked toward the pillar. The bricked-in structure was behind pillar nine. Scarlet flashed in his head. Nine.

Slowly, the tunnel grew darker. The faint glow of the old-fashioned light bulbs faded behind him until he could barely see where he was going. But he didn't put on his night-vision goggles. If Rebar was there with a light, he could blind Joe in an instant. Instead, he counted on Edison to find the way forward.

His heartbeat quickened when he passed the pillar. A slow glance around in the dark didn't reveal anyone, so he switched on his flashlight. His beam picked out a distant pile of broken brick. He'd found the room that Rebar had broken open.

He shone his light around in a circle to see if Rebar was still there. Near as Joe could tell, he was alone. Still, for several minutes he scanned the area. No sign of movement. No unusual sounds.

Slowly, he crept forward to the pile of broken bricks, anxious to see the secret room again but beset with an uneasy feeling. What if Rebar was inside with the light off and his hammer ready?

Joe hesitated before he pulled out his phone. He kept his phone in a special cell phone holder. He called it his pocket-size Faraday cage, because it blocked incoming and outgoing signals. Nobody could reach him, and even the cell phone towers didn't know where he was. As long as he kept the phone in there, he was off the grid.

It didn't matter down here. There was no signal anyway. He filmed the pile of bricks, the darkness beyond, and the floor. Edison touched his nose to his knee, and Joe jumped. He took a deep breath and listened for trouble. He heard only a faraway train, Edison's rapid breathing, his own pounding heart, and rocks rolling underfoot—nothing amiss.

As he neared the pile of bricks, Edison snarled. Joe stopped in surprise—the dog had never made a sound like that before. His hackles stood straight, and a low growl came from deep in his chest. Edison barked.

"What is it?" he asked, wishing that the dog could answer.

Edison barked again, ending with a growl.

Joe swung the flashlight around. Still no one. He stopped and tried to listen, but Edison's growl made that impossible, and he didn't want to shush him. If something upset his stolid dog, Joe wanted him to make noise.

A low rumble grew to a roar. Joe jerked around in time to see a train thunder into the tunnel, across the tracks just past where they'd played fetch, and on toward Grand Central Terminal.

When the noise died away, Edison had stopped growling, but he stared at the broken wall, tail tucked between his legs but head up. Something in there scared him, but he was clearly trying to fight his fear and protect Joe if he had to.

Joe could walk away. He didn't need to know what that room contained, not really. Doubtless, he could lead a happy life without ever looking.

Not true.

He inched toward the hole that Rebar had smashed into the brick wall and stuck his head inside. The beam of his flashlight stabbed into the room, as if eager to show him the secrets inside.

A lot had changed since his last visit.

A handful of small brown creatures moved about in the center of the room. Joe's heart thudded in his chest. Edison's growl changed to a loud bark that echoed around the enclosed space. A few brown bits broke off from the group and ran to the corners. His stomach roiled.

Rats.

He shone the flashlight beam on the object they'd been climbing on. He made out a tan camouflage jacket like the one that Rebar had been wearing hours before. Dark patches stained the collar and sleeves. The jacket covered a corpse. Rebar?

Any hopes that this person had died of natural causes were dashed when he saw the hammer in the dust next to the body. Stains darkened the hammer's silver head. His light played across rusty splashes on the blue train car, lingered over streaks and smears. The man had been beaten to death.

Bile rose in Joe's throat, and he fought it back. This was a crime scene now, and he wasn't going to puke his DNA all over it. He closed his eyes and took a few deep breaths. Sensing his distress, Edison whined.

"Sit," he ordered. Whatever had happened here, it was over now. He should take Edison and go immediately.

But the pull of curiosity was too strong.

He peered back through the hole to examine the rest of the car. Someone had moved the skeletons of the doctor and the soldier, dragging them from the side of the room into the center and piling them on top of each other like pickup sticks. The skeleton on top of the car had been left alone. Someone had also flipped the bodies over and turned their pockets inside out. Rebar, or his killer, must have been searching the bodies of these long-dead men.

Joe pulled out his cell phone and filmed the scene inside from where he stood, hoping that his flashlight would give enough illumination. Then he filmed the whole area, sweeping the light and camera in a circle.

He couldn't shake a feeling of dread. He'd seen enough. He trotted back toward the well-lit tracks and home. He'd have a cell phone signal there, and he could call the police.

They had cleared the tunnel and crossed most of the unused tracks when Edison stopped, turned back toward the direction from which they'd come, and barked a warning. Joe spun, angling the light behind him. A shadow flitted to the side so quickly that he wasn't sure he had seen it. Gooseflesh ran up his arms.

He backed toward the tracks where the trains still ran. A sound that he'd heard only on television cut through the dry tunnel air. The racking of the slide of a gun.

"Stay," whispered a man's voice. "Or I will put a bullet in your back."

Joe's heart raced, but he froze, one foot on the track, the other on a railroad tie. Edison growled and took a step toward the voice.

"I've never liked dogs," the voice whispered again.

"Shh." Joe hushed Edison. "Heel."

This was probably the man who had killed Rebar. Options for escape clicked through Joe's mind—run and hope for the best, charge the gun and pray for a miracle, or try to talk his way out of this. "What do you want?"

"Did the dead man ever give you anything?"

If he told the truth and answered no, would the man shoot him? "I didn't know him."

"I will shoot you first in your left shoulder," the man said conversationally. "You're left-handed, I see, and it will take them months to repair the damage, if they can."

Joe held his breath, afraid to move.

"I can probably shoot you four or five times before you die."

The colors for those numbers flashed through his head—green, brown.

"You look like you're more determined than people would think, and I bet you'll tell me what I want after the third shot, which is quite respectable, as most people talk after one. I'm rarely wrong about these things."

The track vibrated under Joe's sneaker. His mind stayed surprisingly calm, working through the data that he had—Joe was exposed and in the light, the other man impossible to see in the darkness. The other man had a gun and might be a murderer, Joe was unarmed and had to think about Edison's safety, too. The tracks hummed louder. That was what Joe had. Just that. The 5:47 (brown, green, slate) train on the Harlem line.

"Think carefully," said the voice. "And let's start again. Did that man back there give you any documents?"

"No. I didn't know him." Joe remembered the papers stuffed in Rebar's pockets. He hadn't seen them just now when he filmed the body. But, if this man had killed Rebar, surely he must have been the one who took the papers.

The tracks' humming grew to a roar. A train barreled down the tracks upon which Joe stood. The engineer saw Joe, and his eyes widened. Joe was right in his path.

Out of the corner of his eye, Joe saw the shadows that

concealed the man twitch. Joe was certain that he was aiming his gun.

"Heel," Joe yelled. He spun, then jumped to the other side of the tracks mere feet ahead of the moving train. Edison's solid form pressed close to his right leg. Joe ducked against the side of the tunnel before the train reached them, pulling Edison down, too.

The man with the gun was on the other side of the moving train, so Joe was safe from a bullet for now, but not out of danger. Yet.

The train barreled past, cars passing so close that Joe could have reached out and touched them. If he hadn't jumped when he had, he'd have been cut to hamburger by the wheels. His body wanted to flatten itself against the side of the tunnel and wait, but his brain wouldn't let it.

He had to use the train as a shield.

Joe ran. On one side was the unforgiving stone of the tunnel, on the other the moving train. Heat and light blasted off its metal walls. The moving air pushed him sideways, and he fought to stay upright. If he lost his footing, he would be chopped to mincemeat under the wheels.

He snatched a quick glance to the side. He needed a tunnel, an open door, anything that would let him and Edison hide or escape.

No exits.

10

November 28, 5:46 a.m.
Tunnels

Joe ran, arms close to his sides so that they didn't strike the train or the tunnel. The screech of metal on metal as the train braked scraped every nerve in his body. If he'd dared to raise his hands, he would have clapped them over his ears.

Silver cars whizzed by close enough to touch. The smell of metal and electricity urged him on.

Light bloomed ahead. The train slowed.

A platform.

The train arrived ahead of him, stopping with a jerk. Joe threw a glance over his shoulder. He jumped across the third rail, ducked past a pillar, and reached the stairs that led to the platform opposite where the train had stopped. Edison tore up the stairs ahead of him.

A few passengers stood waiting for the next train. Joe barreled past them and up toward the terminal itself. He and Edison didn't stop running until they reached the lobby of the Hyatt.

Once there, he stopped. Sweat soaked his shirt. His heart pounded, and he could not stop shaking. The screech and thunder of the train still rang in his ears. He had almost died down there. A single stumble would have killed him.

Frederick, the concierge, hurried over. "Mr. Tesla, are you

all right?"

"I'll be fine," Joe said.

"Let's sit down."

Frederick led him to his regular chair by the Starbucks stand. Tiffany was setting up for the start of her day, loading a tray full of pastries into the glass display case. Her eyes widened when she saw him.

Joe sat and examined Edison, running his hands along the dog's body from head to tail. He was uninjured physically, but the usually mellow dog pressed against Joe's legs, back bowed with fear.

"It's OK, Edison," he said. "It was close, but we're OK."

Edison nosed his head between Joe's leg and the chair, and Joe petted his back.

Tiffany pressed a warm cup into his hand. "Chamomile. It's calming."

He realized that they thought he'd had another panic attack. They'd seen him have enough of them as he'd tried over and over again to leave the hotel by the front door. But this time his danger was external.

He took a slow sip of tea, then pulled his cell phone from its special pocket. His hands shook so that he could not dial.

Another sip of tea. A round of deep breaths. He was an expert in recovering from moments when he expected to die. The surprise gift of his panic attacks: They had prepared him to deal with real panic.

"Thanks," he said. "We're OK."

Tiffany and Frederick left him alone. He closed his eyes, willing his breathing to slow, his heart to calm.

He started to dial 911, but stopped before he pressed the Send button. In his current state, they'd never believe him. Even if they did, they'd drag him down to their offices to question him. He couldn't let that happen. He couldn't go outside.

Instead, he called his lawyer, Daniel Rossi. Daniel answered immediately, one of the perks of his Pellucid money.

"There's a situation down in the tunnels."

"A situation?" said Daniel. He sounded as if he'd been up for hours.

Joe quietly described everything that had happened, keeping an eye on the nearly empty lobby in case someone might overhear.

"Stay there," Daniel said. "I'll take care of this. For the love of God, don't talk to a single solitary other person about this until I get there."

He hung up.

Joe fed Edison a treat and finished his tea, feeling his heartbeat slow. He was safe. It was OK. Tiffany and Frederick watched him, but they didn't seem too worried. He guessed that was one advantage of cracking up regularly in their lobby.

His phone rang. Celeste. He hoped it wasn't her nurse, Patty, with bad news.

"Joe," he answered, holding his breath until he heard her voice.

"Good morning!" She sounded breathless, as if she had been the one running instead of him.

"You're up early." She never called before ten.

"A little bird told me that you're in trouble."

"How?" He'd barely even hung up on Daniel, and he trusted the attorney.

"I know people who know people," she said.

"Daniel?" he asked.

She laughed. "He would never betray a client. And I would never betray a source."

How much should he tell her? She had enough to worry about. He needed to protect her. "I found something weird."

"A partial truth," she said.

"Are you having a strong day?" Distraction might work.

"Neutral," she said. "Zero."

"Black," he answered automatically. "Like the ocean at night."

"I like that," she said. "I'd paint that if I could."

"It'd be beautiful."

She let out her breath in what now constituted a laugh. "Are you going to hack into God knows where and put up black waves, like the seagull?"

"Do you want me to?" As soon as he finished meeting with Daniel.

"Not this time," she said. "Let's keep it just between us. A secret. Speaking of—"

A hand touched his shoulder, and he jumped.

"Just me." Daniel held up his hands in mock surrender. "Please tell me that's not the police."

"I gotta go, Celeste." He hung up, hoping that she hadn't heard Daniel's words.

Daniel smoothed back his unkempt hair. He looked as if he'd run the whole way. "Have you talked to anyone else? What did you tell Celeste?"

"That I found something weird. That's all," Joe said. "Shouldn't I talk to the police, tell them, too?"

"Under no circumstances."

"There's a dead man," Joe said. "And I was chased by a guy with a gun. Serious stuff."

"I understood that from your call and relayed the information to Mr. Goldstone from our criminal division," his lawyer said. "He'll pass those details along."

"I don't have anything to hide." Joe stroked Edison's floppy ears. They were both much calmer.

"The first rule of a criminal attorney is that you never let your client talk to the police." Daniel fiddled with his shirt cuffs. "Ever."

"I'm not a criminal, and you're not a criminal lawyer."

"You hired me to give you advice. I can tell you right now that it's never in your best interest to talk to the police. Remember how they say 'anything you say can and will be used against you in a court of law'?"

"So?"

"Notice how they don't say it can be used *for* you?" Daniel's voice was low and conversational. No one in the lobby so much as glanced at them. "Mr. Goldstone will report the crime and keep your name confidential."

Joe had been raised in a circus, and it had been drilled into him that he could never trust the police, that people in authority would always rule against you. Maybe the old rules were right. Maybe his time in the world of pure numbers had made him naïve.

"You said on the phone that you can't give the police a description because you never saw him and that you can't identify his voice because he was whispering. There is nothing you can tell them that will help you, and a lot that could harm you."

Joe had to agree.

11

Vivian marched up the stone stairs to the lobby, looking for trouble. She didn't find any. She recognized the short concierge from her last visit. The freckled teenage girl working Starbucks didn't look like a killer. The lobby was otherwise empty, except for her employer, Daniel Rossi, and the man he was talking to. She could see only the back of his head, then he turned slightly, and she recognized him. Joe Tesla.

She checked out the second floor, or at least as much of it as was visible through the atrium. No one stood along the glass dividers that overlooked the first floor. It was too early to see much activity here. She'd been woken from a sound sleep just a few minutes before, swiped deodorant under her arms, jumped into her clothes, and caught a cab straight here. Mr. Rossi had said that it was urgent.

Mr. Rossi resembled an older George Clooney, and usually traded on it, but this morning his perfect salt-and-pepper hair was disheveled. Tesla, on the other hand, looked flat-out terrible. He'd been pale last time she saw him, but now he was practically ghostly. It made sense, since he didn't go outside, but it looked creepy, almost supernatural.

To make matters worse, he didn't just look like a ghost,

he looked like he'd seen a ghost. His eyes were wide, he was jiggling his knee, and he petted the dog at his side over and over with little jerky movements. He was very different from the confident man she'd followed six months before.

She moved into Mr. Rossi's line of sight, but where Tesla couldn't see her. She'd wait there until Mr. Rossi gave her a signal to approach. In the meantime, she scanned the lobby again. A freshly shaved businessman in a blue suit exited the elevators and headed to the escalator. He held a gleaming black briefcase in one hand, carelessly, as if the contents weren't that important. Otherwise, no movement.

Mr. Rossi nodded to her, and she walked over to be introduced.

Tesla had a firm handshake, and he paused for a second when he met her eyes. He scrutinized her face for a second longer than usual, as if he recognized her. Did he? He'd been pretty messed up when she'd met him, barely able to walk.

"I'm assigning you Ms. Torres," Mr. Rossi said. "For close protection."

Tesla's eyes narrowed. "You think that I need a bodyguard?"

"I think one would not come amiss," Mr. Rossi answered. "And I'd advise you to move back into a room at the Hyatt for a few days while this matter is resolved."

What matter? She'd only heard that she was to meet Mr. Rossi here and provide security for a client. She hadn't known who it would be until she saw Mr. Tesla, and she still didn't know why, just that it was urgent.

"I appreciate your concern, but I'm not moving back up here," Tesla said.

Mr. Rossi smiled his lawyer smile that gave nothing away. "Very well. But do please let Ms. Torres accompany you, at least for the next twenty-four hours."

Tesla looked as if he wanted to argue, but he nodded.

"Let's get breakfast."

Mr. Rossi begged off, and she and Tesla and the dog headed out for Grand Central Terminal—a tough place to provide protection.

"Are you sure you wouldn't rather eat here?" she asked. "Or somewhere more secluded?"

"No," Tesla said shortly.

They ended up in the food court at the Tri Tip Grill for breakfast, where Tesla didn't bat an eyelash when she ordered steak and eggs. Lots of men acted surprised to see a woman eat. Tesla ordered steak and eggs, too, and a double steak, rare, for the dog. Privileges of being a millionaire's pet.

She kept her eyes moving around the crowded room. Unless an attacker came toward them in slow motion, she'd have trouble spotting him until he was right on top of Tesla. Still, she searched for people who looked at them too long, people with suspicious bulges under their arms that might be guns, men who moved like they had military or law enforcement training.

Vivian was no good at small talk, but she figured she'd better give it a try. "Mr. Rossi says you're related to Nikola Tesla."

"On my father's side. A couple of generations back." His mouth pursed as if he didn't want to talk about it.

The plates arrived—no more small talk necessary. The waiter seemed to know the dog and put his plate straight on the floor.

"I didn't know that they served dogs here," she said.

"He's not a regular dog," Tesla said. "He's a psychiatric service animal."

A bad conversational trail to go down. "I hear your company makes facial-recognition software. How does that work?"

His shoulders relaxed fractionally. At last, a safe topic of conversation. "We compare pictures in databases to pictures out in the world to match them up."

"Surveillance camera pictures are usually pretty unclear," she said. "How can you recognize a face in them enough to make a match?"

"We use many different factors." He ran his knife across the egg yolk. "First, we measure the distance between your features—how far apart your eyes are, how deep your eye sockets are, how long your jaw is, in millimeters, stuff like that—and we use the information to create a faceprint."

"Are those numbers unique?" She touched her jaw.

"Yes," he said. "If we get a good 3-D image, a faceprint is as unique as a fingerprint. But good 3-D images are hard to come by, so we can't rely on having them. After we get the measurements, we map the surface and texture of your skin. With that data, and algorithms I developed for rotating faces if the subject isn't looking into the camera at the right angle, we can tell you apart from your identical twin. Every time."

Vivian took a long sip of coffee. "So much for all those twin movies."

He smiled. "That's a big market for us, identifying twins in movies."

"I bet."

She concentrated on her steak for a while before speaking again. "So, you reduce the human face to numbers?"

"If you break it down far enough, everything is numbers."

"And you're good with numbers?"

"I see them in my head, as colors, and I can move them around." His eyes shifted past hers, as if he didn't want to admit it. "It's called synesthesia."

"Cool!" She'd never heard of it.

He gave her the kind of shy smile she hadn't expected to see from a millionaire.

"What's it like?" she asked.

"It's just different," he said. "My brain has always been different from everybody else's."

She nodded.

"It used to be a good thing," he said. "It got me out of the circus and into the world of technology."

He didn't seem coordinated enough to be in an actual circus. Maybe it was a metaphor. "That doesn't seem too bad."

He shrugged. "Now that my mind is keeping me trapped inside, being different isn't all it's cracked up to be."

What could she say to that?

After their conversation, the day went better. They wandered the shops at Grand Central Terminal for a bit, and then he said he wanted to go down to his underground house. She'd heard about the house from Mr. Rossi that morning. It seemed too far-fetched to be real, but so did The Campbell Apartment, also in Grand Central, which had belonged to a 1920s tycoon before eventually being remodeled into a bar, so she supposed there was precedent.

Anyway, getting him someplace less crowded would be a good thing. She didn't know why he needed protection, but clearly something had happened to him that had scared him enough for him to call Mr. Rossi at six in the morning. Personally, she couldn't think of a single situation where she would call Mr. Rossi that early. Including nuclear Armageddon.

She let him enter the concourse a little ahead of her, scanning the area. The pillars would give cover to an army, but there was nothing she could do about that.

Straight ahead, people darted back and forth, most arriving for their workdays in the city. Too many to count. Too many to watch. But none raised a red flag.

Tesla made for the center of the concourse and the information booth into which he'd disappeared all those months before. Her niece, Abby, said that the round booth reminded her of a layer cake—waist-high marble, glass windows, glass roof, and the famous clock perched on top like a candle. She remembered watching the movie Madagascar with Abby. The little girl had laughed herself silly when the giraffe got his head stuck inside that clock.

Tesla tapped on the information booth's door, and a chubby black woman with the name tag EVALINE opened the door. This must be the entrance to his underground house. Who had he been visiting down there when he disappeared all those months before?

"I have a guest today, Miss Evaline," Tesla said. "A Miss Vivian Torres."

Evaline folded her arms across her ample bosom. "Unless she's on the authorized list, you know I can't let her go down there."

Vivian braced herself for a struggle. She wasn't going to let Tesla out of her sight, even if it meant that she had to throw him to the ground and hogtie him. Her orders were clear—keep constant visual contact until notified by Mr. Rossi himself.

"I think she might be on the list," Tesla said. "She works for Rossi and Rossi."

Evaline raised one skeptical eyebrow, but typed into a small gray box.

Vivian waited.

"You are authorized, Ms. Torres." Evaline moved aside. "Come on in."

Tesla thanked her and opened a nearly invisible door on the edge of the pillar. Vivian had only ever seen it open once before, on the night when she'd been hired to watch him and had lost him right here.

She followed, surprised that it was so easy. Inside, dingy white paint covered the walls. Like most things, the inside was a lot less glamorous than the outside. She'd expected something grander, but this was ordinary.

Tesla motioned her to stand by the wall and lifted a hatch on the floor. Underneath the hatch a set of wrought iron stairs spiraled down. She went first, judging that an attack from behind was less likely than someone hiding beneath the stairs.

Tesla and Edison waited at the top of the stairs. Tesla looked annoyed.

"Clear," she called up.

They trotted down the stairs, and Tesla pressed the elevator button. Modern steel doors slid aside on an old-fashioned elevator of filigreed wrought iron. Tesla gestured for her to go first and pushed a lever inside to make the elevator go. Was the elevator as old as Grand Central itself— a century? Cool.

Tesla stared up at the ceiling. Machinery was creaking up there, and it clearly didn't make him happy. Luckily, it didn't take too long before they reached the bottom.

She exited first, senses alert. A walkway curved to the side, letting her see a hundred feet ahead. Nothing there. To the right stretched a large empty room, lit by a long string of yellow bulbs. Empty.

"There's a steel door at both ends of this tunnel," Tesla said. "It's operated by an antique key." He held it up. "And an electronic keypad with an eight-digit code. Anyone who wants to come in here needs both. Or they have to get by Evaline to get to the elevator."

With the cops and surveillance cameras in the concourse, no one would get past Evaline without calling down a lot of attention on themselves. "Those are the only entrances to your house?"

His blue eyes darted to the side before he answered. "Yes."

He was lying.

She kept one hand near her gun and walked right down, a short tunnel to a thick steel door. A green light blinked steadily from the keypad. Tesla walked left, and she went ahead of him and checked that door, too. Also clear. Three surveillance cameras—one at each end of the tunnel and one by the elevator. Nobody was going to sneak up on Joe Tesla.

Finally, she turned her attention to the Victorian house. A porch light shone near the front door, but the windows were otherwise dark. Four windows on the ground floor, six on the second.

Tesla started up the stairs, but she stopped him. "Let me go in first, sir, and clear the house. You wait out here with Edison."

Tesla rolled his eyes.

"It's my job," she said. "Just let me do it."

He backed up. She drew her gun and went inside, flicking on lights as she went. The switches were odd, but she got used to them. First, there was a tiny vestibule with a coat rack and an umbrella stand. That led to a hall. Clear. A room on the right with a fireplace and wingback chairs. Nowadays it would be called a living room, but she suspected that the original term was parlor. She cleared it, a library on the other side, then a dining room and kitchen behind those with a tiny bathroom tucked in the corner.

Up the stairs and she walked quickly through three bedrooms, a master bathroom with a claw-foot tub and floor tiles made of tiny pieces of marble, another library, and a room with a giant TV that felt jarring after the impeccably maintained period details. The place was huge, especially when you considered that it was set in solid rock. Unbelievable what people did with their money. But, she had to concede, it was also very cool.

She let Tesla and the dog in, and they went to the parlor

to do who knew what. She spent the rest of the day patrolling the house and the tunnel out front. And wondering about the entrance he'd lied about.

Doors worked both ways. Anyone might come or go through that lie.

12

Dr. Dubois ran a finger inside his collar under his damned designer tie. He found his office too hot, as he always did in winter, but he at least preferred this to the sweltering heat of Cuba. Even before the escape of Subject 523, he'd hated the island. Every time he'd gone out into the humid air, something had crawled on him, flew at him, or stung him. He preferred nature contained and controlled, as it was in his office.

He glanced around the room. It was just the way he liked it—glass desk spotless, ergonomic chair properly adjusted, a purposefully uncomfortable visitor's chair facing the desk, a dust-free computer and monitor, and a few prints of waves painted by an allegedly famous artist. His secretary had picked them out—nature in a frame.

His only personal touch was the putter that leaned in the corner behind the door, a putting cup next to it. Golfing cleared his mind. And, after the distasteful events in Cuba, he liked having something within reach that could be used as a weapon.

He scrolled through his online calendar. Yesterday he'd interviewed yet another unsatisfactory candidate for Dr.

Johansson's job. The woman had proved harder to replace than he had anticipated. Since her death, his workload had more than doubled.

With a grunt, he shifted the position of his wounded leg. The doctors kept telling him how lucky he was that it hadn't been worse. The bullet had missed his artery, or he would have bled out on the foul Cuban ground. The bullet had missed the bone, too, or he'd have needed emergency surgery performed by an underpaid Navy hack right there on the island. Neither of these so-called lucky circumstances changed the fact that the leg hurt like hell, then and now, or that his wife had to drive him back and forth from work, sighing each time she turned on the car, as if he'd gotten himself shot just to annoy her.

Pain pills in his drawer beckoned, but he wouldn't let himself take them. They dulled his mind, and he had important things to do today. He was scheduled to speak to another candidate to replace Dr. Johansson, but first he'd be meeting with a source on the Senate Armed Services Committee. The meeting wasn't on the calendar, so that they both could deny that it had ever happened.

His gaze strayed to the secure cell phone on his desk. He expected a call from Mr. Saddiq today about 523's status, but the phone hadn't rung yet. It would be good news. The deadline he'd worked so many years to achieve was so close. He needed things to stay stable for just a few more days.

His intercom buzzed.

"Your ten o'clock is here," said the nearly mechanical voice of his secretary.

He hadn't given her the name of the man he would be meeting. She didn't need to know it. "Show him in."

Roderick Kirkland swept through the door with a sense of entitlement that surrounded him like a fog. He sat uninvited. "There's going to be a shakeup. December first."

The doctor eyed him with distaste. The man's suit was

rumpled. He reeked of tobacco, and he couldn't sit still for more than a few seconds at a time, but he was the best source that Dr. Dubois had. "Who?"

"The entire division." Kirkland jiggled his muscular leg. "That means a new level of oversight on your Guantanamo Bay trials. Back to the beginning."

"Indeed?" He tried not to look at Kirkland's bouncing knee.

"Will everything pass muster?" Kirkland put a hand on his knee as if to steady it. His dishwater-gray eyes looked skeptical.

"It will." With a bit of luck. He'd eliminated the 500 series, then purged them from the electronic records. Painstaking work, yes, but he'd had little else to do during the weeks that he was laid up with the wounded leg. The official record indicated the lab ran only four series of tests—the 100, 200, 300, and 400 series—all successful.

He'd hired Saddiq to dispose of the bodies of the 500s at one stroke, along with Dr. Johansson and the soldiers murdered by Subject 523. Records showed that they had died in an unfortunate boating accident while returning to the United States.

The only loose end was Subject 523 and the papers that he had stolen. The soldier had confiscated evidence of the 500 series before the campaign of obliteration.

"Doctor?" Kirkland asked. "Do we have a problem?"

"No." He'd worked on this project for most of his adult life. He wouldn't allow the truth to cost him control of it now.

Over the years he'd learned about taking risks, about compromising some principles to keep the work going. It was for a greater good—thousands of soldiers who came home with PTSD or lost their nerve and never came home at all would be saved because of his work. US soldiers would be more effective, and effective longer, because of his work.

They didn't have to be US soldiers, either. The project could make him a fortune if sold to the right allies. He wanted no setbacks.

He touched the disposable cell phone on the desk. Saddiq was overdue to call and tell him that the situation was resolved. Saddiq was very reliable. He'd do the job. But it was impossible to relax until that call came in.

"Subject 523 has been contained?" Kirkland asked.

The doctor rocked back in his chair. How did Kirkland know about that, and what else did he know? He'd better give him a small truth in order to forestall more complicated questions. "The man has been located and will be contained shortly."

"Is there any risk that he will infect others?"

"Minimal." Indeed, risk of infection was great, but the risk that such a catastrophe would be traced back to his project was minuscule, and that was all either of them cared about.

"If you can't get your leak plugged in the next forty-eight hours," Kirkland said, "we'll have to burn the project. We can't move forward."

He had been through reorganizations before. There were worse things than sitting and waiting until they passed. "When will we pick up the trials afterward?"

"Never." Kirkland's nervous fingers tapped his knee. "Your work has been deemed too risky. If you can't fix your problem, trials will be canceled, and the project will be completely disavowed."

"Disavowed? They've funded this project since the beginning—"

"And if you can't get it under control, they'll stop."

"There are records," the doctor said.

"As you know," he smiled, "records can be altered. There is a team in place to paint you as a rogue doctor, hired to conduct fitness trials but secretly performing unsanctioned experiments of your own."

The doctor's leg throbbed. "They would regret it."

Kirkland was already on his feet and heading out the door. "Fix it so nobody has to regret it."

The door closed behind him. The doctor opened his drawer and took out the pain pills. He dropped two onto his palm and swallowed them with cold coffee. He needed to make that clear. Records were more difficult to alter than Kirkland seemed to think.

Before he started in with those calls, the cell phone vibrated. He glanced down at it. A text. Two words.

It's done.

13

Joe stretched his feet toward the electric fire in the parlor and took a sip of coffee from the Victorian teacup on the side table. Cold. The clock on the mantel told him that it was almost four, time to take a break.

He'd been trying for most of the day to find out more about the presidential train car and its grisly contents. Torres's presence in the house distracted him. Floorboards creaked when she walked around, and he worried that she'd find the secret passageway behind the upstairs bookshelf. She had declined lunch, but agreed to help herself to anything in the kitchen if she got hungry later.

Every hour she went out and walked the tunnel, as if someone could break in there without him noticing. But it was her job, and he left her to it. He remembered what it had been like to have a clearly defined job. He missed it.

All day, he'd been racking his brain to figure out why she seemed so familiar. He was good with faces—he'd built a multimillion-dollar company off that talent, and he could not remember where he'd seen hers. By afternoon, he'd developed a suspicion, and he had to know if it was true.

He locked the parlor door from the inside with a long skeleton key, ready to see if he was right.

In his long weeks of confinement at the Hyatt, he'd hacked into the surveillance cameras installed nearby. It gave him something to do, and a feeling that he could watch the outside world, even if he couldn't join it. These days he sometimes flipped through them, as if he were strolling down the sidewalk, like everyone else. Like he used to do without thinking.

He'd been careful with his spying, of course, and he hadn't been caught. In his endless free time, he'd managed to compile a thorough list of the nearby cameras, including what they watched and where they sent the video they obtained. He had a long list now, and, key for his current problem, it included all the cameras at Grand Central Terminal.

Joe connected through a few different computers to cover his tracks and got down to business. He took pleasure in hacking—being able to see what others couldn't, to do things most people were afraid of doing. At the circus, he'd grown up behind the scenes, always knowing more than the marks who'd paid to see the show. Hacking felt the same way.

Edison lay on the floor next to his chair, head on his outstretched paws. He sat up and gazed at Joe with reproachful brown eyes.

"Do you think this is a morally gray area?" he asked, quietly so that Torres wouldn't hear him through the parlor's door. "This kind of snooping?"

Edison lowered his head back to his paws with a sigh.

Joe felt a twinge of guilt. "I don't care what you think, Edison. I have to know."

The dog thumped his tail against the floor. Once (cyan), twice (blue). Joe decided to take that as assent. He was going to do it anyway.

He wanted to find late-night video from the concourse

itself, most particularly the camera that showed the round information booth that led to the entrance to his home. He wanted to try to find out what had happened to him after he'd returned to the concourse on the night before he'd become afraid to go outside.

On that night, he'd come down here for the first time. Leandro Gallo had been throwing a birthday party, and he'd hoped to see Celeste there, or at least find out why she had stopped returning his calls. When he'd found out that she was ill, actually dying, he drank too much and lost track of most of the night, something that had never happened to him before. He remembered taking the elevator up to the concourse, where a person had helped him back to his hotel.

He hadn't cared before, but tonight he was going to find out who.

He hacked into the Grand Central video surveillance database and scrolled through files until he reached the right time. Then he watched himself stumble out of the information booth alone. On-screen Joe closed the door behind himself and then fell flat on his face. He hadn't remembered being so drunk, but he must have been, and he was horrified that surveillance cameras had caught him out, that anyone with access could post him looking like a newb on YouTube for the world to mock. It could have been a media disaster, could still be.

A tall woman with short dark hair helped him to his feet and dusted him off. An uneasy feeling rose in him. She looked familiar, but he could see only the back of her head. Maybe she was simply a Good Samaritan who'd stepped in to keep him from being arrested for public drunkenness.

He switched to the next camera and watched as she helped him stagger across the giant room. He flopped around, his face clear in the video, but she kept her head down as if she were well aware of the cameras.

The quality of the video went up after he switched to the outside cameras. He held his breath when a man entered the frame and drew a knife. How could he have been too drunk to remember that? Damn. The woman on-screen easily disarmed the man, knocked him down, and stomped on his balls. Joe winced.

As the man curled around his crotch, she dragged Joe to his feet and resumed walking him to the Hyatt. Based on her quick actions and her cool response, he guessed that she had specialized training. Probably military.

He rewound, then froze on the image of her face as she confronted the attacker, because for a second she was more concerned about safety than about the cameras. The tall woman with the dark hair and lovely cheekbones was sitting on a chair in his hall. Vivian Torres.

Goose bumps raised on his arms.

He glanced at the closed wooden door, wishing it had a stronger lock. Had Daniel hired her to watch out for him on that night, too? If not, why had she been there? If so, why hadn't he been told about it?

With one finger, he touched the face on his screen. A beautiful woman, but much more than that. He replayed the mugger scene one more time. She was calm and in control. He wished that he could hear what she was saying.

Now that he had an identification, he wanted to find out more. Not a problem.

The Army was the biggest branch of the armed services, so he'd start there. He used the login for Agent Bister, a CIA operative he'd worked with at Pellucid, to connect to the Army personnel system. Bister had led the charge to appropriate Pellucid's software just for the CIA, and Joe couldn't stand him. So, he used the man's accounts often. He had it coming.

Once inside the database, Joe started a search for Vivian

Torres. He got a hit right away. She'd served in the Army, but had been dishonorably discharged a year ago. His unease grew, and he searched for more information, the Victorian parlor around him practically fading away as he moved into the high-tech world on the other side of the screen.

According to her record, she'd served well and earned commendations from her superior officers. As he'd seen on-screen, she was good in a fight, level-headed, and competent. She had been on track to making a solid career when something had gone wrong in an Afghani village where she was on patrol. The details of the event weren't in the file, but whatever happened had resulted in a dishonorable discharge. Since her discharge, she'd worked for various private-security companies and law firms as a bodyguard, including Daniel Rossi's law firm.

With nothing else left to search for, he logged out of Bister's account and broke his connection with the computer he'd used to hide his real location.

"What do I do with this knowledge?" he whispered to Edison. "And why didn't she tell me herself?"

The dog eyed the parlor door. Joe had canceled his daily walk with Andres, not wanting the dog to be out of his sight today. Instead, they'd spent the day with a dangerous woman who had her own dangerous secrets.

Joe stood and paced the ancient Persian carpet. Ever loyal, Edison rose and paced next to him.

The video of Torres and the mugger made it clear that she could take him in a fight, even if she weren't armed. She could have done that when he'd stumbled out of the booth drunk. He'd been completely at her mercy, and she'd only helped him. If she meant him harm, he'd already be dead. Besides, over the course of the day, he'd grown to like her. She didn't seem as if she wished him ill. But it would be stupid to rely on that judgment completely.

He should just ask her, but he was afraid. Overly paranoid, but he didn't care. He wasn't going to talk to her without insurance. He set up his phone to film his conversation, with the video streaming straight back to his laptop, where it would be stored in a file. He set a timer for ten minutes (cyan, black). If he wasn't back to shut it off, the video file would be emailed to Daniel at the highest priority. He'd know what to do.

Of course, he reminded himself, that wouldn't actually save him. It would just make sure that she got nailed for the crime if she killed him.

With only that tiny bit of reassurance, he tapped the screen to start filming, dropped the phone into his breast pocket so that the top of the phone peeked out, careful to make sure that the camera lens was not obscured, and opened the door.

Torres shifted in her chair when he walked into the hall. He'd insisted on moving one of the leather wingback chairs out here for her. If she had to spend her day staring at his front door, she might as well be comfortable. She looked calm and collected, like a competent bodyguard. He balanced his open laptop in one hand, feeling like a waiter holding a tray.

"No activity to report out there," she said. "How's work coming?"

He stood awkwardly in the door frame and stared at her face, eyes traveling across her features to confirm that she was the woman on the video. No doubt.

"First, I want to thank you," he said.

"I'm just doing my job," she answered.

"Not for that. For getting me home safe last spring."

Surprise flickered across her face, but disappeared in less than a second. Microexpressions were impossible to control. Without his training in spotting them, he'd have missed it.

"Were you paid for this service?" The laptop trembled as he pressed a few buttons, starting up the surveillance video of their meeting in Grand Central months before, when she'd brought him back drunk.

"If I were paid for that kind of service, I wouldn't be able to reveal that information."

"Why not?" What was his goal here? To get her to confess? To what, exactly?

"As you know, sir, I work in close protection. Anything I do or see while on the job is confidential." Her dark eyes met his levelly. She clearly was not intending to back down.

"So, you were on a job?"

"I can't say." She squared off her shoulders.

"Does that mean that you were stalking me?"

She laughed. "Not hardly. Maybe I just happened by, helped you home, did the right thing. I'm a Good Samaritan."

Joe didn't believe that.

She pointed behind his head. "What's that mean?"

Joe turned around to look at the round red light recessed above the front door. "It means that the elevator has started going up. But that doesn't make sense, because no one has access to it but me and the Gallos, and they never come down here."

Someone else was coming.

Joe stared at the light that indicated the elevator was right now heading up to the clock and the information booth. He'd never seen it lit before, hadn't known if it really worked, but Celeste had assured him that it did. Evaline wouldn't have let anyone past her who wasn't on the list. Maybe it was Leandro. If not, he hoped no one had hurt her.

"I'd like you to move to the back of the house, away from the windows." Torres's voice was matter-of-fact.

She drew her gun and stood next to the front door, away

from the window, and peeked through the filmy curtains. Her phone buzzed in her pants pocket. Without taking her eyes off the tunnel, she eased it out and glanced at the screen.

"It's from Mr. Rossi. He says that he's coming down with police and two CIA agents." Torres holstered her gun. "They're here to question you about the death in the tunnels. Your fingerprint was found at a murder scene."

Joe stumbled backward. The police and the CIA?

"Mr. Rossi will take care of you," she said.

"They might take me." Joe's heart raced. "They might take me outside. I can't go outside."

He heard panic in his voice, and Edison must have heard it, too. The dog tugged his pant leg, trying to pull him back into the parlor. That wouldn't help.

"Good boy," Joe said automatically.

"I'm sure that Mr. Rossi will explain the situation to them."

Joe didn't think they'd care about his mental issues. If anything, they'd weigh against him. He measured the distance to the doors at the end of the tunnels in his head. He might make it to one of them before the elevator arrived and the men came out, but he also might not.

Edison bumped Joe's knee with his head, reminding him that he was there, that everything was OK. Except that it wasn't.

"I'm going upstairs," Joe said. "Can you buy me time?"

"Yes, sir," she said. "I'll stall them as long as I can."

Joe dropped his laptop in the backpack by the front door, pulling on the hoodie hung there, and pocketing the flashlight. He ran back through the parlor to get his power cord and then sprinted up the stairs, heading for the back bedroom.

He reached into his pocket, fingers closing over a ring of

metal keys. That was something. On impulse, he grabbed the polar fleece blanket from the bedroom floor, the one that Edison usually slept on.

The doorbell told him that they'd reached his front door. Angry voices said they'd be breaking through any second if Torres didn't let them in.

Edison growled.

Joe put his finger to his lips and whispered, "Hush."

He struggled with the heavy bookcase as boots thudded through his house—they were in the kitchen and the parlor. Two separate groups.

If they caught him, they'd arrest him and drag him outside. He couldn't let that happen.

He pointed at the secret passageway, and Edison leaped in.

Joe backed in after him, snaked a hand around the end of the bookcase to pull the rug flat, and closed the door.

The bookcase was barely in place when the bedroom door crashed against the plaster wall.

The heavy steps of several men entered his room.

He didn't dare turn on the flashlight. Light might show around the edges of the bookcase. He should have checked that out on the first day—dropped the flashlight in there, closed the door, and seen if the light leaked through. But he hadn't.

Edison's warm shoulder leaned into his.

Joe scrunched past him and crawled through the darkness as quickly as he could. He had to hope that the dog would follow him and stay quiet. One bark or growl and all would be lost.

He tucked his head low between his shoulder blades so that he wouldn't crack it against the low roof. The tunnel dropped down fast. He forced himself to slow so that he wouldn't lose his balance and face-plant into the rocks.

He hurried toward the end. Was the tunnel on the original blueprints of the house? Was someone waiting for him at the other end?

14

Ozan checked his watch, again, and ordered a refill on his coffee. He'd been here for half an hour already. His contact, a man he knew only as Johnny Tops, was late. The diner was doing a brisk business this early—the waitress bringing food to table after table. Ozan was having coffee and toast.

He held the back of his wrist to his brow. His skin felt hot and damp—feverish. If Erol's forehead felt like that, Ozan would make him stay in bed all day and watch cartoons. No cartoons for Ozan.

Stifling a curse, he shook two aspirin into his hand, chewed them, and swallowed the sharp crumbs. The bitter taste made him grimace, but he'd heard that the painkiller worked faster if you chewed it, and the headache and fever had to go away right now.

A man took the seat across from him, baseball hat pulled low across a square, doughy face. The body connected to that head was wiry and tough.

"Morning, Tops." Ozan gestured to the waitress for an additional menu.

"I'm not staying," said Tops with a strong Brooklyn accent. "But I got something for you."

Ozan slid an envelope with four hundred-dollar bills

across the greasy table, payment for whatever Tops was delivering. Tops slapped a manila envelope into his hand as he stood to walk out.

The middle-aged waitress arrived with a menu and the coffeepot, filling Ozan's cup before bustling off.

The envelope contained reports. Ozan skimmed the pages, learning that the police had named a person of interest in the murder of Subject 523—a millionaire named Joe Tesla. Ozan chuckled. So the tall, awkward man was a millionaire out for a stroll around the tunnels of New York City in the middle of the night. He read further. Apparently, the man had a house down there, but he'd missed a social call from both NYPD officers and agents of the CIA.

Ozan took a slow sip of lukewarm coffee. The CIA? Dr. Dubois must have called in reinforcements, worried that Tesla knew something. Whatever it was, the reclusive millionaire wouldn't last long once he was caught.

He'd have taken him out if that damn train hadn't arrived, and the man jumped across the tracks. He hadn't expected him to act so rashly. After the train had passed, Ozan had followed him up onto the platform, but the crowds had been too thick to do anything to him. Knowing where the man lived, that would eliminate that problem.

Time to pay the man a visit at home.

An hour later, Ozan leaned against the side of the tunnel to catch his breath. He should leave the tunnels, leave Tesla to others. Catching Tesla wasn't technically part of his mission, and he didn't think that Tesla had received papers from 523.

Ozan didn't want to quit. A force he couldn't explain drove him on. Maybe it was stubbornness. Or maybe Tesla was a gift to him. According to the report, the man was unable to go outside because of a mental condition. Which meant that he hid out in the tunnels, the perfect target for a game of cat and mouse. Ozan loved to play, although he rarely let himself indulge in those kind of games. This time, the temptation was irresistible.

He'd return to the murder scene to see if he could pick up Tesla's tracks from there and follow them through the tunnels to find his house. Like everyone, Tesla was a creature of habit. His habits would betray him.

Ozan should have approached him right off, dragged him deeper into the tunnels, but the dog had made things unpredictable. Plus, Erol loved dogs. How could Ozan look Erol in the face if he killed a dog?

But this, this would be fun. Tesla was smart; he was clever. The way he'd jumped in front of the oncoming train and used it for rolling cover to escape was ballsy. And, since the guy couldn't leave the tunnels, Ozan could take his time. He only needed to bag him before law enforcement did, and he intended to use them as hunters used beaters—tools to flush out his quarry and drive it straight toward him.

Ozan slowed and studied the murder scene, his crime scene, from a distance. Floodlights turned night into day. Police and crime scene people walked ponderously back and forth as if their very deliberateness would solve the crime. But he'd been careful, and clever. They'd never catch him.

Hot and cold poured over Ozan in waves, and his head pounded with pain. So much for the chewed-aspirin theory. He ignored the pain and soldiered on like the soldier he had once been, staying as far from the crime scene as he could while he searched for the dog's prints. Tesla's dog was probably the only dog in these tunnels. His ears strained to hear the rumble of an approaching train. He didn't want to end up smeared across the tracks.

Dizziness swept over him. He slumped against the stone wall until it passed. Then he pushed himself upright again and tripped over a broken train tie leaning against the side of the tunnel. Anger took over. He swore and savagely kicked the tie.

"Hey!" called a voice behind him.

Ozan whirled to face the speaker. No one had gotten that close to him without him noticing in a long time. He must be sicker than he thought.

"Police," said the shadow between him and crime scene. "You're not allowed down here."

He should run. Even sick, he was a fast runner. He could get a quick lead. But the officer, too near already, kept coming. Ozan shouldn't tempt fate by confronting him. He shouldn't even be here at all. He should run.

But his head hurt, his muscles felt weak. It'd be easier to deal with this guy right here. If the guy wanted to cause trouble, he'd show him trouble. Why should he be the one who ran away? An alarm bell clanging in his fevered brain told him that this line of thinking was very wrong.

He ignored it.

Instead, he lifted a piece of broken train tie. Solid and heavy, its weight felt right in his hands. The tarry smell of creosote drifted up from the wood.

"I'm sick," Ozan called to the man who had disturbed him.

He lowered the tie so that it was hidden by his leg. Just in time, because the policeman shone a flashlight at him, right in the eyes. Damn bastard. Ozan held his arm over his aching eyes to shield them from the bright light. He managed a weak smile and held up his other hand to show that he had no weapons. Just an innocent guy.

The train tie leaned against the back of his calf. He couldn't use it yet. Where was the second cop? Usually they ran in pairs.

"Keep your hands where I can see them." The cop was young, Ozan saw that now. He had almond-shaped brown eyes, so like Erol's, and short black hair. Chinese? "We're going to need you to step this way."

He'd said "we." Where was the other one?

"Of course, Officer," Ozan called. The meeker he was, the closer he'd be able to get.

The flashlight stayed pointed at his eyes, and Ozan kept one arm up as the policeman moved closer. A telltale vibration under his feet told him what to do next.

"You do look a little under the weather," said the cop. "Would you like us to help you get to medical care?"

Careful not to telegraph the movement with his eyes, Ozan swung the broken piece of wood like a bat, catching the unprepared man on the temple. The man collapsed backward onto the tracks. The thunder of an oncoming train covered the sound of his fall.

Ozan kept a tight hold on the piece of train tie and ran, ducking left into another tunnel, heading for the darkest parts, even though he didn't have a light.

From behind him came the shrill screech of brakes. Simple physics told him that the train wouldn't stop in time to avoid the man on the tracks. The young cop was dead. If the blow hadn't killed him, the oncoming train had. His partner would stop to check, though, and Ozan's lead would grow.

He settled into a quick trot. He could get out of the underground system through a broken access door about a half-mile away, where he'd entered. After a quarter of a mile, he dropped the train tie. No one would ever search this far afield, even if they thought the cop had been murdered. The cop's death would likely be blamed on impact with the train. Ozan was probably in the clear. So close to the scene of 523's murders, though, he couldn't take that for granted. And he had to come back for Tesla.

He cursed himself for his inattention and recklessness. He

counted off his mistakes in his head. First, the policeman should never have gotten so close to him without being noticed. There was no excuse for leaving himself vulnerable. Second, he should have had an escape route planned for every second that he spent down here. That was standard procedure, and he'd violated it. Third, he should have run instead of provoking a confrontation, or he could have played off the man's offer of medical help. He most likely would have gotten away without having to kill a man. The train had been a lucky coincidence, and he couldn't depend on coincidence. At least he had done everything necessary to get home safe to Erol. Erol needed him.

Still, Ozan had made a long list of mistakes, and he never made mistakes.

What was wrong with him?

15

November 28, 8:44 p.m.
Underground maintenance room
Subway system

Joe leaned his back against the rusted metal door. He flicked on the flashlight and swept the room with its beam. The musty space about the size of his first dorm room, big enough to lie down in, but barely. It contained an old mop and bucket, a pile of rags, a three-legged wooden stool, and a stack of yellowed comic books. He pictured a long-ago maintenance man hiding here, reading during his breaks.

He checked the walls and found a light switch. Crossing his fingers, he flicked it on.

Buzzing fluorescent lights washed the room in pale blue. Before he'd moved down here, he had expected the tunnels and rooms to exist in a state of perpetual darkness, but had instead found lights affixed to many tunnel ceilings and working lights in long-deserted rooms.

He sat on the stool, and Edison put his warm muzzle in his lap.

"We're in a bit of a bind, Edison." Joe leaned his head against the wall. A bit of a bind? That was an understatement.

Joe was screwed, but maybe he could find a good home for the dog. Edison, after all, was innocent of everything, and he had good job skills to boot.

Edison whined.

The logical move was to call Daniel, meet him someplace, and go in for questioning. He'd done nothing wrong— everything would be fine. Except that he couldn't do it. It meant that he would have to go outside.

He hated his agoraphobia. No matter what the psychiatrists said, he viewed it as cowardice. He should be able to man up, take a deep breath, and go outside. Logically, he knew that going outside wouldn't kill him. Staying down here and playing hide-and-seek with the police and a killer might.

But he couldn't go outside.

After he'd left his house, he'd run through the tunnels for over a mile and switched from the commuter train tracks that ran through Grand Central to the subway lines at Times Square. They were more heavily patrolled, he imagined, but at least they were patrolled by cops who weren't specifically looking for him.

At the 68th Street/Hunter College station, he'd climbed onto a platform, hoodie pulled low over his face to keep the surveillance cameras from recognizing him, although a man coming out of the tunnels with a golden Lab was already distinctive enough that they didn't need facial-recognition software to identify him. He stared at the friendly blue station sign with its green border and took a few deep breaths before joining a mass of people heading toward the stairs leading outside.

Each step seemed harder, and the crowd shifted him against the right-hand wall, the side reserved for the injured or weak. He fell in behind an elderly woman with a nimbus of thin white hair that shivered like dandelion seeds in the wind coming off the subway. She struggled with each step, but hauled herself upward. When she reached the step bathed in gray sunlight, she neither stopped nor slowed, but moved up to the next step, and the next. Behind her, Joe stopped.

His heart raced. Sweat drenched his T-shirt and ran down his back. His breath puffed out in front of him in rapid clouds. When he grabbed the cold railing to keep from falling, he realized that his hands were numb. A feeling of dread consumed him.

He would die here on the steps.

Edison tugged at his leash, but Joe didn't have the strength to move. The dog took the leg of his jeans in his mouth and pulled him down a step. Joe watched Edison. The dog stood one step below him with a mouthful of wet jeans. He set his front legs far apart and dragged Joe down another step. His implacable strength comforted Joe. He released his hold on the railing and let the dog guide him through the stream of people back into the tiled tunnel and the dark safety of the platform.

He couldn't go out there.

After that, he'd led the dog back down the tunnels to the abandoned janitor's closet where they now sat. A dark, wet circle on his knee showed where Edison had taken hold of him. The dog deserved better than a master who was stuck down here until the cops caught him or he got hit by a train. "You're a great dog, you know that?"

Edison cocked his head. Clearly, he didn't think that this was news.

"OK, Yellow Dog," he said. "Why would the CIA come to talk to me about a murder in the New York subway?"

Edison yawned.

"Don't yawn. That's the most interesting piece," he said. "Think about the jurisdiction, Edison. For a simple murder, the cops would have come on their own. For a complicated murder, like the work of a serial killer who killed in multiple states, they might have also brought along the FBI. But they brought the CIA. Why?"

The dog flopped onto the dusty floor, obviously not interested in analyzing the case.

"Some partner you are." Joe pulled treats from his pocket and handed them to Edison. Soon, he would have to sneak out and get them both real food.

He pulled out his laptop, felt ridiculously thrilled to see an electrical outlet in the corner, and compiled what he knew about the case. Not much, really. One man beaten to death recently, two men and a child bricked in decades ago. In spite of everything, it felt good to be doing something meaningful again.

Rebar was the key. Joe needed to find out why he'd been killed, and why the CIA cared. How had he known that the car was there? Had he found the treasure that he'd expected to find inside?

Joe remembered the footprints in the dust and how the man had clearly searched the skeletons' pockets. The car itself might hold the answer.

He struggled to understand why the CIA would care about an event that far in the past. It was more likely that Rebar had been wrong about the car, that he had been chased because he'd known something from the current day, maybe had had proof about an activity that the agency desperately needed to keep secret. The answer must be in the documents that the man who had chased him had asked about.

The shaky video he'd taken of the crime scene was still on his computer. Maybe the answer was in there. He hesitated before opening it. He didn't want to see the blood-spattered scene again. He hadn't watched much television as a child, or movies, and he still found such images unnerving in a way that he'd never been able to explain to his college peers who'd grown up immersed in a world of simulated bloodshed.

Still, he'd have to fight his squeamishness, because he wouldn't allow himself to be intimidated. He took a deep breath and clicked the Play button. The video started with footprints in the dust and moved to take in the skeletons that had been dragged into the center of the room. The skulls had both fallen off and rolled to rest against the far brick wall. The person who'd moved them clearly hadn't cared about the skulls. He must have been looking for something they'd carried in their clothes.

Joe scanned through the video but didn't see any identifying indicators that would help him to figure out the men's identities. Because of the way that the soldier's body was positioned, he couldn't see the front of his shirt, where his name might have been sewn on. These people must have been important (hence, the train car), and they must have been considered dangerous, maybe because of chemical contamination or biological infection.

As if he'd known his later self would want to know, the film focused on the tiny skeleton, the one that he'd assumed belonged to a child. Unlike the others, this one wore no clothes. And its legs looked wrong. He enhanced the image and zoomed in until the images got grainy. The spine didn't look right. It had several extra vertebrae. A tail.

Joe's heart lightened when he realized that the bones didn't belong to a dead child, but rather a monkey. That explained why it was naked, but it didn't explain why someone had bricked the poor creature up deep under New York City.

Maybe it was a pet. Maybe it was more sinister, like an escaped lab monkey. Had they used monkeys for testing that long ago? If so, then perhaps the men, and the monkey, had been infected with a disease. And, now, maybe Joe was, too. He shivered.

The goal was to identify Rebar, not to solve the crime, but he'd come back and watch the video later and search for more clues. In the meantime, he fast-forwarded past the rest of the room to the part where he'd filmed Rebar's body.

Nausea rose in his throat at the rats cowering in the corners. Edison kicked in his sleep, as if he dreamed of running.

"Good instinct, boy," Joe told him.

He forced himself to look at the battered face. The skull had been crushed. There wasn't enough intact bone to support a face. He wouldn't be able to identify him from that.

But he had more to work with. He could search through surveillance video of Grand Central and get a picture of the man before he'd gone into the tunnels. He could use that to identify him just as he had identified Vivian Torres.

For that, he had to get online. Not tonight.

Instead, he tried to put the pieces together. An hour later, he was no closer to an answer; he kept nodding off. He shut down his laptop and unfolded Edison's blanket. When he'd grabbed it, he hadn't thought about why. Now he knew—he'd need it to get through the night.

The comic books made a serviceable pillow. He bunched them on the floor in the corner and spread the blanket next to them. He turned off the light and pulled the blanket up like a sleeping bag. Edison lay down on the covers next to him. The dog's warm form comforted him, and he had to live up to his no-self-pity rule. He'd gotten himself into this mess, he would get himself out. He just needed to figure things out, and he was good at figuring things out.

He'd better be.

16

November 29, 7:32 a.m.
Underground maintenance room
Subway system

Joe woke to utter darkness. For a second, he wasn't sure if he'd opened his eyes. His back ached, and his right arm was asleep. Edison's relaxed breathing was the only sound. He smelled dog and mold.

Slowly, it came to him. He wasn't home. He was in a maintenance closet somewhere in the subway tunnel system—he wasn't sure where. He wasn't lost, but he wasn't found, either.

No point in dwelling on that. He turned on his laptop to check the time: 7:30 a.m. Late enough to give up on getting more sleep and time to figure out how to get breakfast for himself and Edison without being arrested.

With cracks and pops, he stood. His back told him that it had not enjoyed sleeping on cold tiles all night long, and that it never wanted to do so again. Even Edison made a grunting noise when he got up, as if he'd missed his dog bed.

It took only a minute to turn on the light and gather up his belongings. The blanket, he bunched in his arms. He'd need it for cover in the tunnels.

"Let's go, Edison." His voice sounded unnaturally loud in the tiny room, and he lowered it. "Let's go on a mission for food and Internet, the staffs of life."

The dog shook himself and walked to the door.

"Heel." Joe didn't know what they would face out there, but it would be easier if Edison stuck close. "And stay there."

He reached up and flicked off the light before opening the door. He didn't want to be visible to anyone outside. After giving his eyes time to adjust to the darkness, he walked out the door and down the tunnel. A set of stairs ran up to a metal grate. Shoes walked across over his head, dropping dirt and water down on his hair. Shoes on the feet of people walking down the sidewalk, as he used to do.

He hurried past the grate, keeping to the side of the tracks, searching for side tunnels.

A train neared, white headlights a beacon in the tunnel. Joe pulled Edison in front of him and curled against the wall, wrapping the blanket around their bodies so that nothing showed. He hoped that no one would notice a dark hump against the wall, nearly as much as a man with a dog.

The blanket trick seemed to work, because he made it almost all the way to Grand Central without incident. Almost.

A policeman stood at the tunnel entrance to Platforms 9 (scarlet) and 10 (cyan, then black). Joe shrank back in the tunnel and tried Platforms 7 (slate) and 8 (purple) with the same results. Looked like they'd staked out all the platforms. Hard to believe the cops would expend that kind of manpower for a simple murder investigation.

He ran back toward the track that led to Platforms 16 (cyan, orange) and 17 (cyan, slate), Edison loping between him and the side of the tunnel. He had a chance to get in, but he had only a narrow window of time. Even then, it was risky.

Jogging, he formulated a plan. A quirk in MTA's schedule

meant that one train halted in the tunnel for about two minutes every morning at 8:03 (a purple, black, and red ribbon flashed in his head) while the train in front of it finished loading at the platform. He'd seen the train sitting there one morning on a walk with Edison and had checked the schedule to see why. The tunnel system was his backyard, and he wanted to know why a train would be loitering there.

Maybe today his curiosity would help him out.

He arrived with less than a minute to spare and hunched against a pillar near where he hoped the last car of the train would come to a stop. He held the blanket ready to cover them. The train clattered up close, and he hid them under the blanket. Edison tensed in his arms but didn't panic. Joe fingered one of the keys from his massive key ring, hoping.

He felt more than heard the train stop and pulled off the blanket, standing and running toward the back. He hoped that the engineer wasn't looking. He couldn't do anything about the passengers, but most people kept their eyes focused inside the train, ignoring the subterranean world beyond their metal and glass walls.

In a few strides, he reached the train's back door. The narrow entrance was too high to reach, but he was ready for that. He vaulted onto the coupling, teetered, then caught hold of the metal door handle with one hand. A quick turn of his key, and he was inside. Step one was successful.

Edison whined. He turned back to the open door and the tracks behind him.

"Jump, boy!" He calculated that they had fifteen (cyan, brown) seconds left. If Edison didn't jump soon, he'd have to climb down himself and figure out another way. He'd never seen the dog jump more than a couple of feet high. Had he ever jumped so high before? Could he?

Edison was not one to be left behind.

The dog got a running start, then hurtled up and into the car. Joe put his hands out to catch him before he hit the back of the small compartment that separated them from the main car. Edison lunged to the side as he landed, sliding forward and against Joe's hands, redirecting his momentum. Smart dog.

Joe slammed the door behind him and turned the key in the lock. They were committed now.

"Good boy." He picked up Edison's leash and opened the door that separated them from the rest of the train car. His plan wouldn't work unless he got farther forward in the train.

He walked straight through the car, as if he belonged, hip inches from blue fabric seats. Most people didn't look up from their newspapers, books, and phones, but a woman in her forties eyed him suspiciously. He walked on. Even if she called the police, the call probably wouldn't be routed to the police at the platforms within the two minutes left before the train arrived at the station. He hoped.

In the next car, nobody looked askance at him. They must have assumed that he'd come from the car behind them. A few smiled at Edison absently. He walked until he reached the middle of the train. Here, he would hide amongst the crowd. The sheer volume of commuters might be enough to keep the police at the platform ends from seeing the dog or recognizing Joe.

When the train pulled in, Joe hung back to let a few people by. He couldn't go first. He needed a critical mass of people on the platform before he exited the train. When he judged there were enough people there, he pushed to the door and out. He didn't dare to be the last one off the train, either.

He kept Edison close and let the crowd draw them along the platform toward the exit. He couldn't see the policemen and hoped that he wasn't visible to them, either. As for Edison, all those many legs on the platform would conceal him. With luck, the policemen weren't watching the departing crowd too closely. If they spotted him, he still had a good chance of getting away before they worked their way through the crowd.

Joe and Edison reached the main floor without incident. Joe led the way up the stairs to the west balcony. From on high he took a quick look at the people moving through the giant room below. None seemed to notice him and wouldn't even see Edison from down there. Good.

He headed over toward the elevator by The Campbell Apartment. He hated taking the elevator, with its camera, but he didn't think that anyone would be monitoring that camera. They probably hadn't expected him to get past the platforms. He made it safely to the elevator and pressed the button to go to the floor of the Vanderbilt Tennis and Fitness Club, his workout facility.

Once he got into the gym, Joe felt safer. Inside, it looked like any other gym—a counter at the front to sign in and receive a towel and locker rooms to the right for men and left for women. Across from those were the weight room and tennis courts.

The young man at the desk, Brandon, recognized him. Nothing in his greeting seemed different from any other day. Brandon looked like Joe—the same height and build with the same short dark hair and blue eyes. Brandon, too, was a programmer, working his way through college, and Joe had arranged an internship for him at Pellucid the following summer. He wore a bright blue Pellucid baseball cap to work every day.

"You're up early, Mr. Tesla." His accent was pure Bronx.

"I'm busy later," Joe said. "I thought I'd better get a workout in while I can."

Brandon nodded. Joe normally kept strange hours, dropping in at any time from when they opened at six a.m. to when they closed at one a.m. He was grateful for that now. Nothing seemed out of the ordinary.

On the desk next to the sign-in sheet rested Brandon's phone. It was the same brand as Joe's, but without a cover. If Joe could switch their phones undetected, the phone might inadvertently trick the police into following Brandon. Joe rejected the idea. The switch might get the young man into trouble, and the police would know about Joe's connection to the health club.

"Could you do me a favor?" Joe asked.

"Always, Mr. Tesla."

Joe slid two twenties across the desk. "Get me a bagel and coffee for breakfast and get Edison a steak from Ceriello? You can keep the change."

Not that there would be much change. Ceriello steaks were expensive.

Brandon put a "back in a minute" sign on the desk and headed out.

Joe made for the locker room, dropping the towel over his shoulder. He unlocked his locker and took out shampoo, shaving cream, and a razor. He lingered longer than he probably should have under the water, loving how it washed away the smells of night on the floor with the dog and how the hot water relaxed his tense muscles. Plus, under the shower he could pretend that this was just another ordinary day.

After he got out and dried off, he had to face the reality that, among other things, he had no clean clothes. He sniffed his workout shirt and then the shirt he'd been wearing all night. No contest. The workout shirt smelled better. He pulled it over his head, wishing for clean clothes. No luck there, but what the gym had, which was better than clean, was Wi-Fi. After all, the fully connected businessman had to be able to access the Internet between sets.

Clean and dry, he sat on the wooden bench in the locker room and logged into the Wi-Fi with Edison curled on the tile floor at his feet. He'd gotten through a couple of computers to hide his location by the time Brandon came back with breakfast. He even brought a plate for the steak and a bowl of water for Edison. A good kid.

In a few minutes he had hacked into the Grand Central video surveillance archive. This time he wasn't searching for Vivian Torres's embarrassing rescue. He was searching for Rebar, trying to figure out when he'd come through the terminal, or if he'd come through the terminal at all on his way down to the tunnels. There were hundreds of other entry points—old access doors, the platforms at the subway stations, and who knew where else? Still, it was a place to start.

Joe could download surveillance footage before the approximate time that he'd seen Rebar and then work back in hourly increments to look for a man who'd climbed off one of the platforms and into the tunnels. With forty-four platforms (double greens), it was a lot of footage, but he could automate most of that work.

He started it up, then let it run in the background while he searched for news of himself. Nothing. It was hard to believe they'd blanketed the place with police without explaining anything to the public.

His stomach tightened. Whatever they wanted him for, it must be important and top secret. What secrets had Rebar uncovered?

Joe carried the laptop into the weight room and watched a couple of businessmen play tennis while he tried to think. The men ran across the blue court, each returning the ball with a grim concentration that said it was more war than game. He felt like that right now himself. With a sigh, he went back to the locker room and reclaimed his spot on the bench and searched for news on Rebar's murder.

He started with the *New York Post*'s web site. It didn't skimp on coverage of bizarre murders. The web site featured a brief piece about a body found deep under Grand Central, but it mentioned neither the presidential train car nor the other skeletons. So, the police must not have released those details to the press. If they had, the *Post* would have shouted it far and wide. It was too strange not to, but the reporter made little of the murder—hinting that it was a homeless man probably bludgeoned by another homeless man, identity of both unknown. That meant the media didn't have the juicy details.

The site gave its biggest headlines to the story of a policeman killed by a train while investigating an incident in the train tunnels. Rebar's murder, perhaps? The police called it "a tragic accident." The dead man left behind a wife and six-month-old baby, poor guy. Maybe it was murder, and committed by the man who had almost shot Joe. It was too easy to get paranoid.

A bong from his computer drew his attention to the Pellucid window. He tabbed over. The video showed a tall man in a camouflage jacket climbing off the end of Platform 23. A crush of people filled the platform behind him, but no one seemed to notice his actions. No one threw him a curious glance. The anonymity of the big city had worked to Rebar's advantage.

Joe moved his legs to let a tennis player walk by to the showers. He looked out of place working in the locker room, but he hoped that big-city indifference might help him, too.

It didn't. The man glared at him. Though Joe ignored him, a seed of worry started. What if the guy complained about him or, after reading the news, mentioned the weird guy with a dog and a laptop at the gym?

Probably nothing to worry about, but Joe worked faster anyway. He went back to the picture of Rebar. He couldn't see his face in the shot. He painstakingly backed the video up from that point and switched through other cameras in the station, hoping to find Rebar captured in one of them.

Bingo. He tilted his laptop's screen forward to get a better view. Edison cocked an ear in his direction, sensing his excitement, but didn't lift his head.

Joe moved the video forward a frame at a time. A man in a camouflage jacket entered the concourse with determined long strides, a shadow indicating stubble on his chin. What looked like crumpled papers overflowed from the pockets of his jacket. He walked with the erect posture of the man Joe had met in the tunnel. It might be the same man, but he couldn't get a positive ID unless he could see at least part of his face.

The man pointedly angled his face away from the camera as he crossed the concourse and headed down to the platforms without a glance at the arrivals and departures boards. A man who knew where he was going—and where the cameras were placed.

The entrance to Platform 23 had a camera. When Joe switched to it, he was rewarded by a view of Rebar looking directly into the surveillance camera. A determined expression crossed his face as he stuffed papers deeper into his pocket. Joe didn't remember seeing those papers when he'd filmed the crime scene. Maybe the murderer had taken them, or maybe Rebar had lost them or stashed them on his way to the train car.

He had to stay focused on the identification. He took a screen shot of the facial image and ran it through tools to enhance it. He made a few guesses to clean it up and then started running the picture through Pellucid, starting with military databases because of the jacket, posture, and how he'd called Joe "sir."

Edison sat patiently next to him. The man came out of the shower and glared at the dog.

"Psychiatric service animal," Joe said. "You can ask at the front desk."

"Some of us are here to play tennis."

"I'm waiting on my court time," Joe lied.

"Surely you can find somewhere more comfortable than that."

"You'd be surprised." Joe went back to his screen.

He'd gotten a hit on Rebar's picture. He brought up the window and scrolled down. Rebar's real name was Ronald Raines. He was in the Navy and had been stationed in Guantanamo Bay, Cuba. Currently listed as AWOL. Who went AWOL from Cuba? It wasn't a war zone.

Edison lay down, blissfully unconcerned about these questions.

Even though he had his own accounts with official access to the databases he needed, he used CIA Agent Bister's login and password. He'd cracked Bister's password the first time he'd logged in next to him because Bister typed with two fingers at about the speed of your average chimpanzee. His password, not surprisingly, was *hulksm@sh*.

Joe always masked the IP address of his computer and this morning, for all the Internet knew, he was Agent Bister logging in from Peet's Coffee & Tea in Redwood City, California, where Bister liked to hang out, probably because the woman behind the counter had big breasts and a TV smile. Sunil had often teased Joe for being paranoid, but knowing as much as he did about how data were collected and used, he considered his precautions barely adequate.

Once in, he settled down to read about Ronald Raines, the man who'd introduced himself as Rebar in the tunnel.

Before the man had gone missing, he'd worked in interrogations in Afghanistan and later in Cuba. Did that mean he'd asked clever questions, or did it mean he'd tortured people to obtain information? The files had no answer. Had he gone AWOL because of something he'd uncovered in an interrogation? Had a prisoner bribed him?

The files listed extra combat training. Otherwise, nothing unusual. He memorized Rebar's parents' names and phone number. No other personal contacts were listed. The file said that he was single, with no children, so at least there were no kids growing up without a father.

The man must have known something important to have a killer sent after him. And what could be so important that it would call for so much police presence the tunnels under New York after his death?

17

Stomach seething, Vivian jogged up Fifth Avenue. She maneuvered through commuters carrying coffee and brown paper sacks full of breakfast. Frost rimed the sidewalk, and she watched her footing. Each breath puffed out in front of her, and cold air stung her cheeks. A good winter day for a run. Running was what she did best when angry. And today she was miles' worth of angry.

She'd texted Dirk to meet her by Pulitzer Fountain on the south end of Central Park. A good mile from Grand Central. Had Tesla really stumbled across the body, or had he put it there? Her instincts told her that he wasn't a killer, but she knew better than to trust that assessment. She'd seen enough seemingly mild-mannered men in Afghanistan who'd turned into brutal killers.

She passed the skaters in front of Rockefeller Center, then the spires of St. Patrick's Cathedral. Her footsteps pounding against concrete pushed her on. Not ready yet to slow down or catch her breath.

An email had arrived in her account early that morning that looked like it had come from her mother. Her mother had emailed her only once a year or so, preferring to talk on the phone, so Vivian had opened it immediately. The first paragraph chatted about a family dinner that had never happened. Just when she'd started to worry that her mother was losing it, she got to the second paragraph.

Remember our friend from the tunnel? I just found out that his name is Ronald Raines and he was in the Navy. Maybe he'd be a good match for you?

Tesla. Either he'd hacked her mother's account or spoofed it, and she didn't give a damn which. He had damn well better stay away from her mother.

She was enough of a good citizen to call Raines's name into the tip line from a phone kiosk not far from her apartment. The surveillance camera pointed at it had been vandalized months ago, so no one would be able to trace her. Damn Tesla for putting her in this position to begin with.

So, where did that leave her? Halfway to her daily run with Dirk and with no idea what she was going to tell him. She kept going, hoping that she would run right into the answer. She didn't.

"Yo!" Dirk waved from the empty fountain. The water had been turned off for winter. He wore gray sweatpants and a blue sweatshirt that matched his eyes. A black watch cap was pulled low over his ears, and his nose was red.

She headed over to him, glancing inside the fountain at the black leaves mounded up in the corners. "Nice day for a walk."

Dirk looked at the gray sky and quirked his mouth. "Might snow."

She started a fast jog around Grand Army Plaza, and Dirk fell in next to her, not yet breathing hard. He gave her a long look, like he expected her to talk, then pressed his lips together. He'd wait her out. He always did.

They passed a woman in a long gray woolen coat pushing a stroller so mounded with pink blankets that Vivian couldn't see the baby, but it had to be a girl. Not even old enough to go to school and already suffocating in pink. Vivian had been a tomboy, fighting pink all her life.

Dirk gave her a sidelong smile. He knew how she felt about pink.

"Any progress on the tunnel murder?" she asked.

Dirk slowed his rhythm and put on his cop face. "Why are you asking?"

"I might have an ID on the victim," she said, running faster. "An anonymous tip."

Dirk caught back up before saying anything. "We have a tip line. Call it in there."

"I did. I want to make sure that it gets treated seriously, so I thought I'd tell you, too."

"Then tell me the ID," he said. "I'll make sure."

She hesitated a long time before answering. He knew that she sometimes worked for Rossi and Rossi, and that they represented Joe Tesla. He even knew that she'd been assigned to Tesla once. She couldn't give him details without implicating a potential client. "I can't."

He'd check today's tips now, and he'd be able to say that he hadn't gotten the information from her.

"I see," he said. Frozen leaves crackled under their feet as they ran deeper into the park.

"Any news you can share?"

"We only recovered two sets of prints at the scene," he said. "One from the victim. And one from that guy you worked with—Joe Tesla. That's not been released to the press, but his lawyer knows, so I imagine you already do, too."

She lengthened her stride, as if she could run away from that truth. Dirk kept pace easily. "Is that so?"

Dirk ran on without saying anything else.

"What's the CIA doing?" she asked.

"Why would they be doing anything?"

"I met two of them yesterday at Tesla's house, and I thought I saw a couple of them up in the concourse, too."

Dirk slipped on an icy patch, and she caught his arm. "Dirk?"

"I don't know what the CIA wants with him. We want him for questioning about the murder of the homeless man in the tunnels."

Ronald Raines, she wanted to say, but didn't.

"They seem to think he's got classified information," Dirk said.

"Doesn't his company work with them all the time? I imagine he has a security clearance. A pretty high one."

Dirk nodded. "That's been bugging me, too. You'd think he'd be in the CIA's pocket already, and I can't figure out what contact he'd have with some random homeless guy that would interest them. But they are very interested. Do you know why?"

"I don't," she said. "You know I'd tell you if I could."

"When would that be?" he asked. "We both know he's a client of yours."

"Why don't you guys ask him?"

"He's lawyered up. They say he can't be reached. He can't even be found."

That part was probably true.

"Why'd he do something like that?" Dirk asked.

"Go to ground?" She dodged a slow jogger lost in the music of his MP3 player. "He's terrified that he'd have to go outside, that you guys will make him leave the hotel for questioning. Remember that article I showed you?"

"Jail's inside," Dirk said.

She thought of her mother's name on Joe's email.

"If he did it," she said, "then you ought to put him there."

18

Joe couldn't stay much longer, but he didn't know where else to go. He paced from one end of the small locker room to the other, closed laptop under his arm. Edison didn't bother to pace with him this time. He had curled up on a pile of dirty towels to sleep. He'd clearly had a rough night, too.

Joe knew he had to act fast, but he didn't know why. Rebar had told him that something big was due to happen by the end of the month, and that was the day after tomorrow. Obviously, something more important than Rebar's life, and Joe's.

He hadn't found out anything about Ronald Raines that might indicate why he'd been murdered, much less why the CIA cared.

The information Joe had uncovered about mysterious deaths in Guantanamo Bay might be related. A few days after Rebar had been reported AWOL, one hundred and two soldiers and a doctor were lost at sea when the ship they were on went down halfway between Cuba and Florida. Pretty suspicious, but the Navy had done only a cursory investigation, blaming freak weather conditions. He'd checked weather satellite data for the period in question, confirming the weather had been calm and clear the night the ship was lost. It looked to him as if the boat had been sunk on purpose.

Had Rebar been involved in their deaths? Had he killed them?

Joe leaned against the wall and made a VoIP call on his computer to the number he'd memorized from Rebar's file. The call might be traceable, but it wouldn't be easy.

He settled headphones over his ears and listened to it ring once (cyan) and twice (blue).

"Raines," said a woman's voice. She sounded so tired and defeated that he almost hung up. He hated to worry her further.

"Good morning, Mrs. Raines." He introduced himself and lied about being from the Navy. "Have you had any word from your son, Ronald?"

"Have you?" She coughed into the phone, a deep, retching hack. A smoker.

He didn't dare tell her the truth. "I'd like to go over some facts in his file, ma'am."

"Why?" she wheezed.

"The file doesn't seem to support what Specialist Raines's fellow soldiers had to say about him." He had no idea if that was true, but it seemed like a good starting point.

"What'd they say?" She didn't sound worried that anyone would say anything bad about her Ronald, and Joe wondered what he might have been like before the events in Guantanamo Bay.

She was asking more questions than he was.

"What would you like to tell me about him?" he asked.

"Ron's a good boy," she said. "Smart. Tough. He always wanted to be a soldier like his father, God bless him."

"I see." He kept his voice pitched low.

"He never would have gone AWOL. Never. That's a

mistake."

"His file says—"

"I don't believe it," she said. "And I know him better than you do."

Joe couldn't argue with that. "What do you think he did?"

"I think he's on some kind of special mission, undercover, and that once he's done they'll clear his name and let him come home." She coughed as if to underline her point.

He wished, for her sake, that she had been correct about the last part. "I see."

She laughed bitterly. "I know you can't tell me even if you do know, which you probably don't."

"When did you last hear from him?"

"He called a couple of months ago, like I told the last investigator I talked to."

Last investigator? "How did he seem when he spoke to you?"

She hesitated. "He said that he wasn't feeling well and that he had an important mission, but not to worry about him. So, I'm not."

Why the pause before answering? "Did he say anything specific about the nature of his mission, ma'am?"

"Of course he didn't." She sounded offended by the question.

After a few more minutes of trying, he gave up on getting any other information out of her. He thanked her for her time and closed the connection.

The only thing he'd learned was that Rebar thought he was sick, and that didn't seem relevant. Maybe it was. Joe's suspicions of an infectious disease could be right. That might explain why the monkey was there—it could have been a long-ago test subject.

If that was the case, the cops weren't after him to arrest

him—they were after him to quarantine him.

He'd have to turn himself in.

Maybe he was wrong. How could a pathogen live seventy years bricked in underground? The longest-living spore that he could think of was anthrax, and that lived only fifty years in the soil. Even if the men in the train car had been infected, they couldn't have infected Rebar after all that time.

No. Rebar had been sick before he'd broken through the wall.

Still, it might be worth checking to see if the cops were treating the scene as if it were biologically contaminated.

Just because he hadn't caught anything from the people in the car didn't mean he hadn't caught anything from Rebar. If he had, he'd walked, potentially infected, through a giant crowd of people just to get here. He needed to get away from people until he knew more—a self-imposed quarantine. He snorted. That described his current life, more or less, anyway.

The risks were low that he'd caught anything. Joe was basically paranoid about the world, so he knew a lot about disease vectors. There weren't many strictly airborne diseases—fewer than five (brown)—so it was statistically very unlikely that this one was airborne. He'd had no direct contact with Rebar. He was probably fine and, even if he wasn't, it was improbable he'd infected anyone else. Everything was fine.

But knowing for sure would be even more fine.

Brandon walked into the locker room wearing a blue tennis club shirt and his bright Pellucid cap. "Do you need anything else, Mr. Tesla? I'm only working a half-day today."

Joe sighed. He hated what he was about to say. "I need a giant favor."

"What is it?" Brandon smiled expectantly, a kid willing to go the extra mile to impress his future boss.

"Could you take Edison to a friend's house for me?"

"Of course!" Brandon looked relieved that it wasn't more complicated.

"Much appreciated." Joe rattled off Celeste's address and handed him another twenty.

Joe snapped Edison's leather leash on to his collar. Those brown eyes gave him a betrayed look, his whole furry body pleading. Joe handed the leash to Brandon.

"Don't worry, boy," said Brandon. "It sounds like you're going on a doggie vacation."

"Exactly." Joe didn't know how he'd manage without Edison, but the dog was too conspicuous, and maybe in too much danger, to let him stay.

Edison's head and tail drooped as he obediently followed Brandon out of the locker room. Joe fought down feelings of guilt and panic. Edison would be fine. Celeste would spoil him terribly. And Joe would be fine, too. He'd lived most of his life without a psychiatric service animal, and he'd last a few days until he got this sorted out.

The cold truth was, he'd be in greater danger if Edison came with him.

Joe packed everything up and put his gym bag back into his locker. He'd head down to check out the crime scene, but first he wanted to watch Edison leave. He circled the blue tennis court, likely annoying the players, to stand in front of the rounded window that ran along one wall. The windows were set in sturdy frames, which made it easy for him to look through them without panicking. Ridiculous that such things mattered.

Hiking his backpack up on his shoulder, he looked down on the entrance to Grand Central. People walked in and out, coming and going, a simple thing that he couldn't do anymore. He had been just like them, before his ill-fated trip to New York. What use was he to anyone wasting away here underground?

Maybe Edison should have a real life as Celeste's pet.

He spotted Brandon's bright blue baseball hat, and his eyes lingered on the yellow dog walking dispiritedly next to him. Brandon swung his arms and talked to Edison. The dog looked over his shoulder at the front door as if he expected Joe to come for him. Celeste would take good care of him until Joe could take him back. He'd call her in just a second. It would be good to hear her voice.

Brandon, as energetic and cheerful as ever, made it down the front stairs and onto the sidewalk, where a short man wearing a dark blue parka and a Yankees cap jostled him. Edison's leash dropped to the ground as Brandon turned toward the man. Joe leaned closer to the window. What was Brandon thinking, letting go of Edison like that?

Brandon's legs buckled, and he crumpled to the ground. The man in the dark parka melted into the crowd. Blood spread out from Brandon's body onto the sidewalk.

19

Ozan wiped the blade on an antiseptic tissue and slipped the knife back into his ankle sheath. The time he'd spent sharpening it had paid off—it had slid between the man's ribs with an ease he'd learned to appreciate. Clean and fast.

Happiness radiated from the hand that had done the job into his entire body. His favorite sensation after a successful kill. He'd never taken anyone down in such a public spot before. He'd wanted to wait, known that he should wait, until the man was somewhere private, but in the end he couldn't resist. The blade had needed to slide through the jacket and between the ribs. The man had needed to fall. Right then. And he had, like an actor in a well-rehearsed play. Tesla had, in the end, played his part with perfect timing.

Even the dog had missed the moment.

Ozan paused to watch oblivious passers-by, another first. Why should he, of all people, be denied the aftermath of his actions? That pleasure was always robbed from him because he never stayed. He leaned against a light pole a few feet away and waited, not minding the cold seeping into the soles of his shoes.

The dog suddenly realized that no one held his leash. He

turned and nosed the fallen man as if he could make him wake up. But the dog was smarter than the people around him. He knew right away that the man would never wake up again. He barked, running in a circle around the fallen man, dangerously close to the traffic rushing by on Forty-Second Street.

A child stopped first, of course, because they still saw things for what they were. His mother tugged on his mittened hand, followed his gaze to the fallen man, and screamed.

The scream lanced into Ozan's aching head, and he fell back with a gasp. She screamed again, like an actress in a bad movie. He hadn't thought that people responded like that in real life. It was simply a man lying on the sidewalk, a red pool spreading out from his body, melting the thin layer of frost. He'd seen so many dead men that this one seemed as natural as the yellow cabs driving by or the long green tassel on the child's cap.

A man stopped next to the screaming woman, then another. She choked out another scream, a mitten clutched to her mouth. Soon, a circle formed around the outstretched body, but no one wanted to touch it. Ozan joined the circle, wanting to get close to them, struck by their ordinariness. Had he ever been like them?

A woman in a camel-colored coat knelt next to the body. There was nothing that she could do. Ozan had killed cleanly, swiftly, the man dead before he'd hit the ground. But she didn't know that. She pulled aside the man's coat collar and felt for a pulse on his neck, her dark eyebrows drawn down with worry. The dog whined and paced in front of her.

As she leaned back, shaking her tawny head, Ozan looked to the victim's young, fresh face. It was not Joe Tesla. A stranger lay dead on the ground.

Shock caused him to stumble, to stare, seemingly as upset

by the man's death as those around him. How had he made such a mistake?

Misdirection. Respect welled up in him at his target's ingenuity. He rarely dealt with anyone so interesting. And he had been fooled. The man wore a cap from Tesla's company. He had Tesla's dog on a leash. He was a decoy. He wasn't Tesla.

And, of course, he couldn't be.

Tesla didn't go outside.

A laugh bubbled up in Ozan's throat and burst free. He wanted to clap, but stopped himself as people were already turning to stare at him. But he couldn't stop grinning.

This was extraordinary. Ozan could hunt his quarry in the tunnels as long as he wanted. He closed his eyes from the joy of it. After all, Tesla couldn't leave. And he would have more tricks in store. Ozan didn't remember the last time that he'd been so excited by his work. Part of him knew that his reaction was out of proportion, but he didn't care. He worked hard. He deserved a little fun.

In front of him, the woman unzipped the corpse's navy blue jacket. He wore a bloodstained blue shirt with a silver tennis ball embroidered on the left breast, above his heart. Even from his position a few feet away, Ozan could easily read the words underneath.

Vanderbilt Tennis and Fitness Club

Grand Central Terminal

Ozan's eyes were drawn to the Beaux-Arts-style terminal building. He'd learned the grand old dame's ins and outs while researching the hit on Subject 523. He knew the location of every store and bathroom. His eyes went straight to the third floor, where the tennis court was located. He'd visited it once, but had not been able to find out if Tesla was a member. Apparently, he was.

A shadow moved near the top of the rounded third-floor

window.

Ozan circled the crowd that had gathered around the fallen man, intent on the shadow high above him. Tesla was up there. It had to be Tesla. He had seen Ozan kill the tennis player. He knew what would happen to him.

It was Tesla. Certainty coursed through Ozan. He'd been a hunter long enough to recognize prey. And this prey would be terrified and running. He had to go after him.

The yellow dog streaked past. He wriggled between the legs of a man with dreadlocks and a knit cap in the doorway and disappeared inside the building.

Ozan ran after him. The dog must have sensed the danger that his master faced and had gone to protect him. He would lead Ozan straight to the man himself.

The hunt was on.

20

Joe ran straight across the tennis court, taking a ball to the shoulder. The players cursed, but he didn't slow down. He had to get to Edison before the man in the dark parka did. He could not bear to lose the dog.

And he'd lost Brandon. The young man was dead, and it was Joe's fault. He'd sent him out with Edison, wearing a Pellucid cap. Stupid. There was a killer searching for Joe, and he'd inadvertently used the kid as bait.

He might as well have stabbed Brandon himself.

Joe slammed open the door to the locker room, vaulted the bench, and hit the other side of the room in just a few strides. A naked man coming out of the showers leaped out of his way.

Then Joe was in the reception area, running for the stairs. He had no idea of what he would do, but he'd try anything to keep Edison safe. He ran hard, knocking people out of his way. Where were all the cops he'd had to avoid earlier?

He jumped the last three steps, sliding on the marble floor when he landed. Everywhere, people. Rush hour was over, but they still filled the giant room, talking, walking, getting in his way.

A bark! Edison shot into the hall like a furry cannonball, running full tilt across the polished floor toward him. A beautiful sight.

Yards behind the dog, the man in the dark parka slipped through the crowd like a shark. The killer was almost upon him.

"Edison," Joe called. "Heel!"

The dog altered his trajectory toward the sound of Joe's voice. As did the killer. Edison gained ground on him, running pell-mell between people's legs.

They weren't safe here. Neither was anyone else who got in that man's way. Joe had to draw the guy away from the crowd.

Joe ran toward the passage to the Hyatt, searching for cops. None. Earlier, he couldn't have swung a dead cat without hitting one. Now, nothing.

He whistled. Edison changed course again. The killer, too.

Joe burst into the lobby at a dead run, Edison beside him. He pelted past the front desk. Someone called his name, but he didn't look to see. Whoever it was, they would soon be chasing him, too.

Joe slammed open the door to the employee-only section of the hotel—simple walls, no decoration. He and Edison skidded around a corner and down a dingy hall. His goal lay just ahead. He hoped that he was aiming for more than a rumor.

He reached the corner of the building. On the other side of the wall was Park Avenue, the street that split in two to go around Grand Central Terminal.

Behind him, the door crashed open. Someone else had entered the hall. Joe wasn't lucky enough for it to be a Hyatt employee. It had to be the killer.

Edison barked threateningly, backing up his guess.

"We're in this together, boy." Joe was breathing so hard that he could barely get the words out. That sprint had cost him, but he had no time to be tired right now.

He yanked open a door marked Authorized Personnel Only, entering a small, dark room full of service carts. So far, so good.

With one hand, he pushed a cart to the side so that there was room for him and Edison. Once inside, he closed the door and latched the flimsy bolt from the inside. That'd keep the killer occupied for about a nanosecond.

He moved another cart, then the next, pushing them against the door while he headed toward the back corner. The combined weight of the carts might slow the bastard down. Not much, but maybe enough.

When he got to the corner, he made out the contours of a wooden hatch built into the floor. His spirits rose. He'd worried that the existence of this hatch was a hotel urban legend, or that he'd come to the wrong room, and that he and Edison would be trapped in here.

He lifted the iron ring in the center, and the hatch creaked open. A dark hole yawned in the floor. A thud against the door told him that the killer was right outside. The bolt wouldn't hold against him for long.

Hoping for a miracle, Joe climbed into the hole. With no hesitation, Edison ran next to him. He loved that dog.

Light from the open hatch gave him enough illumination to see metal pipes, now covered in rust. Those were old steam pipes that had once heated a building that stood on this site long before the modern hotel was built in its place. He looked up at the bottom of the hatch to see if there was any way to lock it from this side. There wasn't.

He glanced around the room, finding a door on the other side. He closed the hatch, plunging the room into darkness. He jerked his flashlight out of his pocket.

During his stay at the Hyatt, he'd learned of this room from a bored security guard, and had hoped that it hadn't been filled in or locked off. He'd been lucky so far. He reached a door and shone the light across its rusty surface, searching for the handle. He found it and tried to turn it. Locked.

Above him, carts rattled and smashed. The killer was up there.

Joe stuck his flashlight in his mouth and fumbled with his keys. The Gallo ancestor had specified that he have access to the steam tunnels. Joe hoped that his reach extended to this set of tunnels, this particular door.

He jumbled through the keys, one after the other, hoping for a clue. A metal tab next to a skeleton key had the word Steam embossed on it in Gothic lettering. Joe pushed the key into the lock. With a little wriggling, the rusty tumblers turned.

Joe lunged through, Edison on his heels.

He closed the door and worked the key in the lock as fast as he could. Anyone could pick such a simple lock. Joe grabbed duct tape from his backpack and tore off two strips. Using his teeth, he ripped off a tiny corner and rolled it into a ball small enough to jam into the lock, sticky side in. Then, he stuck that to a second piece. He pushed the tiny ball into the lock and secured it on his side with the strip of duct tape. The man inside would have to fish it out before he could pick the lock, and he might waste time trying to pick the lock before he figured it out.

Or he might just kick it down.

Joe sprinted down the steam tunnel. The guy who was after him would get through the door eventually, and he and Edison needed to be far away when that happened.

Cold, rusty pipes flashed by on both sides. All these pipes must be out of commission, or else he'd have been burning up down here.

He dashed through another door, another tunnel, and another. It was like a rabbit warren down here, and he didn't see how the killer could find him. Lost, and out of breath, he stopped running.

He'd have to hike until he found a landmark, or met a friendly policeman to ask directions. He sighed. Maybe not that last one.

Edison gave him an apologetic look and peed on the wall. Poor thing, he hadn't had his walk. "It's OK," he told him. "You're a good dog."

The dog wagged his tail. A dark splotch marred the golden fur on his chest. Joe scrubbed at it with his hand. It was blood. Joe shone the flashlight on it to make sure that Edison wasn't wounded. He wasn't.

It was Brandon's blood. Poor Brandon had practically still been a kid. He'd had nothing to do with any of this, and now he was dead. That was Joe's fault.

Joe couldn't fix it and bring him back. His family and friends would have to mourn and go on without him. But Joe could make damn sure that his death didn't go unsolved. He would find out the name of Brandon's killer.

Once he had that name, he would see to it that the man met with justice, no matter the cost. He wouldn't get to melt back into the crowd like he had at the murder scene. He'd be exposed as a killer, and he'd pay the price.

Joe owed Brandon at least that.

21

Ozan pulled the hatch carefully closed. Not just for stealth, but also because sharp noises aggravated his headache. The room above was empty. Tesla and his dog must have gone through the door on the far side, although he'd checked the rest of the room thoroughly, in case there was another trapdoor in the floor or secret exit on the opposite wall. But there was nothing like that. This room had been built to allow the building's engineers to access the steam tunnels for maintenance, not to prevent a palace coup.

He stifled a laugh of exhilaration. Tesla had led him in a good chase through the terminal. The police had massed to follow them, but they were at least a minute behind and, in Ozan's world, a minute was an eternity.

He'd lined up the room service carts on his way through, not worried about coming back that way and hoping to stall his pursuers. If they caught him, he had only to identify himself and use his contacts at the CIA to be released. But he would lose the scent here, and he didn't want to do that.

He drew his flashlight and headed down the stairs.

His head throbbed with each step. He'd been eating aspirin like Pez today. It had brought down the fever, but not dulled the pain. His brain felt as if someone was

163

prodding it with hot needles.

A quick glance revealed that the old door would be easy to kick down. Whoever had built it hadn't been worried that someone would want to break into the steam tunnels, or out of them. But he hesitated.

Tesla might be on the other side, armed. He must have led Ozan down here on purpose, probably into a trap. The man had proved that he could be wily, and even a cornered rabbit could fight. They didn't often kill the fox chasing them, but sometimes they got lucky.

Elation ebbing, he leaned against the wall. The needles in his brain were keeping him from thinking clearly. His illness was affecting his judgment. He should go home and rest, come back later when he felt better.

He squeezed his eyes shut against the memory of the grisly sample he'd collected from Subject 523. Dr. Dubois had insisted on a piece of his brain. Ozan had assumed it was just a repulsive proof of death, but it might have been more. What if the doctor was looking for something wrong with his brain?

Thumping overhead brought him back to the present moment. He had been followed back to this room. He didn't have the luxury of thinking it over and taking another path.

He squandered a precious minute fumbling with the door lock before he realized that Tesla had jammed something into it. Clever rabbit. Brute force would have to win out over finesse. Forcing his way out seemed crude, irritating to his sense of order. Worse, it left an unobstructed path behind him, but it had to be done.

Taking a step back, he aimed for just below the door lock and kicked. The wooden door frame cracked. That was the weakest part of this door—metal door, strong lock, but a weak frame. He kicked again, feeling the frame give. One more kick was all he needed.

Then he was through the door, gun and flashlight up and ready. If Tesla didn't take him down with the first shot, he wouldn't get a second one.

The long, dark tunnel was empty in both directions. Ozan stopped and pointed his light at the floor, searching for footprints. He found many boot prints; the tunnel wasn't as deserted as he'd have thought. But he found only one set of paw prints. Following them, he hurried west.

"Freeze," called a voice from behind him.

The idiots from the hotel must have broken through.

Ozan darted into a side tunnel, followed it to a junction, and chose right. A few turns later, he'd lost his pursuers. He'd also lost Tesla.

The dangers behind meant that he couldn't go back and track his rabbit from the hotel's steam tunnels. That was just a waste of time.

Instead, Ozan resolved to return to the murder scene and track him from there. Like all men, Joe was a creature of routine. He must have his favorite tunnels, places where he rested. Ozan would find them, and there he would wait.

22

Joe crept to the end of the tunnel and glanced across the open field of tracks. He had to cross that without being seen. But the lights were all on, and two cops wearing navy blue uniforms and menacing looks were standing around.

He shrank back into the darkness. If he circled around to the west, he could use a tunnel that came out near to the bricked-in train car where he'd met Rebar. It was a much longer walk, but he couldn't think of another way.

Fifteen minutes later, he had a good view of the crime scene. Yellow tape had been tacked across the broken entrance and also in the area around the bricked-in car—forming a large square. A woman stood just outside the tape, smoking a cigarette. She wore a standard NYPD uniform—not a yellow biosuit. A bit of good news.

Another man stepped out of the hole. He wore civilian clothing and, other than latex gloves, he had no special gear.

Joe was so relieved that his knees threatened to buckle. Whatever else they were worried about, nobody was acting as if Rebar, or the skeletons and the monkey, represented a biological hazard. He wouldn't need to go into quarantine. He'd be able to move around and try to solve the crime on his own. Indoors. He could still be of use.

That was all he needed to know. He turned back the way that he had come. He had a new destination now: Grand Central Terminal's Platform 36.

Joe and Edison approached Platform 36 (red for three, orange for six), footsteps quiet on the tracks. He'd never appreciated just how quiet the dog was until today. Several bulbs had burned out in this section of tunnel recently, so they moved in a protective cone of darkness.

On the end of the train platform, right where Joe had hoped to climb the stairs and get into Grand Central Terminal, a man peered into the tunnel. Putting a hand on Edison's head to keep him still, Joe eased behind a pillar and studied the guy. When this was over, he was going to buy a set of binoculars, regular and night-vision.

For now he had to trust his eyes. The man on the edge of the platform wore a dark uniform, details easy to pick out because the light behind him silhouetted his stocky form. He was a cop.

Joe doubted that the man could see far, looking from light into darkness as he was. Still, the man scanned the tunnel every few minutes. He seemed alert.

Joe had to get closer, but he didn't dare get caught.

He slid out from behind the pillar in slow motion. People keyed in on movement, especially quick ones. He took one slow step forward, then another, slipping from pillar to pillar with Edison. The man put his hand above his eyes, shielding them from the light. Several long seconds later, he shook his head and lowered his hand.

Joe crouched behind the pillar. He didn't dare move closer. This would have to be close enough.

He gestured for Edison to lie down, and the dog flopped down on the broken rocks that underlaid the tracks. Joe stifled his automatic "good boy" and lowered himself next to the dog, making sure that no part of his body stuck out from behind the pillar.

Angling it down toward the ground so that no one could spot the glow, he turned on his laptop and crossed his fingers. The station master's office on Platform 36 had free Wi-Fi, and that was just what he needed.

Before he had time to log in, the rumble of an approaching train told him that he'd have to wait. Still hidden by the pillar, he hauled Edison up into his lap, and covered them both with the blanket. They waited.

After running next to a moving train, sitting while one passed didn't seem dangerous at all, just loud and annoying. Funny how he'd changed his assessment of risk with experience. Edison, too, felt more relaxed in his arms.

Once the train passed, he decided to keep the blanket around them. Carefully, he tucked in the corners. It smelled like double dog in his blanket tent, but that couldn't be helped. He pulled the blanket off his head.

"Baths for both of us when this is over, right, Edison?" he whispered.

Edison refused to meet his eyes. He hated baths and knew the word. Joe grinned. No matter what, some things never changed.

He flipped the laptop open again and tried to connect to the Wi-Fi. One bar. No good. A quick glance around the pillar told him that he didn't dare move closer. But he had a Wi-Fi booster in his backpack.

It took only a few seconds to set it up and plug it in. He held his breath and tried again. Still too weak.

What if he tried to create a distraction and sneaked onto the platform? Too risky. He could try to sneak back to a subway station—he doubted that the cops had the manpower to cover them all. But he didn't know of any subway stations that offered Wi-Fi. Another dead-end.

A train approached with a roar, and he pulled the blanket

up over his head. Before the blanket covered his eyes, he saw the train's headlight glint off a discarded beer can, just feet from his position. That should do it.

After the train rumbled into the station, the policeman turned to study the disembarking crowd. Joe took advantage of the distraction and darted out to grab the can.

He upended it. Empty. He popped off the pull tab and dropped it to the stones.

Then he took out his pocketknife and got to work, moving fast so that the noise of the departing commuters covered the sound. First, he sliced off the bottom of the can, impressed at how easily his knife cut through the aluminum. Edison watched, ears up and eyes intent.

Holding the top of the can, Joe stuck the knife just under the thick rim that ran around the top and slit the side from top to bottom. This took some doing, and he wished for a pair of scissors.

Finally, he cut in a circle around the top of the can, under the rim, most of the way around. He left a half-inch section untouched. That should be enough to keep the rest of the can from coming loose in the next step.

Carefully, so as not to cut himself on the sharp edges, he bent the sides of the can outward until the can looked like a miniature radar dish, which he stuck back on top of his Wi-Fi booster.

It wasn't glamorous, but it might work.

He checked the Wi-Fi again, slowly turning his improvised dish until he picked up a signal. A couple more bars. Strong enough. He grinned at Edison. Who said software guys couldn't do hardware? To mark the position, he drew a line next to the edge of the dish.

He quickly connected to the Wi-Fi, and took his standard precautions before hacking into the database for the surveillance cameras outside of Grand Central. His years of careful paranoia had paid off. Without his experience at moving unobserved online, he'd have been caught already.

He was going to use this talent to find out who killed Brandon.

He fast-forwarded through the video until he found the time of the attack. Tears sprang into his eyes as he watched the killer crash into Brandon. He was small and slender, with curly dark hair. He didn't look like a killer.

The man first stepped quickly to the side, as if he had slipped on a patch of ice, seeming to steady himself against Brandon's back. Even knowing that the man had just stabbed him, Joe could barely see it. The killer stepped away and kept walking. The only thing that separated him from the other walkers was his innate gracefulness, belying the ruse that he had slipped. This was a man whose every movement looked calculated and lithe. A dancer.

Then Brandon collapsed onto the sidewalk. He didn't even have time to cry out. Just like that, a promising young life was gone.

Brandon had had a girlfriend who worked in PR and didn't mind a walk in the park instead of a fancy meal, a single mother who had taken on a second job to get Brandon through college, and a little brother who wanted to go to college, too. All of them left behind.

With one hand, Joe stroked Edison's warm back, both to calm himself and to apologize for what the dog had gone through.

Joe could do nothing to comfort Brandon.

But he could make sure that his killer didn't walk free.

Another train passed, knocking Joe off the Wi-Fi. He realigned his beer-can booster to his marks and went back to work. His fingers danced across the keyboard as he worked through the footage until he found a good shot of the killer's face. The man had looked up, past the camera location, toward where Joe had watched him from the tennis club window.

Reflexively, Joe cleaned up the image until it was good enough to result in a match. This was more art than science, but he had practiced with a thousand faces over the months and years it had taken to build the Pellucid software. A seemingly mild-mannered man stared back at him—black hair and dark eyes, a round face, and a high forehead. A Russian ballet dancer.

With a few typewritten commands, Joe had logged in to a backdoor account he'd created in Pellucid at the very beginning. He'd be invisible there, and his movements wouldn't be logged. Sunil would be furious if he knew—as would the government agencies they worked with. Again, Joe was glad that he had done it. It was as if he'd always known that he'd need a secret entrance someday.

Joe submitted the killer's picture to a search of the test databases. The company had cloned them early in the process so that their tests didn't affect the government's databases in real time. What it meant now was that no one in law enforcement would receive notice of his search. It didn't take long to get a match. The man who had killed Brandon, and probably Rebar, was Ozan Saddiq.

A commotion on the train platform drew Joe's attention. He looked cautiously around the pillar to see what was going on. More cops?

The noisemakers were just a group of teenagers, all dressed like old-fashioned barbers—with red-striped vests, red suspenders, and flat straw hats. He did a quick head count, twelve (cyan, blue) kids. Three (red) barbershop quartets. Normal life was going on all around him.

Joe settled back down in front of his laptop, but before he read Ozan Saddiq's file, he hacked into Torres's mother's email account. He used that to send the information off to her daughter—Saddiq's picture and its source in the surveillance video, complete with time stamps, the picture it had matched in the Pellucid database, and the name Ozan Saddiq. That should be enough to nail the man for Brandon's murder.

Of course, if she didn't play her cards right, it was also enough to nail Joe for hacking if they traced it back to him. That didn't matter. What mattered was bringing Brandon's killer to justice, and keeping him from killing again. No matter what happened to Joe now, Saddiq was taken care of.

After he read Saddiq's file, he regretted sending off the material so quickly. Saddiq was a very dangerous man, and he probably had contacts to help him avoid being prosecuted for Brandon's murder. Nothing was ever simple.

After a stint in the military distinguished by careful and methodical performance, the man had worked for the CIA. He wasn't a full-time employee, but rather a contractor employed in an unnamed capacity at different times and in locations throughout the world. He received strong recommendations for his thorough and painstaking work. The file didn't say what he had done, but Joe was willing to bet that he was a contract killer. If so, a logical assumption was that the CIA had hired him to kill Rebar, and maybe Joe. If so, the information he'd sent might have placed Torres in danger, just as he had Brandon.

He and Edison barely noticed the next train as it swept by in a cloud of noise and vibration. The most important thing was that his beer-can antenna didn't lose its Wi-Fi connection. The can was better than he could have hoped. Well, this kind of stuff always worked for MacGyver.

Joe searched the file for Saddiq's next of kin. Both his parents were dead. He was unmarried, no children. The file listed a single name for next of kin: Erol Saddiq.

A rock dug into Joe's butt, and he lifted up an inch to

move it, careful not to disturb Edison's warm head resting on his lap. The dog snored. He'd had a rough day.

A quick search showed that Erol Saddiq lived in an expensive home for adults with special needs in Oyster Bay on Long Island. A hired killer with a handicapped brother. Joe squelched his feeling of pity. Nothing had slowed his hand as he'd killed Brandon, leaving Brandon's brother to fend for himself.

Still, he spent a few minutes studying the home's web site. It was set in a former mansion, with most of the facilities in the main house, including beds for residents. Other residents shared housing in converted stables, carriage houses, and servants' quarters. They wore GPS bracelets and were provided transportation to jobs in the area. It looked like Erol Saddiq lived in comfortable circumstances.

Perhaps he might provide a link to his dangerous brother. A few keystrokes later, and Joe had cracked his email account. Like far too many people, Erol's password was secret. He exchanged emails with one person—his brother, Ozan.

Joe skimmed them. It looked as if Ozan loved his brother. He sent him seashells from around the world, and a local bakery delivered a bunch of cookies for him every Friday night. If Ozan was there, the brothers would eat cookies together and watch movies. If not, Erol ate cookies and watched movies with a member of the home's staff named Melanie. The emails were sweet, but it didn't change the fact that Ozan was a cold-blooded killer.

The last email was most interesting.

> Dear Erol,
> I won't be around this Friday. I'm sick with a fever. But don't worry. I am taking good care of myself and will be better soon. I know that you and Melanie will have a fun time.

Your brother,
Ozan

Ozan was sick, as Rebar had been. Was it coincidence?

Joe closed his eyes. He didn't feel sick. Tired, sad, and frightened, but not sick. Even if Rebar or the train car had some mysterious disease associated with them, Joe had barely come in contact with either. He was fine. Fine.

Fine or not, he needed to know more about why Rebar had been ill. If Joe had had contacts at the police department, he could have tried to ask for the autopsy report, but he didn't. He didn't have the system access to hack in and steal it, so that meant he was going to have to find a different route to that information.

He'd have to break in to the morgue.

23

Dr. Dubois crutched into the room. The lab's blinds were half open, and stripes of sunlight overlay the clean countertops and polished equipment. All the chemicals had been returned to their glass-fronted cabinets, every bit of glassware clean and put away where it belonged, because his assistants had known he was coming. He ran a tight ship.

He drew in a deep breath of air that smelled of formalin and disinfectant. It took him back years, to his days as a lab assistant first exploring the mysteries of biology, fascinated by how most of our lives were determined by forces too small to be seen by the naked eye.

Because he had ordered everyone out, the lab was empty. He relished the solitude and the order. Too much of his life these days was taken up with people and meetings and paperwork. He was a victim of his own success.

He so rarely got a chance to do hands-on work anymore. Usually, his assistants handled such work for him, but this specimen he needed to see for himself.

The sample case lay on the matte-black countertop, cardboard box still sealed on all sides with tape. It had been hand-delivered to the lab that morning. He slit the tape and pulled out a Styrofoam box. It had been well packed. Dr. Dubois lifted the Styrofoam lid and removed a simple glass jar surrounded on all sides by cooling gel packs. Per his instructions, it had not been frozen. Inside the jar, pinkish-beige tissue quivered like a lump of jelly.

He held the glass container to the light. Some decomposition had occurred, but the sample looked better preserved than he'd dared hope. It must have been taken shortly after death and quickly packed away. What he sought could survive a long time, even at room temperature. A full brain would have been better, but he had more than enough tissue for what he needed. He set the jar carefully on the countertop.

He drew a brand new scalpel from a drawer, unwrapped it, and placed it next to the jar. The sharp steel blade gleamed in a shaft of sunlight. Long ago, he'd had his own set of scalpels, regularly sterilized, but in today's throwaway culture, it was easier to buy single-use ones. This refined piece of equipment might make only one cut before being discarded.

Next he pulled a box of glass slides and cover slips from a nearby drawer. They, too, would only see a single use. He located a pair of reusable tweezers and put them next to the scalpel. His tools were all in place.

Although it wasn't strictly necessary, he put on a pair of latex gloves and a face mask that heated up with the first breath. It felt like dressing up for Halloween. He smiled—nasty tricks or clever treats, there were some of each to be found in this special sample.

The jar proved difficult to open, and he remembered again the small man's deceptive strength. Eventually, the lid budged. A quick turn, and he had free access to the ruthlessly gathered sample.

He dipped a gloved hand into the glass container and pulled out a clot. The tissue felt cool and soft through his glove, like aspic straight from the refrigerator. On one edge sat a darker mass, perhaps a cyst.

He set the sample down on the counter and picked up the scalpel. With controlled, deft movements, he sliced the potential cyst into thin samples and placed the first one on a slide with tweezers. Tenderly, he placed the cover slip on top, as if tucking in a baby.

Trying to control his rising excitement, he took a deep breath, studying the new slide that he held flat between his gloved thumb and forefinger. It contained a sample that he'd never thought he would see.

He clipped the slide under the microscope's lens and focused the eyepiece. As the slide came into sharp relief, he stopped breathing. There it was. Even at this magnification, he could see the sample teeming with parasites—parasites he had put there.

He stared down at the swirling mass.

The last troublesome link to the 500 series was severed. Subject 523 had come back to him. The doctor was safe.

He dropped the slide into the biohazard bin along with the scalpel. The tweezers he put into a bin destined for the autoclave. The tissue in the jar itself he carried to the incinerator in the far corner. It reminded him of the one in which Dr. Johansson had lost her life and reminded him that he had to replace her. No rest for the weary.

Minutes later, the lab was clean—tissue disposed of, box packed away for recycling, countertop sterilized. It was as if he'd never worked in here at all.

The last obstacle to tomorrow's larger-scale testing had been removed. He opened the refrigerator to take out the samples stored there. When he opened the door, light reflected off a row of stoppered glass tubes. The contents didn't need to be refrigerated, but this was the most convenient place to store them.

That was the genius of it—the parasite was so hardy that it was easy to store and transport. Simple, too, to administer. The test tubes in front of him contained enough material to infect a thousand soldiers. And, best of all, the parasite was common enough that twenty-five percent of the population of the United States already carried it; other countries had high incidences of it as well. An autopsy of anyone infected with his strain might find the parasite, but they would dismiss it. The parasite was so common as to be beyond suspicion.

He picked up a test tube and held the cool glass up to the light. Over many years, he had refined the sample stored there. He had tested it on rats, on primates, and on humans. There had been many failures that he tried not to think of, but successes, too.

That the parasite changed the behavior of its host had been documented before Dr. Dubois was born. The microscopic creature changed its host to suit its own needs—causing rats to run to cats to be devoured, or humans to behave with increased recklessness and promiscuity. Fine-tuning the parasite to suit the military's needs had taken years. But he had succeeded.

It was hard to believe that it had started with a simple cat, that each one of these creatures had passed through a cat's gut and out the other end. He had truly mined gold from shit.

He studied the gleaming tube, imagining the creatures teeming within. He had built them to make soldiers do his bidding. And they had.

Only a few more minutes of his lunchtime laboratory ban remained. He swung a metal briefcase onto the counter next to the refrigerator. Specially manufactured foam lined the inside. The foam contained divots the size and shape of the stoppered test tubes. They wouldn't clink, they wouldn't rattle, and they wouldn't break, even if the case were dropped. One by one, he pressed the precious glass containers into their manufactured shell.

Tomorrow morning he would take a train to Manhattan. He'd hand-deliver the case to Agent Marks of the CIA, and the trials would start by the end of the week.

In a few days, a thousand men would be infected.

24

Ozan circled the vast building like a hawk waiting for a mouse to appear in a new-mown field. First, he stationed himself in the great hall itself, watching people come and go until he was satisfied that Tesla was not among them. Then he did a quick walk through the glittering shops and yuppie marketplaces. He didn't expect to find Tesla there—loitering would be noticed—and he didn't. Ditto the food court and restaurants.

He'd easily evaded the net of policemen, surprised at the number of men that they had deployed. Why was 523's murder so important to them? Or maybe they searched for the one who had murdered one of their own. Even for that, the numbers seemed excessive. 523 and his documents held expensive secrets.

He checked train platforms. Police were stationed there, so he didn't expect Tesla to be hanging out on them, but maybe nearby. He flashed an old CIA-supplied badge to one of the police officers guarding Platform 14 and was waved in, probably because he looked nothing like Tesla. He went into the tunnels, walking through the platforms on the upper and lower levels.

It was a lot of work, but it paid off.

Circling Platform 36, Ozan saw a gray lump against the back side of a pillar, facing away from the platform. A faint glow emanated from it. He stopped, trying to figure out what it was. The uneven contours made it look like a long, low boulder, but that didn't make sense.

He moved closer, finally able to discern a knob on one end that resembled a head, and suddenly it made sense— someone was hidden underneath a blanket. Clever and cheap camouflage. The person leaned against the far side of the pillar, so that he would not be visible from the platform itself. Only someone coming from the other side or people in a passing train would see him. He bet it was Tesla, sitting there like a kid reading stories with a flashlight under the covers.

Ozan watched him, savoring the moment. Wouldn't Tesla be surprised when he yanked off the blanket and put one right between his eyes?

25

Stalling, Joe fussed with his Wi-Fi booster under the blanket. He was comfortable breaking in to places electronically, but hated the idea of sneaking into an actual building. What if he got caught? Even if they didn't arrest him, they'd most likely throw him into the street. But he didn't see any other options. He'd just have to not get caught.

Edison sensed his disquiet and woke. He wagged his tail once (cyan) as if to check on him.

"I'm all good," Joe lied.

The yellow fur ball snuggled closer to him. Joe tucked the blanket more securely around them both. They needed to stay hidden.

A quick search told Joe that the Office of Chief Medical Examiner for New York City was located at the corner of First Avenue and Thirtieth Street in Kips Bay, a neighborhood about a mile from his current location. If he could go outside, he'd be there in ten minutes, tops. He studied the modern square building—the Milton Helpern Institute of Forensic Medicine. It was blocky, a glass box rising several stories into the sky. Even looking at it made him nervous—too much exposure to the sky. He clenched his jaw. He'd have to go inside it.

Getting there was the challenge. A cab was out of the question.

If he couldn't go outside, he'd have to make do with the underground. He pulled up an old map that he'd compiled from various scanned-in maps. It showed subway tunnels, train tunnels, steam tunnels, and sewage tunnels. They snaked under the city like a web of nerves sending signals throughout a vast brain.

To start, he could walk along the subway tunnel to the Thirty-Third Street Station (two threes flashed in his head— red and red again). After that, he'd have to switch to a different tunnel.

Sewage tunnels ran practically everywhere, hundreds of miles' worth. The map showed a sewage outfall at the end of Thirtieth Street that pumped treated sewage straight into the East River. That tunnel ran right under his destination and was probably big enough to walk through. Not his first choice, but it might work.

He studied the network of steam tunnels that crisscrossed under the city. He'd read that the steam tunnels stretched more than one hundred miles. Built more than a century ago, some of those steam pipes still carried heat and power to New York homes and businesses. They had been built with walkable tunnels, because the active pipes needed regular servicing.

Tunnels ran back and forth like a maze, and the first few trails he traced ended in dead-ends. He'd best start at the end and work backward. He scrolled to the street corner that housed the Milton Helpern building.

He zoomed in on that city block until the tunnels dissolved into pixels, then back out, finally finding what he sought. A narrow tunnel ran right under the medical examiner's building, and a bracket indicated that the tunnel exited inside, probably for maintenance. A quick scroll back showed that it was linked to the Thirty-Third Street station via two tunnels.

It just might be possible to get to the morgue. Breaking in was another story.

Joe hated to go. The tunnels were full of men searching for him, at least one of whom wanted to kill him. He was safe here.

A train thundered next to him. The tiny clock on the lower corner of the laptop screen told him that they had eight minutes before the next train was due.

"Come on, boy," he said. "We need to get a move on."

He stood and shook feeling back into his feet. Edison stretched.

Joe closed the laptop and dropped it into his backpack, adding his makeshift Wi-Fi dish. He folded the blanket so that it would be easy to shake out and tucked it under his arm. Slowly, he backed away from Platform 36 and the cop who served so patiently there.

A few minutes later, Joe and Edison reached the locked door at the end of the maintenance tunnel that connected Grand Central Terminal, the train station, with Grand Central Station, the subway station. He already knew which key to use, as he'd hiked through there several times on his nightly wanderings. Thanks again, Great-Grandfather Gallo.

Once he reached the subway station, he followed the tunnel for lines four (green), five (brown), and six (orange) heading south. He got practiced at sweeping the blanket over them and going into a crouch to hide from trains because they ran through here at intervals of five minutes, more or less. He sometimes walked only a few feet before he had to go into hiding. This was why he routinely didn't start exploring until the middle of the night. Today he didn't have that luxury.

Every time he reached a subway platform, he got on all

fours and crawled underneath it so that no one in the station could see him. His knees were black and blue by the time he reached the Thirty-Third Street Station. If he ever got another chance to pack an emergency bag, kneepads and gloves were going in it. Edison had no such problems.

At the Thirty-Third Street Station, he switched to an old Amtrak tunnel heading east, sweeping his flashlight along the wall every few feet, looking for the door that would lead to a steam tunnel but finding only neat rows of wires fastened to the wall.

He was almost on top of it when he realized that he could have found it without the light. The temperature in the tunnels usually stayed in the mid-fifties, chilly but comfortable with his hoodie, but the air felt much warmer here. At the warmest spot, his light illuminated a simple metal door.

Would his bundle of keys include the right one? Great-Grandpa Gallo had demanded full access to all parts of the subterranean world, but Joe worried that the various underground authorities hadn't always bothered to send updated keys every time they changed a lock in the last century. He fished through his keys, trying first one, then another, and another. The fourth key did the trick. Sometimes, bureaucracy worked.

He pushed the door open with the toe of his sneaker, and a blast of hot air flowed across his face. Inside, it felt like a sauna. Sweat coated his body, and Edison began to pant. Joe put the temperature at around ninety degrees. A big change from the air outside, but bearable.

He peeled off his hoodie and looked around for a light switch. As expected, he found one, and lights flickered on down the tunnel. He clicked off his flashlight, glad to spare the batteries.

On his left ran rusty steam pipes with massive wheel-operated valves. He supposed they still worked, even if they looked rusted shut. Rust flakes littered the floor like decayed snow.

On his right was a long, whitewashed wall. Power cables hung on the ceiling that powered, probably among other things, the fluorescent lights. The tunnel stretched ahead in a straight line.

He stuffed his hoodie and the blanket into the backpack and shouldered it back on so that his hands were free. He didn't expect trouble, but he had to be wary. He walked forward, Edison at his heels.

Steam rushed through nearby pipes with a rattling sound, like rain on a tin roof, and an occasional burble. Heat radiated off the metal. If even a pinhole opened up in one of these pipes, it would cook him and Edison like prawns.

He broke into a quick jog. Sweat poured off him, but he didn't slow down. It wasn't far, less than a half-mile, and he wanted to get through it as fast as he could. It gave him the creeps knowing that he could be cooked alive at any second.

26

A train drove Ozan back away from the blanket-covered form, and he lost precious time identifying himself to a passing patrol. Cursing his luck, he hurried back toward the platform, only to find that the gray lump had vanished. There was nothing on the ground but the pull tab of a beer can. He hesitated. Maybe it had been a drunk curled up under a blanket to sip a beer and rest within sight of other people.

He shone his light in a circle. There it was. A dog's footprint.

At a jog, he followed the direction taken by the dog. They were heading away from the platforms and deeper into the tunnels. It felt as though they had a specific destination in mind.

Within a few minutes, he saw his quarry far ahead. He slowed, barely keeping the man and his dog in sight. He wanted to move closer, but feared that the dog would notice him.

He almost lost them each time that he and they had to flatten against the wall as trains passed. Even if it meant that he might get caught, he had to close the distance between them. If the dog spotted him and things went south, he'd kill them both right here.

When the man opened an underground door, Ozan ran to catch it before it closed, holding it open less than an inch. He counted to fifty, then eased open the door.

The man and dog were jogging away from him. He followed, wishing for cover, but it was one long, well-lit line. He kept his pistol drawn and ran behind them, not worried about noise. The clanking of steam pipes drowned out any small sound he might make.

When the man stopped at another door, he knew he'd never make it in time before it closed. Instead, he flattened himself against the white wall, knowing that the man would see him if he merely turned his head. He didn't.

Once the door closed, Ozan walked up to it. Stenciled on its gray surface was an address: 520 First Street. He knew what could be found at that address. The medical examiner's office. He'd identified his parents' bodies here years before.

Ozan remembered the brain sample he'd taken from Subject 523 and settled down to wait. Tesla might be searching for the same answers that he was. Dubois's request for brain tissue was too odd. If Subject 523 was contagious, Ozan didn't trust Dubois to have warned him about it. The sample he'd scooped from Subject 523's crushed skull made sense only if something horrible had been done to the man.

And what if it was a disease Ozan himself had caught? He'd come in contact with the man's blood—it had even splashed into his eyes. Maybe that had made him sick, made him reckless.

He hated to think that what had been done to him might affect his judgment. His cool and collected brain was the thing that he prized most about himself. Without it, he could not do his work. Without it, he wasn't so different from Erol.

He'd wait for Tesla to come back out and ask him

questions. Tesla would have to come back through here eventually. It wasn't likely that there were other underground exits to the building. And Tesla had to stay inside.

The heat made Ozan drowsy, and the rattling pipes aggravated the pain in his head, but he stayed in position. Sweat broke out all over him. He'd felt terrible since a few hours after the murder, and he had to have answers.

And Tesla might have answers for him. That must be why Tesla had come here. He, too, needed to know about 523. It couldn't be as simple as cause of death. Anyone could see that the hammer had killed him, so Tesla must be seeking something else.

Ozan had to know now. He couldn't kill Tesla. He'd have to wound him, interrogate him, find out if the fever that flowed in Ozan's body had first flowed in 523's. Once he knew the cause, he could find the cure. Once he knew the cause, he could kill Tesla.

But not until then.

27

Joe passed a few locked doors before he found the one that led to 520 First Street. One of his master keys fit into the lock, and it turned easily. People kept these locks well oiled. He hoped that he didn't run into them.

A cluster of pipes turned here—some went into the wall next to the door, and others curved down into the floor to another, deeper level. This juncture wasn't on his maps. Someday he'd explore that level.

He entered the building's sub-basement—a simple room with raw concrete walls. Gray metal lockers ran along one wall, a gray metal table and two chairs stood in the middle of the room, and a sink with a hotplate and an ancient coffeepot sat in the corner. The film of dust coating everything looked at least a decade old. Either someone was a very bad housekeeper, or no one had been in this room in a long time.

Joe opened the first locker and smiled. It contained a tattered orange safety vest with a blue and white Con Edison logo stuck on the left breast. It might as well have contained an invisibility cloak, and he quickly donned it.

He poked around the room and found a wooden clipboard with a five-year-old work order fastened to it, which he scooped up, too. A man wearing an electric-company vest and carrying a clipboard looked like he knew what he was doing. His days in the circus had taught him that people saw what they expected to see, and props set their expectations.

He could never explain a dog. A Con Edison worker with a psychiatric service dog was too memorable.

"Sorry, boy," he said. "You're going to have to stay here."

He led Edison over to the far corner by the lockers, where the air was cooler, and he would be hidden behind the table. He filled the old coffeepot to the brim from a rusty metal faucet that had dripped a red blotch onto the dirty white sink under it.

"Water, boy," he said, setting it down by the dog.

Edison lowered his head and drank greedily. Joe rinsed a thick white cup that he found sitting upside down in the sink and downed a few cups full of rusty-tasting water himself. The jog down the steam tunnels had dehydrated both of them.

"Stay," he told the dog.

Edison cocked his head uncertainly. His job was to accompany Joe.

"Just for a little while," Joe said. "Stay."

Edison understood the tone and settled down, muzzle on his paws, to wait. Joe hated to leave him alone.

He glanced at his watch. Dinnertime. With luck, everyone would be gone home for the day and the building would be mostly empty. He might get through this without any problem.

If not, and he got arrested, he'd tell them where to find his dog. Edison was microchipped, and any vet who read it would return him to the service-dog headquarters. Edison would be fine.

Would Joe?

28

Joe took a last long look around the nearly empty room, wondering if he should check all the lockers to see if there was anything stored there that might help him. He rinsed his cup and set it upside down in the sink for the next guy. No point in stalling. It was already nearly seven. Most of the employees had probably gone home for the day. He hoped.

He gave Edison a two-fingered wave and a final injunction. "Stay."

Edison gave him a dubious look, and he wondered if the dog would stay put.

Joe tried the door that led out of the basement. Locked. Several minutes later he'd established that none of his keys fit the lock. It made sense—the building itself wasn't part of the underground network.

Undeterred, Joe circled the room. The door was the most obvious exit, but the steam pipes themselves left the room and vanished into the ceiling. He placed his palm on both pipes. Cold. Apparently, this building was too modern for steam heat. The hot pipes in the tunnels must have been carrying steam to another building farther down the line.

He studied the pipes. A gap between the pipe and the edge of the ceiling looked promising, but it would be a tight fit. An image of his mummified body dangling there forever flashed through his mind.

With one quick motion, he took off his backpack. He'd never fit through with it on.

"Wish me luck," he told Edison, and he left the backpack by his front feet.

Edison turned his head away, clearly offended at being left behind.

"I don't blame you, boy. But you're never going to make it up the pipe. You're a dog, not a monkey." An image of the monkey skeleton bricked in so long ago flashed through his mind. "And it's just as well. I like you better as a dog."

Edison's tail wagged once (cyan) as if he couldn't help it.

Joe stuck the clipboard inside his shirt and tucked the bottom of the shirt in tightly so that the clipboard wouldn't slide out during his climb. Then he transferred his small flashlight to his front pocket.

Hoping that it would hold his weight, he wedged his toes in the dusty brace that secured the pipe to the wall. He grasped the next brace and pulled himself higher. His sneakers slipped off the metal. He fell downward, but caught himself with his arms. Again, he searched for a toehold in the brace. His foot slid off.

With a sigh he climbed back down to the floor. Edison bobbed his head, looking as smug as possible for such a good-natured dog.

"I've got a plan," he told the dog. "Just you wait."

Edison wagged his tail.

Joe removed his shoes and socks, flattening out his socks and stuffing them in his pockets. His sneakers were a different problem. Where could he put them where they wouldn't be in the way? In the end he tied the laces together and hung them around his neck.

Up the pipe again. He reached out and took firm hold of the first brace, hauling himself up. The metal dug painfully into his palms. His feet sought purchase against the sides of the pipe, slipping before curling like a monkey's. The rusty surface felt rough against the soles of his feet.

He shimmied up a foot, then another, skinning the inside of his right ankle and swearing. If Edison had been a person, he'd have been laughing.

Finally, he got his head through the opening in the ceiling, but the room was so dark that he couldn't see where he was. He pulled one arm up and braced his elbow on the floor. Leaning his weight on that arm, he threaded his other arm up through the small opening.

A few minutes later, he was sitting on the floor. Edison woofed once from below.

"Hush," he called down.

He shone his flashlight around the room—a metal door, a bare bulb with a pull string above, painted concrete walls lined with plastic bottles of cleaning fluid. He was in a broom closet. Just one glamorous stop after another these days.

Sticking his head through the floor, he waved to Edison. The dog was standing at the base of the pipes, looking up.

"Stay, boy. Back soon." He hoped that was true.

Reaching up, he pulled the string to turn on the light. The knees of his pants were filthy, and rust streaked the front of his orange safety vest. If nothing else, he looked as if he'd done a hard day's work underground—the kind of authenticity that money couldn't buy.

He took the clipboard out of his shirt and set it on the floor. When he put his socks and shoes back on, he noticed his ankle was bleeding. He checked the shelves for a first aid kit, but didn't find one. He'd just have to wash it as soon as he could and hope for the best.

In the meantime, he pulled his dirty sock over the wound as gently as he could.

Then he found a dry paper towel and used it to wipe his

face, hands, and arms, leaning forward to shake dust and cobwebs out of his hair and onto the clean floor. Not the equivalent of a shower, but it would have to do.

He tried the door handle. Open. He poked his head through and looked right and left. A darkened empty hallway. Best-case scenario. In he went.

He was inside a new building, one that he had never seen. That was not to be taken for granted. He was over a mile from his house, and he'd come all the way without going outside. The tunnels under New York might be dank and full of rats, but they had given him a new sense of freedom. He had miles and miles yet to explore.

The hallway led to a door that opened onto a grimy set of fire stairs leading up. It was a universal law: Even the fanciest buildings had grungy fire stairs.

He hurried up the stairs. The first floor was marked by a giant number 1 painted in red on the door. The bright red 1 bothered him—it should have been cyan. One was always cyan.

He pulled open the door and entered a well-lit hallway lined with industrial gray carpeting. Offices with tall glass windows and closed doors sat on each side of the corridor. At least he was in the center of the building, away from the giant sheets of glass on the exterior walls that looked out onto the outside.

He had no idea if an autopsy had been completed on Rebar, although he imagined so. If so, he had no idea how to find it. Flaws in his plan bubbled up in his mind. First, he had to find a computer.

"What are you doing here?" asked a voice to his side.

Joe jumped. "I'm here about the problem with the heating."

A woman with dark hair pulled into a bun eyed him sternly over a pair of purple reading glasses. She was tiny, about five feet, in a white lab coat. She seemed a little out of breath, as if she'd been hurrying from somewhere. "The heating? It's about time. My office has been alternating between Antarctic wasteland and jungle swamp for six years."

"Yes, ma'am," Joe replied. "Where's the head of your physical plant?"

He must have gotten the terminology right, because she scowled. "Marcus? Marcus Gruber? He'll be gone for the day, I imagine."

Joe shook the clipboard. "I need to have him sign the work order before I can start. Maybe I could wait awhile for him, just in case? We're running late, and I hate to put this off until tomorrow."

She sighed and glanced at her wristwatch. Joe upgraded her age to at least forty. Nobody younger than that wore wristwatches anymore, except for him. "You can wait in his office. I'll see if anyone knows where he is."

"Thank you, ma'am."

Joe fell in behind her as she trotted off at a good clip, clearly annoyed at him for wasting her time. He hoped that Gruber really was out of his office. Time in an empty office was what he needed.

They ended up inside a nice modern elevator with steel sides, completely unlike the antique rattletrap he rode every day. He thought about the modern safety features it must possess and smiled.

"Gruber's on the third floor. I'm on the eighth." She held out her hand. "Dr. Stavros."

Joe wiped his hand on his pants and shook hers. "Buck Ornish."

He had no idea where that name came from, but she nodded as if it were believable. Really? Did he look like a Buck?

Gruber's messy office was two (blue) doors down from the elevator on the right-hand side. Papers covered a massive oak desk that looked as if it had sat in the same spot for a century. The papers at the bottoms of the piles had yellowed with age. Three (red) half-empty ceramic coffee cups held down a half-curled-up map on the right corner. A computer with smear marks on the dark monitor sat on the left.

Dr. Stavros pointed to an empty chair. "When you see him, remind him about the drain in the second autopsy room. It's been draining slowly for a week."

Joe had a flash of sympathy for Gruber. "What floor is that, ma'am?"

"Ground floor," she said. "He'll know."

As soon as she had closed the door, Joe shot over to the computer and sat down in the creaky desk chair. One key tap brought it out of sleep mode. No password. Wonderful. He started walking through the network. He didn't expect to find the computers that he was looking for, but at least he'd get a better idea of who worked here and what they did.

He got lucky and found Dr. Stavros's computer. A quick search confirmed that she was a medical examiner. It took a few minutes with a password cracker to get her password, *knowthyself*. A literary choice pulled straight from the Temple of Apollo at Delphi. A literary medical examiner with Greek roots.

He figured out how she organized her reports and her notes and, after a few false starts, found the autopsy for a John Doe killed by blunt force trauma on the same date as Rebar. A description of his clothes and location where the body was found told Joe that this John Doe was the man he'd met in the tunnels. Clearly, they hadn't yet confirmed his identity as Ronald Raines.

Joe didn't know what he was looking for, so he downloaded everything onto his jump drive while reading.

The cause of death seemed clear—hammer to the head. Joe didn't care about the time of death or what the man had had for dinner, but one item from her notes jumped out at him.

Brain tissue severely damaged, but there are several lesions present that seem consistent with toxoplasmosis.

The computer finished copying the files. He slipped the jump drive into his pants pocket and closed the files as fast as he could. Time to go. He'd made it. But he'd only started toward the door when a fat man opened it and entered the office.

"What are you doing here?" He glared at Joe from close-set brown eyes set in a bullet-shaped head.

"I'm waiting for Mr. Gruber." Please don't let this be him, Joe silently pleaded.

"That's me." Joe's heart sank. "Why are you in my office? Do you have a pass from security?"

Joe moved toward the door. How could he keep Gruber from having him arrested? His heart raced. He wasn't some glib action star—he was a programmer.

Clearly not willing to let Joe leave, Gruber folded his massive arms. "What did you want from me, Mr. . . . ."

"Buck Ornish," Joe said. He searched for a good lie. "A Dr. Stavros called my department about a slow drain."

As Joe had hoped, an aggrieved expression flitted across Gruber's face. He'd obviously tangled with Dr. Stavros before. "She needs to submit her complaints directly to me."

Joe was glad to see the conversation shift away from him and onto Dr. Stavros. Time to add fuel to the fire. "They sent me right over. I heard she was pretty worked up."

"I bet she is. It still has to go through me."

"Look." Joe tried to sound helpful, like someone who could solve Gruber's problem. "I go off shift in a half hour, and I still have to look at some steam pipes under the building. I can do that now, and put off the drain problem until tomorrow, after a report is filed through proper channels. How does that sound?"

"That'd do," Gruber said grudgingly. "I'll take care of it myself."

Joe shrugged. "If I don't get a report to fix it, I'm happy. I'm on salary."

"I'll walk you down. You can't be on your own." Gruber cast a sidelong glance at Joe. "Who let you in here?"

"Dr. Stavros," Joe answered truthfully. Gruber hadn't asked him for identification yet, or even a name, and he hoped that Gruber would assume that he had checked in with Stavros first because she had filed the complaint. She seemed as if she'd be thorough. He hoped they didn't run into her on the way out.

Gruber gestured to the open door, and Joe went into the hall. He followed the larger man down the hall to the elevator.

"I can get you into the sub-basement," Gruber said. "I don't have keys to the steam tunnel."

Joe held up his massive key ring. "I do."

Gruber raised an eyebrow. "Lots of keys."

"Lots of doors," Joe answered.

The elevator stopped at the sub-basement without a single jump or creak. There was a lot to be said for modern elevator technology.

Gruber led him down a corridor with cinder block walls, coming to a stop in front of a metal door. Joe was pretty sure that he'd left Edison in a room just behind this door. Gruber fumbled through his keys.

"I never open this one," he said.

"If you don't use steam heat, there's not much call to," Joe answered.

Joe was glad that Gruber would let him into the room

and he wouldn't have to climb back down the pipe. Gruber unlocked the door and pushed it open. Joe preceded him into the room and clicked on the light. He'd seen the location of the switch before he climbed up the pipes.

He hoped that Edison would not come running. That would be too much to explain.

"I'll stay down here with the steam pipes," Joe said.

Luckily, the yellow dog seemed to know what Joe wanted, and he stayed put.

"I'll go see about that drain," Gruber said. "So you don't need to bother coming about it tomorrow."

"OK," Joe said. Things were working out for Dr. Stavros.

He was inside with the door closed behind him before he let out a sigh of relief.

"Edison," he called. "Here."

The dog walked over, wagging his tail, and stuck his nose in Joe's palm.

"I think we got what we needed," Joe said. "Let's get home."

Where was home, these days?

He put his hand on the warm door handle, ready to go into the steam tunnels. Wherever home was, it wasn't here.

Edison crowded close to him, aware of his mixed-up state.

"Good boy." Joe gave him one of the last treats in his pocket. He'd need to find food for the dog again soon, and himself, but he didn't dare show his face at Grand Central. The killer must be staking it out.

He opened the door, and the clanking from the pipes pushed into the room. He had a fleeting wish that he could go outside and catch a cab instead of having to leave through the dark and loud tunnel.

No self-pity.

29

Ozan leaned back against the white wall next to an intersection of pipes that shielded him from view. He slid down to a sitting position, legs crossed tailor-style.

The pipes provided the only cover in the tunnel, but it was hotter near them. Maybe the heat would cure his fever. He thought they did that for fevers in the old days. Or maybe they packed people in ice. Ice would feel good right about now. An ice cube glowed blue in his mind, bright as fire. The fever again. Strength sapped from his body with each drop of sweat.

He took off his shirt and used it to mop his forehead. His head felt too heavy on his neck, like it had been turned to steel. He hung it forward until his chin touched his chest. Pain pulsed in his brain to the slow beat of an old ballad.

Get up, Ozan, said a voice that sounded like his mother's. Go home and rest.

He could almost feel her cool hand on his brow. The money is in your accounts, she reminded him. It's enough to keep Erol safe in that beautiful home for another year. You are a good brother. Now, go home and rest.

He struggled to his feet and stood, swaying. But he moved too close to a steam pipe and pain seared along his side. His head cleared. He couldn't go home. Not yet.

He'd heard from a contact at the CIA that the New York Police Department had orders to turn Tesla over to the CIA before interrogating him. That meant one of two things—either they intended to kill the millionaire themselves or they wanted to keep whatever he might say under their control.

Either way, whatever Tesla found out about 523 would not be made public. Ozan might never know. If his illness was connected to his contact with 523's blood, he would never know.

He remembered the one hundred dead men he'd found in the hold of the boat. Maybe they'd all died from this disease. Maybe Dr. Dubois had hired him to cover that up. The doctor would let him die before telling him anything.

Ozan slid down to the floor again and watched his strength leach out in drops on the stone floor, drifting in and out of sleep. A sound woke him with a jerk. It took him a long time to remember where he was. Then his head rolled to the side and he could see around the pipes and back up the tunnel. A man and a dog shimmered through the heat, their figures small with distance.

Ozan stumbled to his feet. His legs had gone to sleep. They tingled painfully and felt fat and cut off from his body.

"Stop!" he shouted.

The man broke into a run. The dog jogged along at his side.

Ozan sighted his gun at the man's back, remembering just in time that he needed to take the man alive. He lowered his gun and took aim at the man's legs. He fired, but it went wide.

Steam boiled from a pipe behind the running man. Ozan's bullet had opened a hole. He'd have to crawl under it.

"I need to talk to you," he shouted.

The man and dog sprinted on, half-obscured by steam. The man ran as if he knew that it was for his life, long panicked strides.

Ozan hobbled after as fast as he could, which was pitifully slow. "It's about 523."

That didn't provoke a response, either, so he fired again. The shot went high and broke a light bulb, raining glass onto the ground.

Ozan's hands shook, and his eyes blurred. He could not let them get away. He abandoned aiming, just fired his Glock empty. The tunnel rang with the sounds of the shots. Steam shot from hole after hole, creating a hot, white wall he could not see through.

A jet of steam hit his wrist. The pain steadied him, made him realize what he had risked. He might have hit Tesla. He might have killed him. He cursed his own stupidity.

Ducking under the scalding steam, he stumbled forward.

He needed Tesla alive.

30

November 29, 8:10 p.m.
Steam tunnel from 520 First Street

Joe's pack bounced against his back as he fled down the tunnel, the laptop battering bruises into his shoulders. Joe didn't care. A killer had just shot at them.

A second shot came, then more. He tackled Edison and huddled against the wall, knowing that he was completely helpless. Shot after shot boomed through the tunnel. Joe couldn't even think. Stay down, stay small, a voice inside him said. Don't be a giant target. He buried his face in Edison's fur and waited.

The shooting stopped. Joe waited for one heartbeat, then another.

A shout echoed down the tunnel.

Whoever had fired the gun was coming toward them, probably reloading. It must be Saddiq. He couldn't see the man through the curtain of hot steam, which meant that the man couldn't see him, either. The steam was probably what had saved his life.

He let go of Edison and ran again.

"Heel, boy!"

It seemed an eternity before they reached the door that led out to the subway tunnels. He had forgotten to lock it when he came through, but he didn't forget to lock it now.

His hands shook so much that he dropped the keys twice, once onto Edison's back, but he finally slotted the key in. It was a stout metal door in a solid frame. That would buy him time.

The cooler air of the tunnel dried the sweat on his skin, but he didn't feel cold. He was running too fast for that. He had no idea how long he ran, wanting to do nothing but put distance between himself and the killer.

Eventually, he slowed down, out of breath. In a few feet they'd be at the first tunnel intersection. Not far after that the tunnels split again. Each turn would make it harder for Saddiq to guess where they'd gone. Once he got to the train track, they wouldn't leave footprints. They could get away.

When he reached the first intersection, he swung left.

"We're OK," he said, looking down to where Edison always ran next to him.

He wasn't there.

Joe stopped dead and looked around. The tunnel was dimly lit, but light enough that he would have seen Edison if he were anywhere close, but he wasn't. Joe was alone.

"Edison," he called, heedless that the sound would draw Saddiq to him.

Silence.

He hurried back the way he had come, calling the dog's name.

Pounding echoed down the tunnel. Saddiq was beating against the inside of the door to the steam tunnel. Joe shut up. If he could hear the killer, the killer could hear him.

He was out of breath, but pushed himself to run faster back to that door. That was where he had last seen Edison. Saddiq might break through at any moment and start shooting. Joe kept running. He had to find Edison, no matter what the cost.

Breathing hard, Joe got to the door. A yellow mound lay

stretched in front of it.

Heart in his mouth, he ran to it and turned it over.

Edison.

"Boy?" Joe's voice cracked.

The dog whimpered, and Joe's heart rose. He was still alive. Joe had to keep it that way.

"It'll be OK," he whispered.

"When I get out of here, you are in a world of pain," shouted a voice from behind the door.

Joe flinched. The killer was a few feet away. If he got through, they were both dead.

Working fast, he slid his hands over Edison, searching for a wound. His right hand came back wet with blood. Joe clicked on the flashlight and held it in his mouth.

Edison had been shot.

The bullet had grazed his right shoulder. Dark, wet blood spilled across his golden fur.

Joe pressed his palm against it. Direct pressure. The first rule of first aid.

The killer kicked the door savagely, and it bowed outward. He would get through it soon, and then he would kill them, probably in a painful way. Joe would fight back as best he could, but he was no match for a military-trained assassin with a gun. That only worked in movies.

Think, Joe told himself. Think.

Years ago, he'd held another wounded dog in his arms. She, too, had trembled with pain and fear. Roxy—a trained poodle and the centerpiece of his act. They had been miles from circus grounds, out on a hike with Farnsworth, the old man who took care of the animals.

Farnsworth drank too much to hold down a real job, but managed to fit into the nomadic life of the troupe. He cleaned out cages and set up tents. He was quiet and smart, and Joe liked spending time with him.

Farnsworth had had the answer then.

Joe dug in his backpack with his free hand, pulling out his dirty T-shirt. It was the cleanest article of clothing he had with him. He folded it into a rectangle and pressed it against the dog's wound. Edison whimpered.

"I'm sorry, boy," he whispered. "I know it hurts."

Another volley of kicks bent the door outward about an inch. It couldn't hold much longer.

With his free hand, he fumbled the roll of duct tape out of his backpack. He scrabbled to find the end of the tape, lifted it up a bit, and held it with his teeth. He wished for three hands as he unrolled it.

He spat out the end of tape, careful to hold it away from the floor, and tore off the strip with his teeth. Carefully, he fitted the tape atop the makeshift T-shirt bandage as he'd seen the drunken vet do years before. Back then, the bandage had held until they'd gotten Roxy back to the trailers. He hoped that this one would hold up as well.

Edison watched him with no hint of reproach in his eyes. He trusted Joe to make him well. Joe hated himself for what had happened to the dog. He should never have been down here playing detective. He should have been able to go to the police and let his lawyer sort it out. Only possible if he could outside.

A thud came from the door. Steam leaked out under it.

Moving fast, Joe shrugged on his backpack, wrapped Edison in the blanket and held him against his chest. He jogged away from deafening bangs from the killer's gun. He was shooting his way out.

Joe redoubled his pace. Edison's seventy-five pounds weighed heavy in his arms. Joe tightened his grip and kept going. He would carry this dog until he dropped.

His original plan had been to lose the bad guy in the tunnels and circle back to Platform 36 to find out all he could about toxoplasmosis and Ronald Raines. But he couldn't do that now. He had to get Edison to help, and fast.

He slowed. Edison grew heavier with every step. Joe's legs and back ached with every step. He staggered to a stop.

He had nowhere to go.

31

November 29, 8:21 p.m.
Central Park

Vivian jogged across the dimly lit park to the bank of phone booths. Phone booths were getting rare in the city, and she had a call to make that she didn't dare make from her cell. Thanks, again, to Tesla.

Frozen leaves crackled underfoot, and the sky glowed dark golden from the streetlights. It was a beautiful night. She swung her gloved hands as she ran, keeping loose and ready in case anyone thought that a woman alone in the dark was easy prey. That anyone would have serious regrets.

The temperature had dropped since the sun had gone down, and she pulled her black knit cap down over her eyebrows. Tesla had told her that most facial-recognition software used the eyes to make identifications—the distance between them, the depth of the eye socket, the color. The old surveillance cameras trained on the phone booths were black and white, low resolution, so maybe they'd be easier to fool.

As she got closer to the camera, she pulled up her black scarf so that it covered her nose. Being bundled up didn't look out of place here, with the cold frost nipping at everyone's nose this time of year.

The phone booths were empty. She aimed for the one on

the end and wished that it had a door so she'd have privacy. Once inside the tiny room, she changed her mind. The smells of stainless steel and urine and cold assailed her—the bouquet of the city. Better to have one side open to the fresh air than keep all this penned up behind a door.

The walls were pocked with dents where people had kicked them or punched them, either because they hadn't liked whatever they'd heard on the other end of the line or to let the metal know who was boss. Any way you looked at it, the phone booth had seen hard use.

Like almost everyone else, she never used phone booths. She had a cell phone to make and receive calls, but she'd turned it off before she left the house. Right now, she was under the radar, like everyone else who used these phones.

A glance into the deformed metal wall told her that her face was still concealed. She dialed the number and faced the opening of the booth again. She had no intention of turning her back on the dark park.

A slender Hispanic man in a denim jacket walked toward the phones, and she tensed. His hands were empty, and his stride was tired. Probably a guy who'd finished work and wanted to make a call. He took the booth next to hers and dialed a long number, somewhere overseas, and dropped quarter after quarter into the coin slot.

The burr of a ringing phone droned on from the plastic handset held an inch from her face. Eventually, her connection went through, and she left a message with the police tip line, the one that she'd called the day before. She relayed the information that Tesla had sent her—the identity of the murderer who had killed the young man in front of Grand Central Terminal and how to find the surveillance footage to prove it.

If Tesla was telling the truth, then the police could verify it. If he was lying, they'd know that, too. Vivian had to tell them just in case. Duty done, she hung up.

The man next to her spoke Spanish in a practically unending stream. It didn't sound like the people on the other end got much chance to get a word in edgewise. Maybe he was leaving a message as she had done. Maybe he was even calling in to a criminal tip line. She smiled. Stranger coincidences had happened.

She checked her reflection again to make sure that her hat was down and her scarf was across her nose before re-entering the cold nighttime park. Once she'd moved out of the pool of light, she let the scarf fall.

Tesla's agenda was opaque to her. He had to know that he couldn't hide out from the police forever without going outside. So, what the hell was he doing?

She pushed him out of her mind and focused on her surroundings—empty paths, drifts of snow against the sides of trees, and quiet. It was too early and too cold for troublemakers, but she kept her guard up until she'd hiked out of the park onto the brightness of Fifth Avenue and over to Madison Avenue.

She turned her phone back on. It had been off for only a few minutes, but it showed a missed call from one of her best clients: Daniel Rossi. She called back.

"Have you heard from Mr. Tesla?" he asked.

She hesitated, wanting for some obscure reason to protect Tesla before realizing that he was better off with Mr. Rossi on his side, whether he knew it or not. "I believe that he sent me an email, sir. It came from my mother's account, but contained information about the knifing that happened this morning in front of Grand Central."

"Details?"

She filled him in on that email and the previous one where Tesla had identified the murder victim in the tunnels. He was proving to be a clever criminal investigator, but it wouldn't be enough to keep him out of trouble. Mr. Rossi listened patiently.

The sidewalks were crowded with New Yorkers in long coats and hats, rushing to catch their trains. She fetched up inside a doorway to avoid the worst of it while she talked with Mr. Rossi.

"Do you know where he might be?" Mr. Rossi asked.

"No, sir." Down there somewhere, unable to come out. In spite of her anger at him for messing with her mother's account, she felt sorry for him. She didn't see how he could get out of this.

"We need to bring him to a place of safety."

"Sir?" She stamped her feet to get blood flowing back to them. Her toes weren't happy that she'd stopped jogging.

"Could you carry him?"

"Fireman's carry. Sure." He wouldn't like it, but it'd work. She bit back a smile. So much for protecting his dignity.

"I'd like you to find him and get his permission to render him unconscious, then bring him to my house."

She didn't have to ask where that was. Uptown. Expensive.

"Do you have any questions?" he asked.

"How should I render him unconscious?" A crack on the head? Choke hold?

"I will provide you with prescription drugs."

Boring. "If he refuses to take the drugs?"

"He needs to be taken out of those tunnels, for his own protection."

Vague answer. "Am I authorized to use force?"

"Try not to let it come to that. If it does, there will also be a syringe in the bag. Two—one for him and one for the dog, in case it acts up."

So, she would be in trouble with Mr. Rossi if she left Tesla down there, and in trouble with Tesla if she injected him against his will and dragged him out. Damned if you do, damned if you don't. Just like the old days in the military. "I see."

"My understanding is that there is a high police presence in the tunnels, and that other government agencies may be involved as well. And who knows if the man who killed the young man in front of the station today is still down there. You should use caution, and avoid contact with these other parties at all cost."

So, she'd have to figure out how to carry him out without being noticed. This just got better and better. "I understand, sir."

What she understood was that this was likely to be a complicated extraction of an unwilling subject under the noses of trained law enforcement personnel and a cold-blooded slasher. A challenge. Vivian loved a challenge.

On the way to pick up the drugs from Mr. Rossi, she bought a simple burner phone and sent an email to her mother from her smartphone.

> *Hi Mom,*
> *I got a new cell phone. It's 212-555-0919. Call me when you get this to see if it works! Remember the number so that you can reach me if you get lost on the subway.*
> *Talk soon,*
> *Viv*

She called her mother to explain but was too late, so she got a tongue-lashing for assuming that her street-savvy mother might lose her way on the subway.

After Vivian explained that it was a code, her mother was angry about that, too. She didn't want her account to be used to pass coded messages any more than Vivian did, but she agreed to leave the message there, so if Joe logged in to that account and read it, he might call.

Vivian couldn't count on him reading the email, or on him trying to cooperate. She needed to track him down.

It couldn't be that hard. He couldn't go outside, so he was limited to the tunnels. Of course, there were literally hundreds of miles of subway tunnels, steam tunnels, and even sewage tunnels that he could be using. She'd never be able to search them all.

Maybe she wouldn't have to. Based on the information that he'd been sending her, he still had access to an Internet connection. That meant that he could be in only a few places.

Most of the shops in Grand Central Terminal didn't provide Wi-Fi. They didn't want their customers to linger. The Apple Store did, but only during business hours. She'd check there.

In the underground platforms, the only one with Wi-Fi that she knew of was Platform 36. She'd comb the platform itself and the area around it, although she might have trouble getting down into the tunnels there, because the place was overrun with cops. Maybe Dirk could help.

If Tesla wasn't there, then maybe he'd gone back to his underground house (or close enough to get into his wireless router). If she made a circuit between those few stops, she'd catch him eventually.

She just hoped that no one else caught him first.

32

November 29, 8:32 p.m.
Thirty-Third Street Subway Station

Joe paused in the darkness next to the edge of the subway platform, studying the people who milled about in the everyday world. Ordinary people, waiting for their train. To them, a trip down into the subway was just a space between their ordinary worlds. They moved through it, not paying attention, intent on their real destination. For him, his whole world now existed in the spaces between.

And right now this interspace was unguarded. That was the essential part. No one was posted at the ends of the platform to watch for him and keep him from getting Edison to safety. Apparently, they'd concentrated their forces around Grand Central. They couldn't be everywhere.

He breathed in the smell of engine oil, creosote, and urine. And dog. Kneeling, he lowered his bundle carefully to the stone-covered ground, wishing it were softer. "How you doing, old friend?"

His heart caught in his throat as he waited for the dog to respond. Was he still alive? Then, the blanket moved as Edison tried to wag his tail.

Edison opened his eyes and looked at Joe, but didn't lift his head. He was weak and tired. Joe had to get him help right away.

First, he needed to make sure Edison could be transported further. Joe eased the dirty blanket from around the warm form, lifting him as little as possible. He needed to see the wound. The dim light of the platform verified that the blood that had once run down Edison's shoulder had dried. He stroked the area around the wound lightly, checking to see if blood had seeped out from beneath the duct tape. Edison's fur was warm and dry. So, the duct tape was holding—no leaks.

"That's very good," he told Edison. "You're going to be OK."

Edison's ears perked up at the sound of his voice, but that was all the movement he had in him.

Joe began to wrap the blanket around the dog's limp body, thinking as he worked, keeping his motions gentle and slow.

He couldn't make it up the stairs and into the outside world. He wished that his life were more like a movie—that his love for the dog would let him overcome his handicap, but he knew better. Whatever quirk had settled into his brain chemistry, wishing that it would go away wasn't going to fix it.

If he tried to go out, he would have a panic attack. Edison would be needlessly upset, and even if people stopped to help Joe, Edison's needs might get ignored. He had to come up with a strategy that was all about the dog.

During his run through the tunnels, he'd realized that he had to call someone for help. His cell phone was surely monitored by now. The second he turned it on, cops would descend on him. For all he knew, Saddiq would receive his location information, too. Everyone would focus on arresting him, and Edison's needs would get lost.

He'd have to try a pay phone. Many stations in the system still had pay phones, although he'd read that more than half didn't work anymore. Maybe he'd get lucky. If not, he'd have to ask a commuter to borrow a cell phone. Maybe that guy would take pity on a man with a wounded dog.

He finished wrapping the dog and picked him up like a baby. Time to go.

In less than a minute, he was up the stairs. He expected someone to yell his name, to come and arrest him, but no one did.

He hurried to the pay phone and gently set Edison next to a metal post painted bright yellow. He tried not to think about how dirty the floor was, how dirty the blanket was. Edison would pull through this. He would.

While he'd run through the tunnels with the wounded dog in his arms, he'd made a list of people who might help him. It was a short list, and made shorter by the fact that the police likely knew most of the people on it—Celeste, Leandro, Vivian Torres. He doubted that any of them had a secure phone line anymore. He could try Mr. Rossi, but didn't want to waste time being lectured about why running and hiding in the tunnels was too dangerous.

That left his dog walker—Andres Peterson. He always paid the man in cash so there would be no credit card trail to link the two of them. Andres never stayed long enough at the Hyatt to talk to the staff. Celeste was the only link, and she would never tell the cops anything.

He rubbed his palms together to clean off the dried blood, watching the flakes fall to the concrete floor, then picked up the filthy handset, and dropped in a quarter. The phone burred once (cyan), twice (blue), three times (red) before it was answered.

"Andres? It's Joe Tesla."

"I came to the Hyatt, Mr. Tesla, but you were not there." Andres's tone was frosty. In all the excitement, he'd forgotten to cancel the dog walker. This was not the best day to have alienated him.

"I'm sorry, Andres." He cut to the most important information. "Edison has been hurt. Badly."

"The friendly dog? No!"

Joe didn't have time to explain, and any explanation might make it less likely that Andres would help him. "Can you come to the Thirty-Third Street subway station to pick him up and take him to the veterinarian? It is an emergency. Life or death."

A crashing sound came through the phone. "I come at once."

Joe gave him directions on where to meet and told him to hurry before hanging up the black plastic receiver.

"Andres is coming, Edison," he told the dog as he lifted him again, happy to see his ears move at the sound of Andres's name. "He's going to help you."

Joe wished, again, that he could help the dog himself. That he could trot up those stairs, hail a cab, and save the creature who had given him more than any other, who had never asked for anything beyond basic care in return. Letting down Edison was worse than letting down the rest of the world.

No self-pity.

What he needed to do was find a way to wait in a busy subway station with a wounded dog without drawing attention to himself, even with God knew how many cops searching for him. That was easy.

Becoming invisible was all about the props. He snagged a Starbucks cup from an overflowing garbage can and made for the exit where he had instructed Andres to meet him. People walked by him, heads hunched into their warm coats, ignoring Joe completely.

Once he was as close to the outside as he dared to get, he put the dog on the cold floor. "Just a minute, Edison. I'll pick you back up in a minute."

Edison's brown eyes followed his every move.

Joe slid the backpack off his back and turned it upside down so that no one could see that it was fairly clean and in good shape. Then he sat down. He emptied the last few drops of cold coffee onto the ground and dropped in a couple of quarters. He sat the cup in front of him, picked up the dog and held him carefully in his lap.

Now he wasn't a millionaire murder suspect on the run. He was far easier to recognize and dismiss—a beggar with a dog. New York City had an army of invisible street people. One more would never be noticed.

People walked by him, eyes averted from the dirty man with the dog wrapped in a blanket. They didn't want to have to think about him, to weigh whether or not they should give him money, or feel sorry for him or the dog. And that suited him just fine.

What he most wanted to do was sit and hold his dog in peace. He wanted Edison to feel how much he loved him, know how sorry he was, and take strength and hope from his touch. It was a lot, too much, to project onto the dog, but he didn't care.

"It's going to be OK," he promised him in a low, crooning voice. "Andres will get you to a vet. Then you can stay with him for a while, or Celeste."

Joe pushed the image of Edison's lifeless body from his mind. Instead, he stroked the dog's head, his soft ears, and stared into those patient brown eyes. Edison didn't deserve this. He deserved walks in the park and steak sandwiches and warm evenings by the fire.

"Once I've sorted this out, I'll get you back. I promise."

He kept up a steady dialogue while petting the dog, trying not to think of anything but the moment. No future. No past.

A figure knelt next to him and Andres's familiar voice spoke softly. "I'm here."

"Thank you." Joe had never felt such gratitude toward anyone. "Thank you."

"I could not let Mr. Edison down." Andres petted the dog's head gently.

Joe pulled all of the money out of his pocket and handed it to Andres. It was more than five hundred dollars. "This should cover the vet bill and the taxi there. If it runs over, Celeste can pay you."

Andres took only one hundred dollars and handed back the rest. "If it is more, I will ask Celeste. I think you need this more than she."

What did Andres know? Who had told him?

Apparently reading the questions from his face, Andres said, "I see it in the evening paper. You are on the front page. Now I know why you did not call me before."

He would look into that later. "There is an emergency vet—"

"I know all this," Andres said. "I researched on my phone on the way. They will take good care of this good dog. Make him jumping for a ball like a puppy."

Edison's tail moved once (cyan) at the word ball.

Joe smiled down at him. He hoped that Andres was right and that he and Edison had many long games of fetch in the tunnels ahead of them, that the dog would sit stretched out by his feet soaking up the warmth of hundreds more fires, that he would gulp down bits of Joe's sandwiches for years to come. He couldn't bear to think of the alternative.

Andres stripped off his long coat. "Take this."

"I couldn't," Joe said. "I don't know when—"

"You can give it back later," Andres said. "But my mother would scold me if I sent you away with no coat and no blanket."

He folded the coat lengthwise and placed it on the floor. Joe didn't want to argue anymore, so he left it there.

Joe eased his arms under the blanket and put Edison into Andres's outstretched arms, wondering if he would ever hold the dog's warm body again.

Andres shifted Edison closer to his chest, and the dog whimpered in pain. It cut Joe's heart to hear it.

Andres, too, looked grave. "I go now. My cab is waiting on the street. Good luck."

"Good luck to you." Joe bent down and kissed the top of Edison's muzzle. "And to you, Yellow Dog."

33

November 29, 9:04 p.m.
Thirty-Third Street Subway Station

Joe watched Andres and Edison until they disappeared up the stairs and into the light. He imagined them crossing under the streetlight, passing people hurrying to get out of the cold, getting into the cab, closing the door, and riding away.

His imagination didn't dare go further than that.

Instead, he shrugged into Andres's warm coat and headed back for the anonymity of the underground. Shivering, he pulled the coat tighter around himself. He hadn't noticed how cold he was until Edison was gone. His teeth chattered, and he silently thanked Andres for giving him the coat off his back, and so much more than that.

A train must have just arrived, because the corridor was suddenly full of people. A man bumped into Joe's shoulder and muttered at him. Joe moved closer to the wall, to stay out of the way of the crowds that surged past him on their way home.

Home.

The mass pushed him to one side, but he limped back into the station. His ankle throbbed, and he couldn't remember what he'd done to it. His arms and back ached, too, from carrying a limp Edison through the tunnels. He only hoped that it mattered, that the vet would be able to heal him. That his pathetic weakness had not doomed the brave and loyal dog like it had doomed Brandon. If Joe could have gone outside and explained everything to the police, Brandon would still be alive, and Edison would be chasing a ball in the park. No self-pity, he reminded himself. But this wasn't self-pity. It was grief and shame.

A man in a dark suit dodged in front of him to drop his newspaper in the recycling bin. Joe held out his hand, and the man slapped the paper in it without breaking stride.

Joe sat down on the subway bench, holding the newspaper. He was afraid to read it and see what it said about him, but he had to know.

He unfolded the newspaper. He hadn't expected the *New York Post*. The man had looked more like someone who read the rarified words of *The New York Times*. A surprise. The scent of ink drifted up, an ordinary smell from his past—a time when he could sit with his coffee and read the paper and then go outside and start his day. He ached for those days.

He shook the paper out and read the headline: MOGUL ON MURDER SPREE? Underneath the headline was a photo of him gleaned from an old version of the Pellucid web site. They were lucky that he'd quit, considering the damage control they would have had to do if their chief technology officer was a crazy killer hunting victims through New York's subterranean world. Mind-boggling.

He read the headline again. He was a mogul now, was he? And a killer. Anger rising, he skimmed the article, gritting his teeth when he came across phrases like *mentally ill* and *chained to a life indoors* and *source of his murderous rage*. They had effectively painted him as a bored rich kook who couldn't go outside and had turned to murder in the tunnels to amuse himself. The last line read,

If he's innocent, then why is this so-called brilliant man cowering in corners instead of accounting for his whereabouts to the police?

Joe tore the paper in half. Yes, the article was damaging, and parts of it were lies, but it contained a grain of truth—he was cowering here instead of proving his innocence. Well, screw 'em. He'd find the guilty parties and get them arrested.

He dropped the pieces of newspaper into the recycling bin.

What was up with Vivian? Had she received his emails and relayed his tips to the cops? If she had, no one on the force was leaking the information to the *Post*. If she hadn't, how else could he get that information out to the public? Everyone needed to know Rebar's true identity. They needed to know that Saddiq had killed Brandon, and probably Rebar as well. Maybe that would be enough for them to put the pieces together. Or not. His best chance of solving this lay in putting together the pieces himself.

A man sat next to him on the bench. He turned up the collar of his camel-hair coat and studied Joe's face. Did he recognize him? With his face covered in stubble and grime, wearing an Eastern European army surplus coat and stinking of blood and dog, Joe didn't see how the man would connect him to the well-groomed and happy millionaire on the front page of the newspaper. He couldn't be sure.

"Spare change?" Joe held out his dirty hand, palm up. He figured this was the last thing the guy would expect from a millionaire.

The man's face tightened. He shook his head and looked away.

Joe stifled a smile and reached down for Edison. His hand landed on empty air. He looked at the spot and saw a dirty tile floor with dark spots of gum stuck to it. He was alone.

Worry for Edison rose up in him again, and he pushed it back down. Edison was in the best possible hands now. Andres would see to it. And once he got out of the vet's office, he would lie by Celeste's bed—Joe envied him—and be petted and spoiled until he could come home to Joe again.

For both of their sakes, Joe had to restore their world even though he'd been branded crazy. Starting with finding the truth, and then sharing it. He'd have to do it without Edison's support, on his own.

What he wanted to start with was a warm shower, a soft bed, and a hot dinner. He knew where he could get some version of all three.

Home.

34

November 29, 9:38 p.m.
Grand Central Terminal

Vivian passed the shoe-shine boxes where she'd tussled with that kid six months ago. On the last day that Tesla had gone outside. A black man in a dark blazer stood where she had sat Tesla down while she subdued the attacker. The man held a wooden brush and a rag, about to shine the brown leather shoes of a businessman in a navy blue suit. The businessman stuck his foot out and opened his paper.

Tesla's face stared at her from the front page. That man was in more trouble now than he'd been the night she met him. She'd read the article and didn't envy him his notoriety. He couldn't catch a break. Maybe once she delivered him to Mr. Rossi, they could start rebuilding his reputation and persuade the police to search for the real killer.

Maybe they'd already gone after Ozan Saddiq. She hadn't dared to ask Dirk about it, needing to keep herself, and by extension Tesla, out of it.

A man at the top of the stairs held open the heavy front door for her, and she gave him a quick smile before stepping through and into the terminal building. Warmth enveloped her as soon as she got a few steps from the door, reminding her how cold it was outside on the streets tonight. She hoped that Tesla had a warm place to hole up.

Then she began her sweep of the station. It took over an hour to hurry through each open shop, making sure that Tesla wasn't hiding in a fitting room trying on pants or picking through produce at the marketplace or waiting for a latte at Starbucks. In fact, she got in line at Starbucks to get herself a plain coffee, eyes scanning the other patrons for a tired-looking software engineer and his dog. Nothing.

She took her coffee and headed back toward the main concourse. Her feet were sore, and she was tired. She'd seen no sign of Tesla. What she had seen, between commuters, were police and government agents—in uniform and undercover. They loitered in the food court, waited on the balconies, patrolled the entrance to each set of platforms, and stood by the passageway to the Hyatt, near the elevators.

If Tesla showed his face here now, they'd nab him in a minute. And she still had no good plan for getting him out of the tunnels with such an interested audience. She had a vague idea that she could persuade him to hike to a subway station, a place far from here that wasn't watched, then either persuade him to take the drugs or inject him and get him on a train. She'd brought along gin to pour on his clothes, so it would look like she was walking a drunk guy out to a cab. She had experience maneuvering a drunken Tesla.

Then what? Three men had died suspiciously in the area—the man beaten to death underground, a cop who had fallen or been pushed in front of a train, and a young tennis instructor knifed out front. If you believed the news, and Vivian usually didn't, Tesla was responsible for them all. Mr. Rossi had his work cut out for him.

She walked up the stairs to the west balcony, cradling the warm coffee cup in her hands. It smelled like early mornings and breakfast, but instead of that she was experiencing an evening of futility.

The Apple Store was closed, but she managed to catch an

employee in an Apple shirt while she was locking up.

"Vivian Torres." She flashed her badge. She'd bought it online. As long as she didn't say that she was a police officer, she wasn't technically breaking the law.

The red-haired girl gave her a skeptical look. Her name tag said GINGER.

"I was wondering if you'd seen a man in your store today."

"I saw lots of them." Ginger pocketed her keys and pulled on an orange parka that clashed with her hair.

"This guy would have had a dog with him, a yellow Lab."

Ginger fiddled with an iPhone. It looked like she was selecting music to play. "Why?"

Because if I find him I might be able to save his ass, Vivian thought. She had to think up a story that would make sense to someone who might know Tesla and his dog. "He comes around here a lot, practically lives at Grand Central."

Ginger's finger hovered over a title on the phone. Vivian wanted to slap her to get her attention. "Don't know him."

"He might have come in today to use the Wi-Fi."

She gestured to the empty space in front of the store. "Lots of folks do. It's not a crime. We offer it for free."

"I don't want him for a crime," Vivian said. "I want to help him."

"I don't know who you are talking about." The girl dropped the phone in her pocket and turned up her collar. "Can I go now?"

Vivian couldn't hold her. And she still had no idea if Tesla and Edison had stopped by. Even if they had, they were clearly gone now.

Coffee cup in hand, Vivian stood at the edge of the balcony and watched the people ebb and flow in the main hall, always looking for a man with a dog. Had the police followed up on her calls to the tip line? The press had not reported on the identity of Ronald Raines. Maybe Tesla was wrong. Maybe the police didn't believe the connection. Maybe they hadn't released that information to the press. Too many maybes. But Mr. Rossi wouldn't let that information go to waste. He'd figure out the best way to work it.

Tesla had to come up for air sometime. He'd need food, information, money, and Wi-Fi. Tesla didn't strike her as a regular computer nerd—he had a difficult past. She'd read that in his eyes and his body language. Whoever was messing with him was going to get more than they'd bargained for. Hopefully, that grit would be enough to carry him through.

She threw away her empty cup. She only had one place left to try in the terminal: Platform 36.

After that she'd head down to Tesla's house, assuming that she was still on the approved-visitors list, and wait there. She couldn't shake the feeling that he'd come back home. If he did, she wanted to be there if they caught him, to help if she could. At the very least, she might be able to keep him from being shot. She could notify Mr. Rossi the second he was in custody and spike him with the drug if he panicked. Because if they caught him, he would be cornered, he would be scared, and he would be unpredictable.

35

November 29, 10:20 p.m.
Tunnels

After more than an hour of walking and doubling back to avoid transit cops, Joe was finally closing in on his own house. He'd never expected it to take so long, but the tunnels were crawling with patrols. One of them even had a dog, reminding him again that he didn't.

As much as he wanted to open a round steel door and walk down the hall to his front door, he didn't dare. If the police hadn't breached his alarm system, they were certainly monitoring it. He wouldn't be surprised if there wasn't someone in his house right now, sitting in his warm parlor, drinking his coffee and pawing through his leather-bound books.

But he still thought that they didn't know about his secret passageway. If they'd known of its existence when they'd come to arrest him, they would have stationed someone there before they'd come down the elevator. Sure, they might have learned about it since then, but he doubted it. Probably, only the Gallos knew of its existence, and they hadn't even told Joe its whereabouts.

He circled the area by the western-most armed door. No one. That made sense. It'd be easier to station someone on the other side. He checked neighboring tunnels—also empty.

He listened for a long time and didn't hear anyone nearby. He almost turned to tell Edison to heel. No need.

Donning his night-vision goggles, he glanced around the dark tunnel intersection. Nothing moving in any direction. The patrols all used flashlights, and he'd see them coming from far away.

He crept slowly down the tunnel that led to his hidden door, stepping on the ties so as not to leave footprints. Here of all places he did not want to be followed. So close now.

The secret passageway ended in the middle of a tunnel, about four feet off the floor, with the door cleverly concealed by the stone. If he hadn't known exactly where to look, he would have walked by it.

As it was, he went straight to it, felt about until he found the divot that was used a handle, and pulled it open. It swung easily, silently, on hinges that he'd oiled himself right after he'd found the door. Even someone standing next to him would not have heard it.

He ran his fingers along the rubber seal that lined the edges. The door had been designed to be watertight in case the underground tunnels ever flooded. Nor would light leak out. He'd tested it by leaving a strong flashlight pointed at the door, then closed it and studied it with his night-vision goggles. Not a shimmer had passed through.

He climbed in and pulled the door closed behind him, carefully drawing the bolt across. Right now he was the safest he had been since the police had driven him out of his house the night before. He was also hungry, smelly, and lonely. But he had the cure to all that in his backpack—his computer.

Wedging himself with his back against one side of the round tunnel and his feet against the other, he started up his laptop. As a supernerd, Joe didn't tolerate network lag. He had a router downstairs in the parlor and one upstairs in his bedroom on the bookcase that served as the interior door to the secret passage.

Wi-Fi strength should not be a problem here. Quickly, he connected and accessed his surveillance cameras. Nobody was at the elevator or in the tunnels right now. Unfortunately, he hadn't installed cameras inside his house, so he couldn't verify that it was empty. He bet that it wasn't.

To find that out, he needed to track movements in and out of the house since he'd been driven out of the house the night before. He connected to the server that stored the surveillance videos and loaded the corresponding one. Four men (green) had left in the elevator late last night, about half an hour after their arrival. Vivian Torres had gone with them. Two (blue) men had stayed.

Every half hour the two men went through his front door. One went down the left tunnel to check the elevator and the door that closed off the tunnel in that direction. The other went right and checked that door. They must have assumed the only way into the house was through one of those tunnels, because they didn't bother to leave someone inside. Each check took them between five and six minutes.

Eight hours later, they had been relieved by another two men who followed the same routine. Eight hours after that, another two men came on shift. It looked like they'd settled in to stake out his house for the long term.

He'd been afraid of that. That left him only the five- to six-minute window when they went out to check the tunnel doors and the elevator. If he was quick and careful, that ought to be enough.

A glance at his watch verified that the men wouldn't be going out on their foray any time soon. No point in wasting the free Wi-Fi. He left the surveillance camera views up on his laptop, hid his IP address, then searched for toxoplasmosis.

The first site brought up a cross section of a human brain with bright yellow dots in it and arrows pointing to the marked cysts.

He read the text below it.

Parasitic protozoans, called toxoplasmosis, infect all mammals on Earth. About 25% of all Americans currently carry these parasites in their blood and brains. Although once thought to be harmless in children and adults with healthy immune systems, new research indicates that the parasite is related to both mental illnesses, such as schizophrenia and Parkinson's disease, and reckless behaviors, causing higher incidences of automobile accidents and promiscuity.

Toxoplasmosis is incurable.

So, Rebar having toxoplasmosis might be unremarkable. Millions of other people had it, and they hadn't been targeted by a contract killer. Joe checked the time at the corner of the screen. Twenty more minutes before his guards left the house. He kept searching.

The symptoms of toxoplasmosis are minor in most people—muscle aches, fever, tiredness, sore throat, and nausea.

He remembered when he'd met Rebar in the tunnel. The man had been flushed, thin, and feverish-looking. Toxoplasmosis could have caused that. Not in someone with a healthy immune system, but toxoplasmosis could be deadly in those with compromised immune systems, such as those infected with HIV, organ transplant recipients, or the elderly.

He hadn't seen AIDS or HIV mentioned in the autopsy or any mention that Rebar might have received an organ transplant or chemotherapy, so his immune system might or might not have been compromised. But maybe the parasite didn't need a compromised immune system to take over anymore. Maybe the parasite had become more virulent.

Joe researched it further.

The toxoplasmosis parasite causes rats to not only lose their fear of cats, but to become attracted to the scent of cat urine—leading them to be killed and ingested by cats. It is only in a cat's digestive tract that the parasite can complete its lifecycle and reproduce sexually, forming eggs that are expelled in the cat's feces.

Joe read that paragraph twice. He grimaced. If a microscopic parasite could persuade rats to run willingly to their deaths, what could it do to humans?

In humans infected with toxoplasmosis, studies show that men behave with greater recklessness, becoming more involved in fights and car accidents than their statistically similar peers. Women, on the other hand, become more compliant and sexually promiscuous.

In addition, patients with some mental illnesses, including schizophrenia and bipolar disorder, have higher than average infection rates. Women infected with toxoplasmosis have been shown to have twice the suicide rate as non-infected women.

A microscopic parasite could have a very profound influence on a person's brain. A seemingly trivial creature could cause someone to hear voices, be depressed, or even take his own life. Feeling paranoid, he checked for a link between agoraphobia and toxoplasmosis, but didn't find one. So, whatever had sent him over the deep end, it wasn't this tiny parasite. Although that didn't mean it couldn't be a different one.

He did a quick search to see how it was transmitted—to make sure that he couldn't have caught it from Rebar.

Toxoplasmosis is usually transmitted by eating undercooked meat from an animal that contains the parasite.

This can include beef, pork, venison, etc.

In rare cases, toxoplasmosis has been transmitted via blood transfusions or organ donations.

He hadn't eaten Rebar or come in contact with his blood, so maybe he was safe. Joe took a deep breath and let it out. He was likely not infected by a killer parasite that made you do crazy things. That might be the best news he'd heard today. He checked the time. Five more minutes.

What about Saddiq? Unless he'd worn a full CDC contamination suit to bash in Rebar's head, he'd probably come in contact with Rebar's blood. If it had come in contact with an open wound or his eyes, there was a chance that he'd become infected, too.

It would explain his reckless behavior—killing Brandon in the street, randomly shooting his gun empty in the steam tunnel. None of his actions jibed with the deliberate, professional man described in his military files.

It made him an even more dangerous opponent.

Joe checked the time. 10:45. He crawled up the tunnel, laptop tucked inside his hoodie. When he got to the top, just inside the door that led to the house, he opened his laptop and checked his surveillance cameras. His watchdogs were leaving—one was fat with straight black hair and the other was skinny with big ears. He named them Abbott and Costello. Abbott went right, Costello went left, and Joe set his watch alarm for four minutes. That gave him a minute of cushion in case Abbott or Costello decided to speed things up.

He pushed the bookcase open slowly, glad that he'd oiled those hinges, too. His bedroom smelled wonderful—like wood and lilacs, remnants of the previous occupants and a reminder of his everyday world.

There was no way around it. He had to take risks now.

He ran down his stairs two at a time and went straight for the kitchen. Here, he gathered food: bottled water, Dr Pepper, MoonPies, trail mix, an unopened block of cheese from the fridge, and a bag of tortilla chips. He didn't have time to be choosy—he just grabbed whatever was at the back of the cabinets and unlikely to be missed.

Then he raced back upstairs to the master bedroom. He took a set of clean clothes from his drawers—black jeans, a black T-shirt, and a black hoodie, clothes that would be hard to see in the tunnels. He threw everything into the passageway and went back to his bathroom. Two minutes. He stripped off his clothes, but didn't put them in the hamper—the smell might get noticed.

Instead, he wet a washcloth with cold water—no time to warm it up—and took the fastest sponge bath in history. Then he brushed his teeth, opening a new toothbrush and taking that and the toothpaste with him. He dried everything off with a towel and took the dirty washcloth, towel, and wet soap with him, opening a new one and leaving it in its place.

He grabbed gauze and ointment for his ankle, and had just bent to look at it when his alarm beeped. Time's up.

He made it back to the bookcase with five seconds to spare, but even so, he heard steps on his front porch. A short round for Abbott and Costello.

He climbed into the tunnel, closed the bookcase door, and realized that he hadn't had time to dress. Stifling a curse, he fumbled around in the dark for his clean clothes. He hadn't checked the bookcase to see if light leaked through, so he couldn't turn on his flashlight.

It took longer than it should have, and he was thoroughly chilled by the time he was done, but eventually he was dressed in his new clothes and Andres's long coat. He packed everything he'd taken from the house into his old hoodie and dragged it down to the stone door that opened onto the tunnel.

He turned on his flashlight and studied his scraped ankle. It looked worse than he'd expected. He didn't like the way that the skin around the wound was red and hot to the touch. The wound itself was deeper than he'd thought, and rust flakes were embedded in it. Clenching his jaw against the pain, he scrubbed the flakes out with the wet washcloth. He covered the throbbing wound carefully with ointment and wrapped the gauze around his ankle, wishing he'd had a better first aid kit with him when Edison was shot. Then he leaned his back against the wall, hoping that the pain would subside and that the ointment would be enough to fight off infection.

Eventually, he gave up on the pain going away and had an impromptu dinner, repacked his backpack, and settled down for the night.

His ankle throbbed, the rocks were rough, and it was cold. Andres's coat gave him a little protection, but he was still uncomfortable. He missed Edison's warm body and steady presence. Hopefully, his dog was OK. Hopefully, he was out of the vet's office with a couple of stitches and was eating steak at the foot of Celeste's bed.

With or without Edison, he had one more clue to follow up. When Saddiq had spotted him in the tunnel just after he'd left the crime scene, he'd had asked if Rebar had given him documents. That meant that the documents were important, and Saddiq didn't have them.

Joe shifted the old hoodie into a more comfortable position as his pillow and stared into the dark.

Rebar hadn't given those documents to Joe as Saddiq had assumed. But Rebar had possessed them—Joe had seen them in his pockets when he'd been breaking the hole into the wall.

If those documents had disappeared by the time he'd

been killed, Rebar had hidden them himself. He hadn't had much time, so they must be close to the bricked-in presidential train car. If Rebar had hidden them in the car or the room itself, the police would have found them, and they would, presumably, have pointed to other suspects in Rebar's death besides Joe. That meant that they had been hidden somewhere else.

In the tunnels.

Joe pulled Andres's coat up under his chin. Tomorrow, he would find those papers.

Maybe they held the key to set him free.

36

November 29, 11:40 p.m.
Carrie Wilbur Home for Adults with Special Needs
Oyster Bay, New York

Ozan eased the window latch to the side with his knife. He'd disabled the motion sensor on it a long time ago. He lifted the window and climbed through it, careful to close and latch it from this side. Sometimes the staff did late-night bed checks and also checked the windows. He could hide under the bed when they came, but he didn't want them to see an open latch. If they asked Erol about it, he'd tell them the truth.

"Ozan?" asked a soft voice from inside the room.

"Just me," Ozan whispered. "Remember, it's our secret."

A few seconds later, he stood next to his brother's bed, looking down at the peaceful manatees on his bedspread. Slow, fat, and happy, they munched through an endless sea of blue. He bet they never got headaches.

"You came to tell me a story?" Erol tucked the blanket under his armpits.

"I did." Ozan sat on the edge of the bed.

In a voice hardly louder than a whisper, he told Erol the story of "The Rainbow Fish." He'd never particularly liked it. It was wrong that the fish had to slice scales off its own body and give them away to make friends. But Erol loved the story, so he told it to him every time he visited. Erol was asleep again before he got to the end, so he stopped telling it, leaving the fish with most of its shiny scales intact.

Ozan wished that he could have told his brother about his day—his good kill of the tennis instructor, his fruitless pursuit of the computer genius and his dog, how he'd finally gone back aboveground to shower and shave and nap. How a quick nap had restored most of his strength.

Whatever bug he'd been fighting off, he'd conquered it. Maybe that sweat bath had been good for something. Or maybe it was just getting solid sleep. Either way, he felt like his old self again.

Once he'd gotten cleaned up and fresh, he'd contacted an old friend with the CIA, Rash Connelly, and told him what he knew about Tesla and Subject 523. Dr. Dubois had links into the CIA, so Rash probably knew most of this stuff anyway. What he didn't know, he'd keep to himself.

"Why didn't you get this Tesla after you killed 523?" Rash asked.

"Not my orders." Ozan didn't mention that he'd failed to kill Joe twice, or that he'd taken out the kid in front of the station.

"The police say that the tennis player was killed by a professional, but they won't give us the name."

Ozan counted to three, thinking it over. "That was me. New orders. I thought the kid was my target—he looked like the guy, he was wearing the guy's company clothes, and he had the guy's dog. It was an accident."

Rash sat silent on the other end, probably trying to decide how much sympathy to have for the accident. He must have decided that the tennis instructor wasn't worth fighting over, because he said, "Why are you calling me now?"

"I want on the team. I want to bring Tesla down."

"That's unorthodox."

"I'm on the job regardless." Ozan let him think that those orders came from Dr. Dubois. "And I think it'll be easier for everyone else if I'm in the loop. It'll keep accidents from happening."

Rash had hesitated again, longer this time. "I'll see what I can do."

It turned out that he could do a lot. He'd called Ozan back during dinner to tell him that he was officially on board. The CIA's orders were not to apprehend Tesla—they were to kill him. He was considered armed and dangerous, having killed two civilians and maybe a cop, and was believed to be in possession of sensitive classified information.

Ozan found that the perfect ending to a difficult day.

Tomorrow he'd go back underground with the morning shift. He'd find Tesla, interrogate him, then kill him, and be done with this job. After that, he'd take a long break, enjoy his restoration to health. Maybe take Erol on a trip to Florida to see the manatees. He smiled down at his brother.

He couldn't tell Erol of the possible vacation until the job was over and the trip was a sure thing. So he watched his brother sleep and ate some of the pink marshmallow snacks that Erol kept in a box by his pillow. He envied Erol his happy, simple life.

Eventually, he took a spare blanket from the closet and stretched out on the carpet under Erol's bed to get some rest. He didn't mind the floor—he'd camped out on worse. He slept best when he could hear the regular, untroubled sound of his brother's breathing.

His days might be filled with cold death and bloodshed, but here he had an island of peace. He set his watch alarm for seven a.m. That would give him plenty of time to leave before the staff came to wake Erol.

Tomorrow he would take care of Tesla and finish this chapter of his life.

37

November 30, 4:11 a.m.
Tunnels behind the Gallo House

Joe woke up feeling worse than he had the day before. His back was in open rebellion. He'd slept outside on the ground often as a kid, but clearly his back was too old to put up with that kind of nonsense anymore. Stifling a groan, he sat up and promptly cracked his head against the roof of the tunnel. He felt like he'd barely slept at all.

Every hour or so throughout the night he'd woken up reaching for Edison, remembering each time with a lurch that the dog was gone. He didn't even know if his best friend was dead or alive. Alive. Edison had to be alive.

He checked the time on his computer. Too early, but he wasn't going back to sleep. The best plan was to give up, have breakfast, and figure out where Rebar had hidden those papers. Maybe then he could put the pieces together and show the finished puzzle to the police. His life would go back to normal. Or as normal as it got these days.

Rifling through his food supplies, he came up with a MoonPie and a can of Dr Pepper for breakfast. Celeste, a vegetarian who only ate organic, would have been appalled. Although, technically speaking, the chocolate-covered marshmallow pie was vegetarian, and so was the Dr Pepper. He raised them both in an imaginary toast to her, and thanked her silently for taking in his dog.

After he finished his healthy breakfast, he packed most of his food back into the hoodie and stashed it up in the tunnel. The packet of trail mix and a bottle of water went into his backpack. That should get him through the day and, with luck, he could come back here tomorrow for refills. But he couldn't hide here forever.

Now, to work. First, he checked the surveillance cameras. Nothing new on them—Abbott and Costello had performed their regular tunnel checks all night long—but, around eight p.m., Vivian had showed up.

Abbott must have seen the red light, because he'd hustled out to meet her at the bottom of the elevator, gun drawn. She'd stepped out, hands in the air, and had a long, animated discussion with Abbott, who had finally let her into Joe's house. He wished that he had audio to hear what they had talked about. But he didn't, and without cameras inside the house, he had no idea what she'd done in there. What she hadn't done yet was leave.

She knew that he must have a secret exit, because he'd escaped while she'd stalled the cops and CIA agents sent to apprehend him. Had she told someone? He shuddered. At least she hadn't done so last night. If they'd found his hideout, they would have pulled him out, and they hadn't.

Instead, they'd sat around inside his house, cozy and warm, sleeping on his bed for all he knew, while he was consigned to the cold rocky tunnel. It was starting to piss him off.

Keeping the window with the surveillance video running, he opened the video he'd taken of the murder scene. As he remembered, no papers were in Rebar's pockets, and Saddiq had asked Joe if he had "documents," which meant that Saddiq didn't have them then either.

So, Rebar had been in possession of those papers when

Joe had met him at around four in the morning, but he hadn't had them by the time Joe had found his body at 5:30 or so. He'd hidden the papers, searched the car, and been murdered, all in an hour and a half.

The logic still held.

All Joe had to do was find those documents. The car itself and the brick room were out. If he had hidden them there, it seemed likely that Saddiq would have found them. He was a thorough guy, and he'd clearly been interested in them. Even if he hadn't found them, the police would have, which meant that if they'd been there, they were gone now.

There was an access tunnel that led to the street a few hundred yards from the railroad car, but Joe didn't think Rebar would have gone up there and, if he had, Joe certainly wasn't going to follow in his footsteps. The most likely hiding place was in the tunnels themselves. It was dark, and no one ever came down there—it was perfect. Even something as big as the train car had stayed hidden for seventy years.

He had to think like Rebar. He had been ex-military. He had been ill. He had not introduced himself by his real name, but as Rebar and as Subject 523. Rebar sounded like a street nickname—most of the homeless guys Joe had met had one. Subject 523 was a different thing entirely. That sounded like a specific identifier, as if he were part of an experimental group, maybe something down in Cuba that had caused him to go AWOL in the first place. Maybe something related to the toxoplasmosis.

Joe brought up surveillance video of Rebar entering the concourse and climbing over the end of Platform 23 (blue, red). Twenty-three again. Maybe a coincidence, but maybe not.

He went back to the video he'd shot of the murder scene, hoping he'd filmed footprints. Rebar's big boots had tramped all over the inside of the brick room. Joe was glad he'd done that quick panorama outside. He identified Rebar's prints once coming, heading away toward the tracks that led north to south, unused nowadays, and then coming back.

It was a place to start.

Joe slipped on Andres's coat and his backpack and pulled back the bolt that held the tunnel door closed. If someone happened to be passing by or looking, he was caught. He swung it open just wide enough to fit through and dropped to the ground, landing with a scuffing sound.

The tunnel around him was empty and dark. He didn't dare turn on a flashlight, so he donned his night-vision goggles. He hated to do it, as anyone with a flashlight could blind him, but he'd never find his way through the dark tunnel without them, not without Edison. He missed the yellow dog.

Joe made it all the way back to the murder scene without seeing another soul. Maybe the patrols had gone home for the night. Or maybe they were due back any second. Moving stealthily, he hurried to the tracks that Rebar had stepped onto the night he was killed.

He glanced back toward the open area behind him, full of track. Rebar wouldn't have hidden anything there—trains were constantly moving through there. No privacy. If he hadn't chosen the car, then maybe he'd chosen the abandoned tunnel next to it. No one was likely to go down there.

He'd search it inch by inch if he had to, but Joe had a theory about where Rebar might have hidden those papers. Rebar was a counter, just like Joe. And he had been obsessed with the number 523. He hurried down the tunnel, counting each tie as he stepped on it. Cyan, blue, red, green, brown, orange, slate, purple, scarlet, and cyan plus black for ten. He crept along, keeping track of each number, head swiveling around, hoping that the night-vision goggles would let him pick out the hiding place.

When he reached five hundred and twenty three (brown, blue, red), he stopped. There was nothing obvious here, but just ahead was a dark mound. He hurried over. The track had been ripped up beyond this point, and the ties had been piled in an untidy stack. It was the perfect place to hide something. Who would ever think to look here?

Joe would.

He looked back down the tunnel for a trace of moving light, like from a flashlight, but saw nothing. It was as safe as it was going to get. He tipped up the goggles and risked using his flashlight. Several minutes of careful digging, which was louder than he would have liked, produced a flat briefcase. It had been fine leather once, but now the surface was cracked. The hinges were broken and someone, probably Rebar, had tied it together with a belt.

Joe tucked it into his backpack. He itched to open it, but it wasn't safe here. The police patrolling the tunnels might be back at any second. They might have heard the noise that he'd made moving the train ties and be on their way to him right now. He had to get to a safe place.

He turned off his flashlight, put on the goggles, and jogged back the way he'd come, wishing that a tunnel branched off, but none did. He reached the brick room without incident, but when he looked off to the side, he saw a couple of men heading across the wide tunnel where the tracks converged—where he liked to play fetch with Edison.

He ducked back inside the dark tunnel and waited.

The men got so close that he could hear them talking. Not exactly stealthy.

"How are we supposed to find him? There's miles of tunnels down here, assuming he didn't just get on a private helicopter and fly to Canada," said a man with a gravelly voice. He sounded as if it had taken fifty years of smoking cigarettes and drinking whisky to perfect that growl.

"He's a nut," the other man said. "Can't go outside, my ass."

"I bet he could if he was properly motivated, like by having the whole damn tunnel system crawling with cops."

Joe wished that were true.

Their voices grew louder. Joe shrank back against the tunnel wall. He didn't dare retreat farther for fear of making a sound.

"I say leave him until we get another superstorm to wash him out," said Gravel Voice. "My feet hurt."

"He might've killed Officer Chin."

"Or Chin might've fallen in front of that train."

The other man grunted.

"Either way," said Gravel Voice, "I say we shoot first, so we don't have to chase him."

"Amen to that, brother."

The voices moved closer. Joe held his breath. If they saw him, he wouldn't be able to get away. He was trapped.

38

Vivian gave up on sleep. She'd dozed a little in Tesla's bedroom, after insisting on sleeping on his bed, but too shy to do more than lie down on top of the quilt. She didn't know exactly where his bolt-hole was, but it was up here somewhere. She'd prowled around, but one or the other of the cops had shadowed her every move, and she didn't want them around when she found the secret door.

Eventually, she'd told them that she was going to bed, and they'd reluctantly left her alone. When the men had done their hourly exterior patrols, she'd searched the house for Tesla's bolt-hole, but she hadn't found it. She'd also found no evidence that Tesla had come back into the house, but she couldn't shake the feeling that he had. He needed food. He needed Wi-Fi. And she'd noticed that the cops left the house together every hour for about five minutes. If she were Tesla, she'd sneak in during that time and gather whatever she needed from inside.

She looked up at the plastered ceiling above Tesla's bed. The plasterer had done an excellent job—the ceiling was perfectly smooth, coved at the edges. A hairline crack ran along one corner, probably from the house shifting when the trains went by. All in all, the house was solid, the kind she'd only read about in books.

She fingered the antique quilt. Her mother would have loved it—tiny stitches formed intricate patterns. The seamstress had spent a long time getting it just right. The quilt and sheets smelled like lilac. Where had Tesla found a lilac-scented detergent? It fit the room perfectly.

The agents downstairs, and they were agents, not police, closed the front door. Time for another circuit of the tunnels. She didn't think Tesla would come in that way. He'd come in through the entrance he'd escaped out of, wherever it was.

She'd lied when she told them that Tesla had slipped down the right-hand tunnel when he'd seen that the elevator was coming down, leaving her behind to answer questions. He had been under her protection at the time, so she'd felt obligated. If they caught him and charged him, her deceit might come to light.

If they caught him? When they caught him. She'd heard that today they were going to start searching the tunnels in a grid pattern with trained bloodhounds. Even with hundreds of miles of tunnels to hide in, Tesla wouldn't be able to avoid them forever.

She sat up in the bed, ran her fingers through her hair. She might as well look for him again. She'd do a round of the station, especially the restaurants, looking for the dog. She wished that she had the easy, and illegal, access to the surveillance footage that Tesla so obviously enjoyed. She'd have been able to monitor him from the comfort of her own home—or his.

As much as she'd been taken aback by the house when she first saw it, it had started to grow on her. She could see why he liked living in the sumptuous antique quarters completely isolated from the noise and bustle of the city above. His bedroom was bigger than her whole apartment and, she hated to admit it, it smelled better, too.

First stop, coffee. Then breakfast and a quick pass of the Wi-Fi stations in Grand Central. After that, she'd see if she could talk her way into searching the tunnels around Platform 36 on her own. She hadn't managed to last night, but there would be a new officer on duty, and that would give her a second chance. If not, she'd come back here and poke around. He was close. She knew he was.

She'd use the syringe first and ask questions later. Joe might hate her for knocking him out, but if she could get him out of these tunnels safely, she'd take the heat.

39

Joe leaned back against the cold steel pillar and made himself a blanket tent. It smelled like dog. In the yellow dog's absence, he found it comforting. He'd dodged patrols for the past few hours. After he'd almost been caught near the brick room, he'd tried heading for home where he could have examined the contents of the briefcase in peace, but there were too many people in his way. Men with dogs.

He didn't know if he'd ever make it back.

Trying not to think about it, he turned on his flashlight and finally unbelted the old briefcase. Slowly, he lifted off the top to reveal yellowed papers, some handwritten, some typewritten.

Gently, he lifted out the first sheaf of pages. The handwritten ones were impossible to decipher. He tried to read the unusual script, but it appeared not to be English to begin with. Maybe German, but he couldn't be sure of that. He wasn't even sure about the individual letters.

Anchoring the blanket tent under his feet, he made space to sort the contents. He set aside the handwritten pages, finding beneath them a slender typewritten report, in English, dated November 1949. That made it almost sixty-five years old.

He began to read:

Prepared for CIA Project Bluebird: Mind Control
Through Parasitic Infection
By Dr. Paul Berger

A chill ran down his spine. A doctor, maybe the one in the car, had carried out deliberate mind-control experiments just after World War II. After having lost control of part of his mind, the idea horrified Joe in a way that he couldn't have imagined a year ago. A person's mind was his most fundamental possession. It was not meant to be toyed with, or experimented on.

Yet it had happened. If this report was accurate, the CIA had sponsored mind-control experiments right after World War II. Using parasites. He immediately thought of the toxoplasmosis that had infected Rebar. That was the link.

Blotches of dark mold obscured most of the first paragraph. He read the second.

Primate trials have been most encouraging—with the toxoplasmosis parasite taking hold easily and well. After a week-long period of illness, the rhesus monkeys seem to subdue the physical symptoms. Their behavior, however, is radically altered.

There it was in black and white. This scientist had been injecting monkeys with toxoplasmosis experimentally to control their behavior.

Formerly docile specimens can become quite aggressive, even reckless, and seem to have no recollection of actions that they commit during their aggressive bouts (See Chart 15.6).

The practical application of this kind of treatment to soldiers in wartime is clear—soldiers can perform dangerous and reckless missions and then have no recollection of them afterward, thereby making it impossible for them to reveal mission details even under the most extreme duress.

Joe read it again. This was an attempt to make supersoldiers who did what they were told and didn't remember it afterward. No vulnerability to interrogation. Or the debilitation of conscience.

> *Once we have the volunteer soldiers in place, we can begin human inoculations. I propose three groups—Group 1 knows they are being exposed to the parasite. Group 2, a control group, believes they are exposed but are not. Group 3 is exposed but without their knowledge or consent. We will measure the following:*
>
> *Suggestibility: How far can we control what these soldiers do.*
>
> *Recklessness: How far can we push the soldiers in stressful situations.*
>
> *Selective amnesia: What will and won't the soldiers remember.*
>
> *I suggest one hundred soldiers for each group, initially. As per established protocols, we need not receive explicit informed consent as these are active-duty soldiers who have volunteered for this program knowing that there might be certain risks involved.*

Joe stopped reading. They had planned to inject soldiers without their knowledge or consent. All that he had suffered since his agoraphobia seemed trivial in comparison.

He fired up his laptop, hid the IP address, and searched for Project Bluebird, growing more horrified with every word that he read. Project Bluebird had actually existed. It had been a large-scale project initiated after World War II, sometimes using Nazi scientists, to research mind-control techniques.

Joe studied the antique, typewritten pages. They provided evidence that a scientist had planned to infect soldiers against their will with a parasite to control their behavior, but compared with the horrors already well documented online and in books, it wasn't a revelation. Why had it mattered to Rebar?

The next layer of papers explained that. They weren't typewritten. They were laser-printed—modern day.

They described a recent trial in Guantanamo Bay, Cuba, also using the toxoplasmosis parasite. Initially used as an aid for interrogations of hostiles, infections had been introduced to volunteer troops in order to study their reactions.

Initially, the trials had gone well—the subjects had shown no reluctance to take on the most dangerous missions, they had not been troubled by post-traumatic stress disorder, and they had acted with cunning and ruthlessness under stress. In short, they had become better soldiers. But something had gone wrong with the soldiers who'd taken part in the 500 series of trials. That must have included Subject 523— Ronald Raines, aka Rebar. Those soldiers had become very aggressive and mentally unstable. The report said the project scientist, Dr. Francis Dubois, had managed to destroy the parasite in the 500 series subjects. They had suffered no long-term effects.

Except for Rebar, who had been murdered not far from where Joe sat. And who knew how many others? This part of the report, at least, was a lie.

With an uneasy feeling, Joe remembered the boat that had sunk in Cuba the day after Rebar had gone AWOL. The press had reported that it had contained one hundred and three people. One of them was a doctor. A few minutes of research produced the name of a doctor who had died in Cuba at around that time—Janet Johansson—and a curriculum vitae. She'd reported directly to Dr. Dubois as a research assistant.

Joe kept reading. Dr. Dubois explained that the trials had gone well, making soldiers braver, more biddable, and less prone to post-traumatic stress. He'd even infected soldiers and sent them to war zones to document their reactions.

Because of this, Dr. Dubois felt the project was ready for widespread trials, with over fifty thousand men, using the standard double-time structure with no consent issues. Fifty thousand men? That was the population of a small city. All of them infected by a mind-altering parasite without their knowledge.

Injections were due to start on December first. Joe checked his online calendar.

Tomorrow.

Where was Dr. Dubois now? Joe checked online. The doctor lived in Tuckahoe, a city on the Metro North line, about forty minutes from Grand Central by train. He worked at a lab not far from his house.

Joe studied the picture on the lab's web site. He looked so ordinary. Ordinary guys were easy to find. Joe went to the list of hacked phones he'd used for his seagull prank, hoping he'd get lucky. He did. It didn't take long for him to locate the doctor's phone from there. The little blue dot that represented the phone's location was heading south. He waited a few minutes to make sure: Dr. Dubois's blue dot was following the rail line. He was on a train heading to New York, which meant that he would arrive at Grand Central.

Joe ran over the schedule in his head. Based on his current location, Dr. Dubois had boarded the Harlem line train (color coded as blue) in Tuckahoe at 8:24 (purple, blue, green), which meant that he would arrive at Grand Central Terminal at 9:07 (scarlet, black, slate), probably on Platform 112 (cyan, cyan, blue).

Every platform would be crawling with policemen. Joe

would never get a chance to get near him there. He could try to send the information that he had out to Torres, but so far as he could tell she wasn't passing that information along. He didn't want to involve Celeste or Leandro—it was too dangerous. He could try to leak it to the press himself, but he'd have to persuade a reporter to meet him underground, after the media had painted him as a crazy murderer.

He needed more proof.

Maybe he could intercept the doctor before his train arrived at Grand Central. Maybe he'd get lucky and the doctor would be carrying incriminating files, or even the serum itself. After all, how else would he get such a dangerous biological specimen to New York City? If he found either files or the serum, that would give him enough proof to back up his assertions. He could convince people.

So, to get to the doctor before his train arrived, he had to figure out how to hack the train, stop it just before it got to the station, and get aboard. And he had thirty minutes to figure it out.

He bundled the files back in the briefcase, slipped it into his backpack, threw off the blanket, and began to run.

40

Ozan watched the commuters rush in through the Lexington Avenue entrance. They left wet footprints on the stone floor. A slipping hazard, an easy way to disguise an accidental death. Not that he needed one right now, but he was always on alert to add to his repertoire.

He sipped his hot black coffee. He was due to meet Rash Connelly at nine sharp by the clock in the concourse. They were going down to Tesla's lair to see if they could find another way that Tesla could have gotten out of his house. Ozan bet that Tesla had a back door. He was too smart not to.

He took a long sip of his strong coffee. He felt better today than he had in a long time—stronger, more clear-headed. A good night's sleep on Erol's floor was all he'd needed.

His cell phone rang.

"Saddiq." He smiled at a blonde ordering a ridiculously complicated coffee that seemed to consist more of things being left out than added.

"Verifying that you have not located the papers."

"I have not." It was Dubois. Ozan recognized his voice and his impatient air. "But we're closing in on Tesla, and I understand that it is imperative that he not speak to the police."

"I doubt that he knows anything. But the orders stand." A familiar clattering in the background gave Ozan pause.

"Are you on a train?" Ozan asked.

"Yes. I have an important meeting in the city today."

"When do you arrive?"

"How is that relevant?" Dr. Dubois's voice sharpened with suspicion.

"If Tesla knows something, he might come after you."

"Ridiculous!"

"Probably." Ozan smiled at the blonde, and she gave him an insulted look. He faced away from her. "What would it hurt if I were to meet your train and escort you safely to your destination?"

He'd have to call Connelly and reschedule their meeting.

"How would Tesla know where I am?" Dubois sounded impatient.

"I don't know," Ozan admitted. "He's smart. I don't think we should underestimate him."

Dr. Dubois didn't say anything. Ozan listened to the sounds of the train.

"He's a software engineer," Dubois said finally. "Not an assassin."

Ozan did not tell him the software engineer had bested him, a sought-after assassin, at every encounter so far.

"Stick with your original duties." Dubois hung up.

Ozan dropped the empty cup in the garbage can and joined the throng heading toward the trains. He checked the arrivals board for Dubois's train. The board said that the train was due in at 9:07 on Platform 112.

He'd meet it. If Tesla didn't show up, no harm was done. If he did, Ozan would be ready for him. Today was a good day, and he would not fail.

41

November 30, 8:57 a.m.
Starbucks, Grand Central Terminal

Vivian took her tray with four coffees from a professionally chipper teenager with buck teeth. He wished her a good day like he meant it, wiping his hands on his black apron as he turned away to help someone else have a good day. She was not a morning person, and didn't trust people who were.

As she added sugar, wooden stirrers, and napkins to the tray, she kept her eye on a slender, dark-haired man. He was on the phone, speaking in measured tones, drinking a coffee and minding his own business. Something about him put her on edge.

She couldn't analyze it, but it was a feeling that had saved her life more than once. When he ended his call and left the coffee shop, she followed. The terminal was packed with commuters, so it was easy to put enough space between them to keep him from becoming suspicious.

He walked at an easy pace, not too slow and not too fast. He wasn't in any hurry, but he had someplace to be. As he stepped to the side to let a couple of teens holding hands pass, his jacket flipped open, and she saw the gun tucked into a neat shoulder holster.

She switched the coffee tray to her left hand so that her right would be free if she needed to draw her own gun. Until now, he'd seemed like an ordinary guy heading through the concourse after having his coffee. But he wasn't.

The way he looked from side to side, studying faces, how people walked, and where the exits were spoke of an elevated situational awareness that most people didn't possess. He was expecting trouble, or about to cause it.

When he went to the middle of the concourse and headed straight for the clock, Vivian closed the distance between them. If he took the elevator down to Tesla's, she'd never let him go alone.

A barrel-chested man with graying ginger hair who was standing next to the north face of the clock shook the man's hand. She recognized him—Rash Connelly. Connelly was part of the CIA team looking for Tesla. She'd met him when she came out of the elevator earlier that morning. That meant that the guy talking to him was probably part of the team—law enforcement or someone who worked for the agency. That explained his gun and his behavior. He was looking for Tesla, too. Not necessarily a good guy, but probably not a bad one, either.

She relaxed and hung back to watch. The small man and Connelly exchanged a few words. Connelly seemed irritated by whatever the man had to say, but nodded as if he agreed with the logic. Both men checked their watches, and the slender, dark-haired man headed over to the walkway that led to the arriving trains.

He looked like he had a train to catch.

Nothing unusual about that. Anyway, he wasn't her problem, after all. Tesla was.

She headed over to Rash Connelly and smiled her best girlish smile, ready to be ingratiating. "I brought coffee."

He took a cup and two packets of sugar. "Did you find your client?"

She sipped her own coffee and shrugged.

"Guess you wouldn't be here if you had," he said.

"Looks like another long day," she said.

"Maybe not."

"Got a new lead?" Maybe the slender man had told him something.

"Maybe I'm just optimistic."

She laughed. "You work for the government. You can't be optimistic."

He ripped open a packet of sugar and dumped it in. "You're in the private sector. Do you have some optimism to spare?"

"I used to be in government," she said. "My supply ran out early."

"What's your plan?"

"I'm going to bring this coffee down to the guys, check the tunnels."

"You think he'll show up down there? He has to know that we've got it covered."

"People surprise you sometimes," she said. She added another sentence, hoping it made her sound lazy: "And sitting in a nice, cozy living room beats stomping around underground not finding anything."

When she turned toward the information booth, she saw a flicker of irritation cross his face. He wasn't excited about a day in the tunnels, either.

"Good morning, Evaline," Vivian said to the black woman behind the counter.

"Good morning, Miss Torres." Evaline gave her a friendly smile. Her eyes flicked across Connelly, but she didn't say anything to him. "Are you going back down?"

"I am indeed," Vivian answered. "But I brought you a coffee."

Evaline's smile widened. "Thank you."

She opened the door to the concourse and ushered

Vivian aside. Connelly stayed outside, drinking his coffee and staring moodily in the direction that the dark-haired man had taken.

Vivian handed her one of the coffees, and Evaline set it on her desk. As she unlocked the door in the pillar, Evaline spoke in a low voice.

"I hope you find him first, Miss Torres. Mr. Tesla isn't a killer, like they say, and I worry for him."

Vivian fingered the syringe in her pocket. "Me, too."

42

November 30, 9:03 a.m.
Harlem Line train

Dr. Dubois leaned forward in his blue seat, watching the other early-morning passengers in the well-heated train car. The other seats were full. The car was standing room only this early in the day, but a young man with four piercings in his eyebrow and a nose ring had given up his seat for the doctor when he'd hobbled into the car on his crutches. The doctor had taken the seat as his due.

He shifted his aching leg to the side. After his meeting today, he would allow himself some Percocet to dull the pain, but not before. He was so close now.

The gray winter sun and bare tree trunks passing by outside couldn't dampen his mood. He looked around the car. People sat reading, playing with their phones or staring out the window, all stuck in their humdrum lives. Today, for him, was a culmination.

He would hand off the serum to put his parasites into a massive trial that would prove he was a visionary. Soldiers would not have to worry about fear as they did their jobs, and they would not have to deal with long-term stress afterward. His work would spare them that.

Saddiq's call had put him on edge. He studied the relaxed figures around him. None of them spared him a second glance. They all seemed as innocuous as they had before the call. Tesla was not here.

The doctor drummed his fingers on his metal briefcase as the train rattled toward the long low entrance to the tunnel that would take them underground and down to Grand Central Terminal. He pulled the briefcase up farther on his lap, keeping it close.

He'd feel better once he'd handed everything off, and the trials were underway. At that point, everyone would have too much to lose to expose him. And the parasite worked. Maybe not perfectly, but every war has casualties, and every drug has side effects. Overall, everyone would be better off.

Especially him.

The train slowed as it headed underground, darkness washing across the outside of the car. Inside, the fluorescent lights shone brightly. Dr. Dubois studied his reflection in the window. Bags under his eyes made him look tired. He should look tired—he hadn't slept since Subject 523 had shot him. Not real sleep, anyway, just narcotics-induced unconsciousness. But his leg was healing, and once this trial got underway he could relax. There would be plenty of time to sleep then.

He leaned his forehead against the cool glass and peered into the darkness that lay beyond. The train slowed still further. Other sets of silver tracks joined with his. They were just slowing for the approach to the platform. The train always did that.

In just a few minutes the train would arrive, probably at Platform 112. He had a long trek up ramps and across treacherously smooth floors before he could get a cab. After that he'd be able to rest again on his way to his meeting.

One long finger stroked the top of the cold briefcase. He had held it tightly the whole trip, as if it might spring from his hands and leap out the window. Or be stolen.

Unthinkable, and unlikely.

When he'd left the case unattended in the lab while he'd gone to the toilet, an overzealous postdoc lab assistant had plastered yellow biohazard stickers on both sides, as regulations required. The doctor had been furious, thinking that it might make it more difficult for him to board the train, but none of his fellow passengers had seemed to notice or care. If they had, who among them would have wanted to steal a biological hazard?

A woman with a poison-green scarf leaned her hip against the edge of his seat, a paperback novel open in her hand. She'd barely looked up from its pages since she'd boarded. Next to her, a businessman in a pinstriped suit crackled his *Wall Street Journal.* The young man with the piercings looked toward the dark windows, swaying in time to music that was piped into his ears via tiny black earbuds. Everything was normal.

He returned his gaze to the window. Nothing—just a wide room with faraway stone walls and lines of steel girders to hold up the ceiling. He'd seen the view a thousand times on his way to the city. Nothing to cause concern.

Then the car stopped.

Dr. Dubois pulled the briefcase closer to his chest. Despite his earlier assurances to himself, his heart fluttered. This felt wrong.

No one else seemed concerned. The woman with the green scarf licked her finger and turned a page in her paperback. The businessman's eyes kept scanning down his newspaper. The kid with the earbuds didn't pause in his rhythmic swaying. This kind of thing happened all the time. Probably just a train ahead of them in the station.

A shadow drew his attention outside. There was a man in the tunnel, walking next to the train. He was tall and thin and dressed all in black except for an orange safety vest. Clearly an MTA employee. Perhaps he knew the reason for the delay. Likely a mechanical problem that wouldn't keep them stuck for long. His meeting must commence on time.

The train worker stopped next to the car ahead of theirs and looked inside for several seconds before moving slowly to the doctor's car. The man seemed to be examining each seat, glancing quickly from one part of the car to another as if searching.

Anxiety tightened Dubois's muscles, making his leg throb.

The man stopped directly outside the doctor's window. He continued his examination until he reached the doctor's seat. Their eyes met. The man looked at him for a long time before shifting his glance to the next passenger. The doctor squirmed in his seat, eyes darting around the car. There was nowhere to go.

Saddiq's caution had been justified. Dr. Dubois glanced at his watch. 9:10. The train should have already arrived at the station. Maybe Saddiq had defied him. He would worry when the train didn't arrive. He would come.

The man in the tunnel smiled.

Dr. Dubois knew what he was looking for now.

The man was looking for him.

43

November 30, 9:09 a.m.
Tunnels under Grand Central Terminal

Joe stared up into the lit train window. The smell of metal and electricity surrounded him. Trains shouldered by on other tracks, none concerned with the blue and silver train sitting stock still on its tracks. Trains stopped all the time to wait for a train to clear the station ahead.

But this train's stop had nothing to do with the schedule. He had caused it by resetting its digital wireless signaler. The signaler gave each train permission to move forward. He estimated that he had about five to seven minutes before the central switching center noticed and reset the signaler again and the train moved forward to Platform 112.

He'd better make it count.

Dr. Dubois was in the second car. He looked just like his photo on his company web site, except more tired. Everyone looked more tired in real life than on the Internet. A silver briefcase with a biohazard sticker on the front rested on his lap. It looked as if he had brought the serum with him after all. Joe needed to get that case.

Joe ran to the side of the train car and pulled himself up in the space between the first and second cars. Taking a deep breath, he opened the door and entered. The car was full, standing room only, and he elbowed his way forward through the passengers.

The doctor was near the far end of the car. When he saw him, the doctor struggled to his feet, fumbling with his crutches. But he had nowhere to go.

Joe reached him and took hold of one of his crutches.

"Help!" Dr. Dubois wobbled on the other crutch.

A guy with a face full of piercings reached for Joe's arm. "What do you think—"

"Careful, buddy," Joe said. "I'm just here to save your life."

The guy grabbed Joe's elbow. "How?"

"I'm from the railroad." Joe pointed at his orange vest. "They sent me down to get this case before it gets into the station."

The doctor goggled at him.

"Are you Dr. Francis Dubois?" Joe asked.

"I . . . no," said the doctor.

"You're the only one on this train carrying a biohazard," Joe said, "into a crowded railway station."

"Nothing's infectious," the doctor said. "It's just tissue samples."

Dubois wrapped both arms around his briefcase.

Joe could tell that he was lying and, clearly, so could the man with the piercings. He let go of Joe's elbow.

"I need to get that case off the train," Joe said. "Please hand it to me."

"Under no circumstances," the doctor screeched.

The passengers edged away from them, except for the man with the piercings, who looked ready to pick a side and pile in. Joe hoped that the man would be on his side.

"Whose tissue samples?" Joe asked quietly. "The ones for the hundred and three people whose boat sank just off the coast of Cuba—"

"No." The doctor regained his dignity. "I don't know

what you're talking about."

Joe held out his hands. "Give me the case. The officers in charge of quarantine can decide what to do about it. You can come with me, if you'd like."

"Give him the case," said the guy with the piercings.

A woman wearing a green scarf nodded.

The businessman looked confused, and the people around him began to mumble to each other. No one was sure if Joe was a helper or a threat. He didn't have time to win anybody over.

"You will regret this," said the doctor. "You think you can take this case? Hold me here?"

Joe'd had enough. "Of course I can. You know the contents of that case can infect thousands of people. To keep people safe, I can take it. And I will."

"Those are brave words from a murderer," said the doctor. "What newspaper would print your allegations, Mr. Tesla?"

The man with the piercings looked uncertain now. He must have read the *New York Post*.

Joe didn't have time to argue. He reached for the case.

The door at the other end of the car slammed open and a thin, dark-haired man stood in the doorway. Joe recognized his silhouette and his walk. Ozan Saddiq.

"Step away from that man," Saddiq called down the train car. He drew a gun from under his coat and pointed it at Joe.

Panic erupted in the train car. People threw themselves to the floor and tried to crawl under the seats.

Joe kicked out Dr. Dubois's crutch and grabbed his aluminum case as the man fell. The doctor wouldn't let go until Joe twisted it in a fast circle and smashed it into his face.

The doctor stared at him, aghast.

"I'm not done with you," Joe said. "Not by a long shot."

The doctor brought both hands up to his streaming nose. "Saddiq!" he called.

A gunshot echoed in the tiny space. Heat seared Joe's ear. He dropped to the floor, still holding the briefcase, and dove the last few feet to the door at his end of the car. He leaned against it and pulled the door open one-handed. He fell more than jumped forward.

The ground jarred his ankles when he landed.

Joe looked back at the train car. The engineer had left his post at the front of the car to investigate the commotion. He wasn't far from where Joe had been standing.

Saddiq jumped out of the rear of the car, and Joe ran around toward the front. He needed to keep the train between them as long as possible. The case bounced against his knee. He hoped the contents wouldn't turn the area into a biological waste site if it or something inside it broke.

The train lurched ahead. Joe sprinted forward a few yards, then cut in front of the engine as the train gained momentum. He heard another gunshot.

Pain blasted up his right arm.

44

Ozan saw Tesla stumble. He'd hit his arm. He didn't want to kill him. He had questions that only Tesla could answer.

"Stop!" called Ozan. He sent another shot just wide of Tesla's head.

Tesla stopped. He held the wounded arm against his chest, but he wouldn't let go of the case. Braver than he looked.

"I just want to talk to you," said Ozan. "I want to know about what's in that case."

"It's full of parasites called toxoplasmosis, Mr. Saddiq," Joe said. "He was going to inject it into soldiers."

Ozan wasn't surprised that Tesla knew his name. The man knew everything. "Does it make you sick?"

"It gives you a fever, headaches, muscle pain."

Ozan's head throbbed. He'd had all those symptoms. He moved to a track next to the stopped train. "Then what?"

"It makes you reckless."

He recognized that, too. This parasite was inside his body. Worry for Erol flashed across his mind. His brother would be alone without him. "Is it curable?"

The track points shifted with a clack. Ozan screamed as the bones of his foot were ground together. The train had been switched to the track on which he stood, catching his foot between the two tracks.

He dropped his gun and yanked at his foot. Hot pain flooded up his leg, but his foot didn't budge. "Help me!"

Tesla put the case down and ran to him. He kicked away the gun before bending down to try to grab Ozan's foot.

"Work the switch!" Ozan tried to push his foot straight back, but it was stuck tight.

The train rolled toward them, ready to go down the new track and run over him.

Tesla leaped up. He waved his arms over his head. Blood ran down his forearm from the gunshot wound.

Ozan looked up at the cabin to see if the engineer saw them. He could switch them back to another track and release his foot. The cabin was empty. The engineer must still be in the second car with Dr. Dubois.

There was no way to get his foot out.

And there was no way to stop the train.

Tesla saw it, too. He tore at Ozan's leg with bloody fingers. Bones scraped together in Ozan's foot when he lurched to the side. Panic tamped down the pain. He fumbled in his pants pocket. He had a knife in there. He could cut his foot off.

The train bore down.

Even as time slowed down, Ozan realized that there wasn't enough of it. He straightened to face the oncoming headlights. The vision of Erol sleeping peacefully under his manatee blanket flashed through his head.

Tesla crouched next to him, still working on his foot. The man would die trying to save him. That was who Tesla was. The clarity that often came to Ozan on the battlefield came to him now. He grabbed Tesla's shoulders and threw him away to safety.

Tesla sprawled on his ass and stared up at him with round

eyes.

Ozan could trust him.

"Take care of my brother, Erol," he called.

The train struck.

45

Joe turned away, holding his bleeding arm. Ozan had been a bad man, but what a brutal way to die. His last thoughts had been for his brother. He'd trusted Joe to find him and look after him. And he would. His brother shouldn't be made to suffer for Saddiq's misdeeds.

A man in uniform shouted at Joe, but he ignored him.

He snatched up the case with his good hand and ran. Speed was all he had, and he poured it on. His legs fell into his familiar stride for running on train ties, but faster than he'd ever moved in his life. He gripped the case to his chest and ran.

Another shot. The cops must be shooting at him now.

A train bore down on him. Not the 9:07, the one after. Joe jumped the third rail and kept going.

Barking told him that he'd captured the dogs' attention. And their handlers.

They all converged on him.

He fled toward the tunnel that led to his house. If he got in, he'd have only two guards to deal with. That sounded like a picnic compared to the mob around him.

He made it to his tunnel, punched in the code with his left hand, waited an eternity for the light to blink off, and turned the key. Once inside, he slammed it behind him.

Three figures ran toward him down the tunnel. Abbott and Costello. And Vivian. Oddly enough, fat Abbott led the pack.

"Freeze!" he called.

Joe froze, lowered the case to the ground, and raised his hands over his head.

Behind Abbott, Vivian lifted an arm, lightning fast, and drove something into Costello's back. He pitched forward and lay still.

"Cuff Tesla," Abbott called over his shoulder.

"Not today." Vivian stuck what looked like a syringe in Abbott's left buttock.

Eyebrows frozen in surprise, he half-turned before collapsing on the ground.

She bent and picked up his fallen gun. "Please tell me whatever you've got in the case is going to save my ass."

"Maybe." Thumps sounded against the tunnel door. Joe felt light-headed. Was he losing a lot of blood?

"Where do you want to go?"

"Elevator," Joe said. "Hold it open."

She ran like a deer, easier and much faster than Joe ever could.

He straightened his backpack and ran after her.

She waited inside the elevator, holding the doors open with her hand. "Someone's calling it to go up."

46

Vivian moved to the side as Tesla stumbled in next to her, clanged shut the gate, and activated the lever to send them up.

"Cops on the other end," she said, calmly. "Lots."

Tesla released the lever, and the elevator lurched to a stop. "Don't let it start again."

"Your arm is wounded." He was losing blood out of what looked like a bullet wound in his forearm. He'd come into the tunnel with that. Nobody had got a shot off once he got through the door. That meant, even though the men she'd disabled hadn't raised the alarm, someone else must have.

"I know."

He threw his backpack on the floor and pulled out his laptop. "Hot damn! Wireless!"

Vivian knelt next to him and pulled off her scarf. "Really? You're going online now?"

"Give me one second." He fumbled with the keyboard, typing slowly with his left hand.

"How about I bandage up the right one?" she asked. "It'll only take a minute."

He held up his hurt arm without looking away from the computer. She pulled up his sleeve and began to wrap the wound with her scarf. She had enough left over to tie around his neck as a sling.

"Can they override the elevator?" she asked.

"I checked on that once. They can't." He reached into his backpack. "The only way they can get us moving is by cutting the cables and dropping us down."

He glanced quickly at the ceiling. She remembered the last time they'd been in the elevator together. He'd been nervous then. She hoped he didn't lose it.

She helped him pull a brown leather box out of his backpack. It was an ancient briefcase, fastened with a modern leather belt. He tried to open it one-handed.

"Tell me what to do," she said. "I don't want them cutting the cables, either."

He smiled gratefully at her. "If you could take out the papers in there and lay them out on the floor."

He fiddled with his phone while she worked. The papers talked about a disease. Some were old, some new. She didn't take time to read them.

Joe whistled, startling her.

"I'm in." He struggled to his feet next to her and photographed the papers. He had to stand on one foot because something was wrong with his leg, but he wouldn't let her look at it.

She put the documents away after he took the pictures and laid out new ones until he was done. He also opened the metal case with the biohazard stickers and took pictures of glass tubes inside of it. "Those pictures are going to save us?"

"Maybe not us," Joe said, "but lots of other people."

"Great," Vivian said. "What about us?"

Joe sat cross-legged on the floor and pulled his laptop onto his knees. "Maybe."

Vivian's phone rang. Mr. Rossi. She put him on speaker.

"I'm up here in the concourse of Grand Central Terminal," he said. "I'm with an agent named Connelly. Do you know Tesla's whereabouts?"

"I'm in the elevator," Tesla said. His fingers zoomed around the keyboard. Even left-handed, he was a faster typist than she was.

"Connelly would like to negotiate your surrender before anyone else gets hurt."

"If I surrender right now," Tesla said, "thousands of men will get hurt. Soldiers. American soldiers."

"They say that they have dispatched a crew to cut through the elevator cables," Mr. Rossi said.

That was probably a lie, she thought. But if it was true, and assuming they lived through the crash, she didn't think the two agents at the bottom would be happy to see them.

She drew her gun. If Tesla had ever needed a bodyguard, the moment was now.

47

November 30, 9:37 a.m.
Elevator

Joe looked up at the ceiling. It wouldn't take long to cut through the cables.

"Please put that away, Ms. Torres." He pointed to her gun. "I think I have another solution."

She holstered the weapon, but scowled while doing it. Clearly, she didn't like being trapped here helplessly any more than he did.

His right arm hurt like hell, but he kept typing. "Danny, please put Mr. Connelly on the line."

"Mr. Tesla," said a deep voice a second later. "You're in a world of trouble right now."

Joe checked the upload bar. The pictures of the research papers were off to an online leak site. All but one of them. "I'd say that you're in more trouble than I am."

"Doesn't feel like it. Let's talk about what you need to do—"

"Let's talk about what *you* need to do," Joe interrupted. "You might not be aware that your agency is tied to a dangerous rogue."

"If you mean that man who died in the tunnel a few minutes ago, you—"

"Ozan Saddiq is not the man I mean." He typed in an

encryption code with his left-hand. "Dr. Dubois is."

A slight hesitation, then Connelly spoke again. "Who?"

"I have information linking your Dr. Dubois to a hundred murders in Cuba." Not exactly true, but he kept going. "And a medical experiment that's scheduled to infect thousands of soldiers tomorrow."

"I'm not sure where you get your information, but—"

"I have uploaded all of it to a site similar to WikiLeaks. Journalists are even now being notified." Joe tapped Send on an email, the one that might save their lives.

The elevator lurched to the side.

"Mr. Connelly," Joe said. "But one page that I uploaded is encrypted so they won't be able to read it right away."

"Let's talk about this up here." Connelly was losing his bluster.

"I've given a friend the encryption code," Joe said. "He'll release it to journalists unless he hears otherwise from me personally."

"Your life is in no danger, Mr. Tesla. There's no need to be so dramatic."

"Aren't you curious about this last sheet of paper?" Joe asked. "It links the toxoplasmosis program to your agency and makes it impossible for you to disavow the actions of Dr. Dubois."

Another pause. "A clever theory. I'd be very interested to discuss it. Up here."

The elevator trembled. "Tell your men working on the cables to desist. Tell your men at my house to stand down. We can discuss your proposal in my home."

"I think that would be an excellent way to de-escalate the situation," Connelly said.

Diplomatic to the last.

A minute later, Connelly said, "I've stopped the men on the cables, can't reach the men in the tunnels by your house.

Are they all right?"

Joe pressed the mute button and looked at Vivian.

"They'll be out for at least an hour," she said. "I injected them with a sedative."

He made a mental note to ask her why she'd been carrying two syringes of knockout juice around. Instead, he pressed the mute button again.

"They're just napping," he said. "See you soon!"

Joe packed up the case with the serum and the battered briefcase with its damning papers.

"What now?" Vivian asked.

"We go down." Joe reached for the lever. "At the bottom, hold the doors open. I don't want Connelly coming down here until I'm ready for him."

He had one more thing that he needed to do.

Vivian helped to lift the backpack onto his back, threading it carefully over his wounded arm. It hurt with each heartbeat. He hurried to his front door, glancing at the two agents stretched out in the tunnel. Vivian had guided them down to lie on their backs, then rolled them onto their sides so that they wouldn't choke. Thoughtful of her.

He entered his house, breathing in the familiar smells, and went into the parlor. He gritted his teeth against the pain and set up his laptop and phone, careful to make them both untraceable. Then he went to the iPhone database he'd used earlier and found phones in Times Square. He'd be sending more than a seagull this time. He turned his phone's camera on his face. Vivian's phone he set on the edge of his lap. He expected it to ring soon.

"I'm Joe Tesla," he said. "And I have something to tell you."

48

Dr. Dubois struggled out of the cab into the crush of humanity and honking horns that was Times Square. Billboards shouted for his attention, ads for musicals he'd never want to see, and junk food he shouldn't consume. He stuck the crutches under his armpits and hobbled toward the hotel.

He was scheduled to meet Agent Marks at the Marriott Marquis hotel at 10 o'clock. He could still fix this. Tesla had the serum, and he had some information about it, but he was contained underground. Saddiq might already have killed him. If not, there was a good chance that he'd been caught by the police. The doctor had heard the gunshots as the train had started to move again. They were after Tesla. They would get him.

If not, he needed to get to his meeting right away. He intended to record it and use the recording as insurance should the CIA try to cut ties with him. Since the 500 series debacle, they had distanced themselves from him, but they knew that they had enough on the line to fill the tunnels with agents looking for Tesla. They'd back him up, especially if he had a little insurance.

The noise level in the square dropped, and several people

turned to look at the Jumbotron. It looked dark among all the glittering lights. He stopped to catch his breath, straightened his glasses, and looked up at the giant screen.

A familiar face looked down on him. His crutch slipped, and he almost fell. Pain rippled up from his leg. He caught his balance and looked back up at the screen.

Joe Tesla's image stared down at him, large as a building. His lips moved as if he were speaking, but there was no audio, of course.

Subtitles appeared against his shirt.

The doctor read them. They told how Joe Tesla was trapped underground in New York City, how he had uncovered evidence of a terrible series of experiments. The image changed to show the doctor's briefcase, one of the yellow biohazard stickers standing out brightly.

He staggered back, crutch dropping to the ground unheeded as he read his own name.

Around him people had stopped moving. They stared at the Jumbotron. A man with a red hat held up his phone to film it. They knew. Everyone knew.

Tesla was giving Dr. Dubois all the blame. But he hadn't done it alone.

A hand cupped his elbow and steadied him. "Dr. Dubois?"

Agent Marks looked down on him.

"I . . . yes. Let's get off the street," said the doctor.

Marks's phone beeped, and he pulled it out of his pants pocket.

The doctor gripped his remaining crutch.

A flicker of surprise passed across the agent's face.

"What?" The doctor fought to keep panic from his voice. "What?"

"Nothing at all." Marks handed him his dropped crutch. "Let's get inside. We have a lot to talk about."

The doctor's galloping heart slowed. They would be able to find a solution.

Marks draped an arm across his shoulders. Something stung the doctor on the side of his neck.

His heart convulsed inside him, and he fell to the dirty asphalt.

"This man is having a heart attack!" called Marks. "Someone call 911."

He'd never survive the wait for the ambulance. Pain radiated out from his chest, down his arm, but it wasn't from a heart attack. He tried to reach the spot where Marks must have injected him, but his arm wouldn't move.

Darkness crowded around the edges of his vision.

The last thing he saw was Tesla's earnest face, with the doctor's name printed beneath it. His own damning name.

49

Joe climbed up an old-fashioned stepladder to place an antique star ornament atop his Christmas tree. He'd discovered a box of Victorian decorations in the attic and brought them out. Hand-blown glass balls, cut-tin shapes, and heavy lead tinsel glittered from every branch. The homey smell of pine filled the room. He bet it looked very much as it had for the first Gallo Christmas. He placed the star atop the tree awkwardly with his left hand. His right arm was healing nicely, but he didn't trust it to hold the fragile glass.

The fireplace crackled cheerily. He'd cleared off the mantel and covered it with pine boughs and holly. Two stockings hung there. A red one with Joe stitched on it and a larger, yellow one, emblazoned with Edison.

"Does this star look straight?" Joe asked Vivian. She was across the room, eying the tree.

"Mostly."

Joe climbed down and scrutinized the angle himself. Crooked.

A warm nose nudged the back of his knee. Joe grabbed a doggie treat off the corner of the mantel. Edison cocked his head, looking festive in a Santa Claus hat. It had been given to him by the residents of the Carrie Wilbur Home for

Adults with Special Needs. After taking over Erol Saddiq's bills, Joe had set up an animal therapy program at the home. Andres would be taking Edison there weekly.

The hat slipped to the side when Edison tilted his head and brushed it against his inverted plastic collar. He was healing without complication and was already outrunning Joe during their morning tunnel jogs. Joe was healing more slowly. His ankle had become infected and took two courses of antibiotics to start healing.

"He loves it!" said a breathless voice from one of the wingback chairs. It was Celeste, on Skype, beaming at the dog. Even though she would deny it, her hair looked perfect.

"Of course he does," said a deep voice with an Eastern European accent. "He is a dog."

Andres balanced a bowl of popcorn on his knee. He had plugged his iPad into Joe's speaker system and Estonian Christmas carols played softly in the background. At least Joe thought that they were Christmas carols—they could have been lullabies or funeral marches, for all he knew.

Andres had insisted they create garlands of popcorn and cranberries. Joe had tried until he'd poked himself under the thumbnail with a needle for the third time. Vivian claimed she hadn't heard that much swearing since she'd left the Army.

Joe's cell phone blared "Jingle Bells," and he hurried to silence it, but not before Celeste gave him a mocking look for having a holiday ring tone.

He'd barely answered before the man on the other end launched into a complicated question.

"Hang on." Joe glanced around the room. "I have to take this, but it won't take long. It's work."

Taking the stairs two at a time, he went to his upstairs office to get his laptop. He'd gone back to work the last time that Pellucid had asked him. It felt good to be using his brain again, solving problems, setting up systems to catch bad guys.

Making a difference.

It didn't take him long to answer the programmer's questions, but he hesitated for a moment, thinking back to a conversation he'd had with Vivian when she'd first arrived at the party. He hadn't seen her since the night that she'd knocked out the agents and held the elevator for him.

He'd put a mug of warm mulled wine in her hand and taken a sip of his own.

"Why didn't you release the encrypted page?" she'd asked. "The one that you said linked the doctor to the CIA? They got off scot-free."

"I know," Joe said. "And I would have released it, damn the consequences, except for one thing."

Her voice sounded skeptical. "What was that?"

"The encrypted page was blank."

Her eyes widened. "It was a bluff?"

"It kept them from shooting us when the elevator got to the top floor," he said. "And it's still keeping them cautious."

She'd grinned and clinked her cup against his. "Well played, sir."

Joe smiled, remembering, and turned to return to the party, but before he could go back downstairs, his phone rang again.

"I'm sorry to disturb you so late." Joe recognized the voice. Dr. Samuels.

His heart skipped a beat. "Yes?"

"The test results are in."

"And?" Joe asked.

"We've definitely established that you do not have toxoplasmosis."

Joe could tell that more news was coming. "That's good."

"Some of the results seem to indicate that you might have

been dosed with certain experimental substances that may have triggered your agoraphobia."

"You mean, someone did this to me on purpose?"

"We don't know."

When Joe ended the connection a minute later, he stood in his darkened office, staring at the drapery covering a window that opened to nowhere.

Who would poison him?

He had to know.

ACKNOWLEDGEMENTS

Putting down Joe Tesla's adventures took a lot of help. Thanks goes first to my wonderful writing group who, as always, helped make the story shine: Kathryn Wadsworth, Judith Heath, David Deardorff, Karen Hollinger, and Ben Haggard. You guys are so talented at writing and editing. I'm proud to know you.

Thanks also to my writer friends, who provided advice and sanity checks—Andrew Peterson, James Rollins, Sean Black, Kelli Stanley, and CJ Lyons. Writing can be a lonely journey, and I'm grateful for the way stations you guys provide.

The book would not be what it is without the care of my agents, Mary Alice Kier and Anna Cottle, and my copy editor, Joyce Lamb; plus a shout-out to Kit Foster for the great cover. I received advice about the workings of the subway itself from Joseph Brennan. I'm sure I've managed to sneak some errors in despite his help, but that's not his fault.

And last, and most important of all, thank you to my husband and son for being kind, supportive, and thoughtful while I slipped away to my underground world. I'll be topside again for a while, but then I have this idea . . .

ABOUT THE AUTHOR

Thank you for reading *The World Beneath*. I hope that you enjoyed the story!

I'm REBECCA CANTRELL, the award-winning and *New York Times* bestselling thriller author of this book. My other novels include the Order of Sanguines series, starting with *The Blood Gospel* and the award-winning Hannah Vogel mystery series, starting with *A Trace of Smoke*. My husband, son, and I just left Hawaii's sunny shores for adventures in Berlin, Germany.

If you'd like to find out more about my novels, visit my web site at http://www.rebeccacantrell.com/. I have them all listed there, in order, plus some extra content about researching them and the worlds in which they take place.

If you'd like to receive advance notice of my upcoming books, please sign up for my newsletter at www.rebeccacantrell.com. I put it out a few times a year, and I promise never to sell or trade your name.

Or, if you want to see what I'm up to day to day, you can find me on Facebook and Twitter.

CPSIA information can be obtained
at www.ICGtesting.com
Printed in the USA
FSHW02n1112150518
48270FS